Payback is Time to die … Again

Book II in the Payback Trilogy

By Douglas Ewan Cameron

A-Argus Better Book Publishers, LLC

For information:
A-Argus Better Book Publishers, LLC
9001 Ridge Hill Street
Kernersville, North Carolina 27285
www.a-argusbooks.com

ISBN: 978-0-6158753-0-9
ISBN: 0-6158753-0-0

Book Cover designed by Dubya

Printed in the United States of America

Acknowledgments

When I finished *Payback is a Bitch* I knew there was a sequel but I had no idea how it would turn out. As it happens there is a third book in this series (*Payback is Bitter Vengeance*) and I hope to have it published in 2014.

This book would not have been possible without the help of long time friend and fraternity brother Bill McClellan. I don't own guns and don't fly planes. He does both and is very knowledgeable about them. In this book, he is my Beecher McFalls.

I must thank my stepson Gary A. Bokas, Esquire, who gave me Michel Villar's insight into Stuart's culpability in the deaths of his wife and brother-in-law.

Also I must thank an undertaker in the Cleveland, Ohio area for the details of the cremation of the body.

And Steven L. Pyatt, Firefighter/Paramedic of Copley/Bath, Ohio, for the extraction and treatment of Michel Villar at the accident scene.

Further, thanks to Dubya (design team at A-Argus Books) for working with me to get the cover I wanted.

All the French and Dutch in this book are translations provided by Microsoft Word for the Mac (Microsoft Office 2011). I trust that they are accurate.

As usual, I must thank my team of proofreaders and editors: David Buchthal, Mary von Zittwitz and, most especially, my wife Nancy Calhoun Cameron.

Finally, as I will do in all my published works, I must acknowledge two writers who have influenced me. First (and only chronologically) is Mary Higgins Clark whom I heard speak at a Book and Author Luncheon (or dinner) sponsored by *The Plain Dealer* of Cleveland, Ohio. She said that many of her works got their genesis with the words "What if?"

The other writer is the late Philip R. Craig, author of the Martha's Vineyard based J.W. Jackson mysteries. My wife and I met he and his wife Shirley on a riverboat trip from Constanta, Romania to Amsterdam, Netherlands in 2005 and shared many a happy meal together including my wife's birthday dinner. He told me that in his writing, while he knew the story line, he often didn't know how it was going to come out and let the characters lead him. Often that is what I do, and I did in this book.

To Elaine and Jack Szabo of North Ridgeville, Ohio because Elaine could hardly wait to read more about Michel Villar.

Part I

Here Comes the Judge

Chapter 1

"Daws, someone is coming."

"I know, Tres," I replied, "Thanks."

I released the intercom button on the remote I carried and looked at the picture. The car was proceeding toward The House at the End of the Road at a normal speed. My backside motion detector system had been first to acquire the intruder, but the camera would have captured him a few seconds afterward. I had two motion detector units (one on either side of the road) at the far extremities of my property that communicated with the house wirelessly and were solar powered.

I had been living here about six months and the first thing I had done after moving in was to install a security system. It wasn't mine by any means, but I knew how to run it. The system was super high tech, some of the stuff I don't even know if the military had. The windows and doors were all equipped with sensors that would detect them being opened. The windows all had glass breaks. I don't know why I put the glass breaks on because all the glass was bulletproof. All the locks were armed with pick sensors. My keys had chips in them and if the wrong key or a lock pick was inserted, then the alarm would sound. I had given up my landline four months ago and all my communication was done by satellite. A security station in the states would pick up the signal and call me. And if I did not respond, they would contact the St. Nantes gendarmes at the same time as Beecher McFalls, my security man who lived on St. Martin. He was an hour away by private plane but I could not do much better, at least in what he could do for me. The plane could land on the road and he would be at my door in sixty-five minutes tops. We know because we tried.

I had four motion detector systems at the house to pick up any intruders, one under the front deck that watched the front yard down to the slope which dropped down to the Caribbean, one on each end of the house concealed in vegetation and one on top of the carport on the back of the house. But it was the backside motion detector that had found the current intruder – I don't know what else to call him. I am a semi-recluse – except for Tres. I don't get mail delivery and my housekeeper Lynette Duprey had been here only yesterday. "Why no mail delivery?" you might ask. Because there wasn't anyone to write me. All my bills I get on line so all that could possibly arrive by snail mail is crap.

I had an automatic backup generator run on natural gas backed up by a fifty-gallon underground gas storage tank. A wind turbine in the front yard generated the majority of my electricity. It was over to the right side where it couldn't be seen from the front windows or from the deck unless you leaned over at the right end and craned your neck. Anyone who wanted to knock out my security would have to start in the house. I still had landline power but if that supply was severed, I wouldn't even have known it except for the alarm which would sound on my monitor remote which I always had with me, even when I was not home.

I was in the basement exercise room when the current alarm sounded and had just completed my workout. As usual it had started with the weights and ended with the treadmill. Treadmills are basically boring. Well, let's face it, all exercise is basically boring. I had a flat panel TV on the wall and watched CNN International when working with the weights but the treadmill I had in front of the slider and I looked out across the front yard at the beautiful Caribbean, which is basically all I could see from my house or at least the front of my house. I owned seafront property and, as with most of the people who own such, my front yard was between the house and the Caribbean. My "front" door (where any of my few and far between guests showed up) was in the middle of the back of my house.

My exercise room was under the laundry room that was at the far west side of my house, accessed by a staircase that came out at a semi-concealed door next to the kitchen on the front side of the house. I had missed it the first time I was in the house over a year ago when I was not in any shape to really notice hidden passages. I had just survived a grueling, tortuous, unending, terrifying (you pick the adjective) sixteen hours in the water after being "drowned" and left for dead by my no-good brother-in-law Howard and his equally no-good friend Keith. Fortunately, I wasn't drowned and I managed to survive.

Wondering whom the visitor was – let's call him or her that until we know more – I ran up the stairs and almost knocked down Tres, who was coming to get me.

"It's a man. He's driving a Porsche. I don't recognize him."

"Okay, then I probably don't either because you know all the people on St. Nantes that I know. Get your pistol and get down to the control room. If there is any shooting, get into the safe room. Lock it and don't come out until I tell you to."

She didn't question me, just stood on her tiptoes, threw her arms around my neck, gave me a big kiss, turned and ran toward the great room. I was right behind but not at a run. I had a towel around my neck that I had used to wipe the sweat away from my workout. Entering the great room and turning left, I stepped behind the bar, dropped the towel on it and hit a panel on the wall. The door popped open to reveal a safe door about the size of a safe deposit box. I pressed my index finger of my right hand and then the thumb of my left against the security panel, which turned blue, and the door popped open and the drawer slid out. I took the Beretta and its magazine out of the drawer and slammed the mag into the gun with the heel of my hand. I closed the door to the safe and the panel door. There was nothing else in the safe. I racked the slide back, seating the first shell in the chamber.

Thus armed, I went through the great room into the foyer. On my left was the stairway entrance to what was now my control center, formerly a theater. I crossed the foyer and looked at the flat panel screen to the left of the door. I could see a man out there, pacing. He was wearing sandals, white tennis shorts, a black emblem-less tee shirt, a matching black baseball cap and reflective sunglasses. I was about to press the talk button to ask what he wanted when he stopped, looked up at the camera, and removed his sunglasses.

I stared in disbelief. I had been wrong. Tres didn't know everyone on St. Nantes that I knew.

The man was Judge Michel Villar.

Chapter 2

In 2009 there was a trial on St. Nantes, the island I had visited and then lived on, that drew international interest.

Since the island is so important in this story, let me tell you a little about it before I explain about the trial. St. Nantes lies approximately 55 miles east southeast of St. Barthelémy and St. Maartin/Martin. It was named after Saint Amandus of Nantes, the founder and the first abbot of the monastery at Nantes, France, from which most of the original group of inhabitants came.

It is composed of two islands; the largest is approximately six miles long with two miles at the widest part (just before the harbor cove) and one and one-quarter miles at the narrowest other then the ends. The northeast side and southeast end of the main island rise to several hundred feet above the water and its slope is sometimes vertical and often hard to climb. The House at the End of the Road where I lived is located at the southeast end. The high part of the island ends at the harbor and there is a somewhat flat and inhabitable area about one-half mile deep along the southwest coast and the slope behind it is suitable for housing. The heights above this area, where the city of Genivee is situated, is flat enough for a small airport permitting small commuter jets which connect the island with St. Martin. On top of the heights overlooking the harbor is the Croix Lighthouse, so named because of the huge cross that sits atop it.

About one-quarter mile from the shore on the northwest and southwest sides of the harbor lies Guerre Isle, named because of Fort Rideau, which was built there. Guerre Isle is about a mile long and half a mile wide with a wide beach running around the southeastern end and wrapping about half the length of the island on both sides. The northwest end is a steep promontory atop which Fort Rideau is built to protect the island's harbor. Guerre Isle almost appears to have been pulled away from the main island, the fit into the harbor outline is that close.

Now back to the trial. Elise Blake Andrews and her brother Howard Blake were accused of murdering her husband Stuart Andrews. The murder was by drowning while he, Howard and Keith Mitchell, a friend of Howard's, were on a fishing excursion off St. Nantes when the Caribbean Isle, their cruise ship and flagship of the fledgling Caribbean Cruise Lines, was in port. They faked Stuart's reboarding the ship and then faked his suicide two days and five hundred miles later in the southern Caribbean. Apparently the pressure of this had gotten to Keith and he had committed suicide leaving a note that implicated Elise and Howard. They were extradited to St. Nantes to stand trial, were convicted and hung. Michel Villar was judge at that trial.

Why does this concern me? Because my name is – make that was but I guess it actually is – Stuart Andrews. I survived that drowning, spending sixteen hours at sea and finally coming ashore near this house. I managed to get inside (nobody was home) and spent twenty-four hours here recovering. Then I went after Elise, Howard, and Keith. I first convinced Quentin Baston, the skipper of the fishing excursion boat who had been paid to be quiet, to fake his death and be a witness at the trial. He had produced the packet of ten thousand dollars – blood money – that had Elise's and Howard's fingerprints on it. He also had my camera, which somehow Keith had used to take a picture of Howard swinging a Heineken bottle at me. The camera had been forgotten when the murderers left the boat but Quentin found and kept it. I then managed to get Keith to confess and convinced him that suicide was the only way to escape the St. Nantes guillotine. Of course, St. Nantes didn't have a guillotine but Keith didn't know that and considered a public death by beheading a terrible fate. I also anonymously told the authorities about an offshore fund to which Elise had access and had used to pay a hit man known as The Facilitator to kill Quentin. He never had even tried, but the money trial marked the conspiracy. Elise also used it to pay for her defense. The evidence had been overwhelming and Elise and Howard never had a chance in a trial that was skillfully and legally manipulated by Michel Villar.

After the trial he had come aboard my yacht Zàkpa and told me that he knew who I was, but he wasn't about to tell anyone. Truth be told, the reason was that he was too involved. He admitted to me that he was the front man for a cartel or syndicate – I never knew exactly what group it was – for which I had been laundering money. In the process of that arrangement, I had amassed a small fortune myself. I would say that over one hundred million dollars was a small fortune. I could do this because I was an investment advisor and Andrews Investment Management was my company that almost went under when I was killed. However Alan Murphy, my former business partner, had surfaced at just the right time and bought the company for about ten cents on the dollar and it was doing fairly well.

Another thing that Michel Villar had given me during that visit was a picture I had taken of the harbor of St. Nantes and sent to Keith Mitchell with the inscription "Four Went Out. Three Came Back. We know what happened." I think that was the straw that broke the camel's back for Keith and nearly mine because I had forgotten to get it from Keith when I visited him the night he committed suicide. How it had not fallen into the hands of the Los Angeles police and how Michel Villar had gotten it, I have no idea but he did have it. I think that it would have made a difference in the trial but I am not certain.

Anyway, that is the background of the relationship between Michel Villar and me. But that doesn't explain what he was doing here. I could ignore him but there are two cars parked in the carport, mine and Tres, whose real name is Treshauna Lee Jones. That's a mouthful just like my name Dawoh Mbayo. That's a fact. That's my Sierra Leone name. I have dual citizenship because my mother was from there. She met my father Kevin Andrews when they were in college. I was an only child. That's another thing. Michel Villar knew my name. That man knew a lot about me. Maybe too much!

I looked at the security panel screen. Michel Villar was still standing there. I knew he wasn't going to leave.

"Who is it, Daws?" Tres asked over the intercom. "Daws" is what I had decided people should call me. It's easier than Dawoh.

"It's someone I know but you don't. I think it will be all right. However just for safety, stay there. Turn on the recorder though."

"Right, be careful."

With my heart in my left hand and the Beretta in the right behind my back, I opened the door.

Chapter 3

"Hello, Daws," said Michel Villar.

I wasn't surprised that he knew my name. After that trial he told me he knew more about me than I thought anyone ever would, except me. That is one reason I am so paranoid about security. Even though he said that my work for the organization was free and clear and that the group accepted the fact that I was dead, I couldn't be certain. Better safe than sorry and I could afford it.

"Hello, Michel," I said, my left hand holding the door and my right behind my back holding my gun. "What can I do for you?"

"Well, for starters you could invite me in."

I didn't move.

"Look, I am unarmed." He pulled his tee shirt out of his shorts and turned around showing skin between the tee shirt and shorts, both being so tight there was no question of a gun.

"I can see that," I said.

"You can't be too cautious," Michel said. "Even with your metal detector, I could have had a composite weapon of some sort."

Another jolt. How had he known?

"You could still have a knife or something else. For all I know you are a martial arts master."

"If I was, you'd be dead now." He looked around. "Seriously, Daws. I need to talk to you in private where we can't be heard. It's a matter of life and death – mine."

I stood there motionless.

"Look, you're the only one who can help me. The Cercle des Frère thinks I have taken their money. Please," he looked at me pleadingly "…Stuart."

With that I had to let him in. It was either that or kill him then and there and for me that was not an option. At least not standing where the world could see. At least not yet.

I stood aside and he came through the door, which I quickly shut. He turned to face me and stopped dead still. My gun aimed pointblank between his eyes.

"Assume the position, Michel. Even as a judge, I am certain that you know what I mean." I indicated a wall of the foyer with my free hand.

"I'd rather not," he said, not moving.

"Then you'd better leave."

"I cannot do that."

"Then …" and I indicated the wall with the Beretta.

"But I have this problem."

"We'll get to that. Now assume the position."

"No, I mean I have a problem with people touching me."

I stared at him not comprehending.

"It's called Aphephobia – fear of being touched."

"Well, you'll just have to put up with it."

He didn't move.

"My way or the highway," I said indicating the door with the Berretta.

Michel shrugged, turned to the wall, placing his hands on it above his head and about a yard apart, and his feet at least that distance from the wall and spread. I used my left hand to pat him down, the gun in my right against the back of his head. He didn't move but I could feel the tenseness in his body and an occasional tremble. I couldn't have done this as expertly six months ago but both Tres and I had spent time with Beecher McFalls learning to use weapons and the basics of self-defense and body searching. This was the first time I had to use this knowledge. I hoped it was the last. Satisfied I stepped back.

"Okay, Michel, you can relax."

He straightened up, stepped away from the wall and faced me.

"I told …" he started.

"Proceed into the great room," I interjected.

He did so.

"I'd say I love what you've done with the place, but you haven't changed it outwardly."

That didn't surprise me. The prior owner had hobnobbed with the elite of St. Nantes society and I was certain Michel, being the island's and the Caribbean's première jurist, had been here before. He was correct; I hadn't changed the great room. When I had purchased the house, it had come with all the furnishings; only the personal items of the Hollywood personality who had owned it had been removed.

The light aqua tile of the foyer ended at the great room entrance and turned to a deeper greenish aqua and then deeper hues of blue ending in a dark blue at the sliders. It was one of the things that I first loved about the house. It looked like the Caribbean as viewed from the deck of the house and that pattern continued throughout. To the left of the entrance was a semi-circle of black leather and chrome furniture. A three-person couch faced the TV and on either side at a 30° angle were two large chairs. On the wall in front of the seating (the guest bedroom wall) was a large flat panel television underneath which was an entertainment center announced by a bevy of green and red lights which gleam through the glass doors. To the right and closer to the sliders, which run the entire length of the front wall, was a modern glass-topped dining table that seats six. To the immediate right of the entrance was a bar with three stools where my guests could sit and behind it there was a sink and refrigerator and almost any type of alcohol you could desire.

Chapter 4

"Can I buy you a drink?" I asked moving behind the bar and picking up a tumbler. I looked around, tumbler in one hand and pistol in the other. Then I set the pistol on the bar and turned to the refrigerator. I opened the door and filled the glass with ice. Turning around to the bar, I discovered Michel Villar seated on the middle stool and holding the pistol.

"Like I said, Daws, if I wanted to kill you, you'd be dead."

"Not with that pistol," I replied.

"Oh, the safety's off, I checked," said Michel.

"True, but it's not loaded."

Michel pulled the trigger and nothing happened.

"You mean you met me at the door with an unloaded weapon?"

"No," I said reaching behind me and pulling my Beretta out from my back pocket. "This is the pistol I had at the door. I changed as you led me into the great room. You see, I didn't and still don't know if I can trust you."

Michel laughed and then gave me his great sardonic smile I remembered from the trial.

"Daws, you can trust me. I hope I can trust you. Now about that drink. I know it's early but how about a Luksusowa on the rocks."

I stared at him.

"It's a Polish potato vodka."

"Don't have any but I'll get some for your next visit."

If there is one.

"It's actually very good. I read a lot of American crime fiction and was a big fan of Phil Craig who wrote mysteries about Martha's Vineyard. His protagonist JW Jackson drank it so I tried it. Now it's my vodka. However, I will settle for Three Olives. I know you have that."

Of course he knew and that's how I became a drinker and lover of Luksusowa. Next he would tell me that I had on blue boxers.

As though anticipating, Michel Villar said, "Haven't any idea what color your boxers are."

This guy was beginning to creep me out. I set his drink in front of him and said, "Okay, Michel. Let's get to the point."

"First, tell Tres to turn off the recording devices and I'll be happy to tell you my problem."

I stared at him, but hell, he knew everything else. I pulled the monitor-intercom out of my pocket and it spoke to me "Already did it, Daws. Can I come up?"

I looked at Michel who was shaking his head. "No, stay there and watch for intruders. I don't know whether to trust this guy or not."

I turned the monitor-intercom off and put it away.

"Okay, no recording, and no one can snoop. I have the best money can buy."

"I know of Beecher McFalls and I believe you."

He took his first sip of vodka. "Anyone else I might not trust not to have spiked the drink, but I don't think you would. Okay, the truth.

"I, and Stuart Andrews, indirectly worked for a French syndicate or cartel – whatever you wish – called Cercle des Frères or Circle of Brothers. It's been in existence about twenty years but only started pulling in the cash about twelve years ago and that's when I was asked by a friend to become the financial intermediary."

"This friend …"

"Let me finish first."

"No, Michel." I said adamantly. "Today you are in my courtroom and just like in yours, the judge asks the questions when he wants and about whatever he wants to know. If you choose not to answer or if I don't believe you, I will show you to the door."

I still had the pistol in my hand and wiggled it at him just as I had at Keith Mitchell that terrible night in Los Angeles when I had learned what my wife and her brother had perpetrated.

"Very well but I reserve the right to appeal," and there was that sardonic grin of his.

Chapter 5

"The friend was Émile Bertran. We had been to law school in Paris together and, admittedly, we were more than friends. And honestly I don't know how she became involved. She came to me because I had always shown an interest in the money markets and they wanted someone in America to handle their sources. I had gone to school in America ..."

I nodded because I knew some things about him.

"And she felt that I might be the person they were looking for. I was having difficulties at the time. In the middle of a divorce that was taking me for every penny. I can't complain, it was my fault but the reasons for the divorce aren't important here."

"You might have stayed married if you had kept it in your pants unless you were at home."

It was his turn to stare.

"Yes, I have some sources also. Continue."

"So I started looking and after several weeks, you were my choice. I had several different agencies in the states investigating people for a French investment group. The group does exist but hadn't any interest in going big time.

"I was impressed with your ability to make gains for your clients and your honesty was above reproach. At least then." Again that sardonic smile.

"After you were on board, I kept as close tabs on you as I could. With my background checks, I knew about your parents and when Sierra Leone offered dual citizenships, I knew you would jump at the chance and you did. I knew that and, as far as I knew, no one else did."

"And now?" I questioned.

"I still think that I am the only one but I can't swear to it. Anyway, I knew about some of your offshore accounts and I knew of your skimming, but you were not taking that much and you were giving Cercle des Frères more than they expected.

"When Stuart Andrews died, things began to fall apart but very slowly. First I went back over your itinerary and discovered that you had made port here and learned of your fishing excursion. That took some doing but I did. In the process of a normal monthly financial survey of the local banks, part of my duties as judge believe it or not, I found the account opened by Dawoh Mbayo. It didn't take much then to find the airplane flights and track you to Amsterdam, then back to Paris where you disappeared.

"I lost you for a while and then Quentin Baston's boat exploded mysteriously. Those fishing boats just don't do that. I checked records and learned that the Zàkpa was in port and thought it was a strange language for a South African named Josef Viljoen to use to name a boat. A thorough painstaking web search led me to the name; so at least I thought I knew what it meant.

"About that time I had a call from a friend in the Los Angeles Police Department."

"Juliet Mills."

"Yes," again his turn to look at me disbelievingly. "I was third-year law ..."

"Wait a minute," I interjected, "you said you were in law school in Paris with Émile Bertran!"

"True. As you know French law is different than American law so I had to pass the French Bar and spent a year studying French law."

"Accepted. Now Juliet Mills.

"Yes. I was third year law and she was a sophomore at The University of Virginia. We were friends."

I waggled the gun at him.

"Okay, more than friends. I had contacted her after I began to believe that you weren't dead and asked her to watch for anything about two people..."

"Howard and Keith," I said.

"Yes, and she just fortunately happened to get the Mitchell suicide, otherwise ..."

"The picture would have been part of the case."

"Yes, she found the picture and didn't say anything until she had talked to me. I immediately knew what was going on and asked her, in the sense of true justice, to send it to me and I would make certain that the guilty would be prosecuted and convicted."

"And why did you really want the picture?" I asked.

"I just told you ..."

"No, you didn't. I want to know. Actually I do know but I want to hear it from you."

Michel Villar stared at me.

"I have had a long time to think about this, Michel. I figured that Juliet Mills was the conveyer of the picture in some form and for the longest time I couldn't figure out why. Now I know but I want to hear it from you."

Michel looked at me and then took a drink, drained the glass and then gestured for more. I complied.

"First of all, if I wanted you out of the way, I could do it legally. I would simply notify the gendarmes that Stuart Andrews was really alive and living on St. Nantes."

"And why would they be interested in me?"

"Conspiracy to commit murder in the first degree and murder in the first degree."

Chapter 6

"What!" I exclaimed "Murder! Conspiracy! How do you figure that? "

Again that sardonic smile, a sip of his new drink, and then the explanation.

"Conspiracy requires an agreement between two or more people to commit a crime. Murder is the intent to kill, and you – and Joaquin by the way – killed Elise and Howard. It doesn't matter that Joaquin and you weren't present at the time of death, or that Elise and Howard died pursuant to a court order. Joaquin's and your actions and intent were the direct cause of the death of Elise and Howard.... at least that's how I would argue it."

"I ... didn't think ..."

"Of course not. No one in your shoes would have, and given the chance you would do it all again. I can only surmise what happened to Mitchell, but even if the picture had been brought into the investigation, it would not have led very far. I am certain that your tracks were well covered and without knowing the personas involved, the police would have had a difficult time.

"Which in a round about way brings us to your guess. 'Why did I give you the picture?' To let you know that I knew, that other people could know, so that you would be cautious as you have been."

I started to say something and he held up his hand

to stop me.

"And because I wanted you as ally if and when I needed one and I do now."

I studied him for a moment. He was right. If he wanted me out of the way, I would have been. The least I could do was listen.

"Okay," I said. "Point made and I'll listen but first one question if I may."

Michel Villar nodded his agreement.

"Was the trial fair and square and by that I mean 'Did you guide the verdict?' "

"No, I didn't cheat. I bent some rules, I was a little one-sided perhaps, but the jurists were not coerced in any manner. This verdict surprised me as much as anyone. I thought it would be six guilty/three innocent or a hung jury.

"But, let me tell you something. That day after the testimony ended, while the jury was deliberating, I had a call from the Liberian Embassy in Washington, D.C. They told me that if Elise and Howard got off, they wanted them to stand trial in Libya for the murder of Stuart Andrews in the southern Caribbean. They could do that because the ship was of Liberian registry. There is no such thing as the battered wife defense in Libya. And, from what I know of Liberian law, they would have been guilty as sin just based on their own testimony in the trial. So for them it was a no-win situation."

He finished his drink, put the glass down and said, "I'd love another but I have a story to tell and then I have to drive home. Can't get a DUI. Wouldn't look good on my record."

"No, it wouldn't but first I have another question. Are all your friends women?"

"Only the ones I go to bed with." And that statement was punctuated by his sardonic smile.

"But seriously, why I am here. The picture, yes, was to make an impression on you in two ways, one of which you have already discerned. If I know about you, then others can and you must be prepared. I think that you are well on the way in that regard.

"The second reason for the picture is to show you that I am a friend because otherwise I could have used it to get you into trouble. However, for right now you are not in trouble, I am.

"While you were doing you laundering for Cercle des Frères, I was also doing a little investing of funds which were not my own. I shouldn't have. I was foolish and I admit it. But I wanted a lifestyle I couldn't afford without that. My revenue was nowhere close to yours but I had to be careful because I knew who my employers were and what they were capable of doing. That should have been my warning and I should have desisted but ... enough said.

"What has happened is that somehow someone determined how much money was missing from the transactions and someone, maybe the same person or maybe not, is truly pissed. He or she – I don't know the sex of the person or anything else – believes that, based on my own investing, I took all the money. They want it back."

I stared at him.

"I am not giving back any of the money. Over half of it came from my own investments. Of course, like you it was with their money but their money that I had earned. They were well compensated."

"Does not matter, my friend, if I can call you that," I

said. "What does matter is that they need to know that I didn't take the money."

"How are they going to know that?"

"Stuart Andrews has to tell them."

Chapter 7

It was sometime later that I closed the door behind a slightly inebriated Michel Villar – yes, he had more than the two drinks. I should not have let him drive, but then I wasn't going to let him stay here. As I turned from the door, Tres came up from the control room.

"So what's that story, Daws?" she said.

Tres had come into my life about a month after I had moved into The House at the End of the Road. I had continued my jogging, preferring to be outside in the cool of the morning to using the treadmill in my exercise room. I would jog into Genivee, get a couple of papers and jog back. I much prefer the newsprint in hand to reading off the web. On that particular morning a car had come toward me and at the last minute seemed to swerve at me. I had jumped to the side and landed poorly. I thought I had done some serious damage to my left ankle. I was limping back home to get my car when a passing motorist stopped and asked if he could help. I accepted his offer and had him drop me at the emergency room of the Genivee hospital.

I was on a table in one of the curtained rooms waiting on the evaluation of the x-rays when Tres had come in to do some additional vital work. I don't remember what she said but was certainly stunned by her beauty and the way her uniform accented her ample breasts.

She had taken my pulse and then turned my hand over. "My," she had mused, "you certainly have big hands."

"The better to massage big breasts," I had blurted out and then regretted it.

I think she had blushed but with most people of color, it is often difficult to tell. We had made some small talk after that while she did some other things and she had gone off. An hour later I was discharged in the care of a taxi driver with instructions to stay off the ankle as much was possible, and keep it iced.

I had been home no more than ten minutes when there was a knock on my front door. I was in the kitchen making up an ice pack and preparing to retire to the deck for a while when that interruption happened. I grabbed the crutches given to me at the hospital and made my way to the door. All I could see through the peephole was black hair. So I opened the door and was face-to-face – well, not really as she was six inches shorter than my six feet two – was Tres. She was dressed as I had seen her at the hospital.

"Hi," she had said. "I came to make certain that you have everything you need." Saying this she had squeezed by me into the foyer. I pulled the door shut and turn around to see her unbuttoning her uniform top.

"I want you to know that I don't do this as a rule." The top was unbuttoned and coming off her shoulders revealing that she was wearing nothing underneath. "But I just had to know if those hands are really as good as you indicated they were."

The dress had slid off her body and was lying in a white puddle around her bare feet. Somehow her shoes had come off on the way in. I just had a glimpse of red bikini panties before she stepped up to me, removed the crutches from under my arms and had placed my hands on her solid firmly-nippled, scorching-hot breasts. In what seemed to be one continuing movement she was against me, her arms around my neck pulling me down to her. Her kiss was smooth and yet passionate, demanding. Her tongue was a flickering darting snake and I found that I was returning the kiss and the tongue investigations of my mouth.

I don't know how, but we made it down the hall to the master bedroom, first having turned into the guest bedroom, but I had managed to get her on down the hall until we fell onto my unmade bed. Between the foyer and the bed all of our clothes – what little of hers remained – had been removed. I placed my hands on her breasts but she had pushed me onto my back and was astride me, lowering herself onto my erectness.

She signed deeply as it entered her and said, "The massage can wait. We have to be certain that everything else is functioning correctly."

A few minutes later we both climaxed simultaneously and as she collapsed upon me she said, "Apparently they are."

We didn't get out of bed for a while and spent most of that day and the next exploring each other. We talked about ourselves and why we were on St. Nantes. Of course being the Doubting Thomas I had become, I had her checked out but everything she told me was factual. Of course if she had me checked out, she wouldn't have found much and what she did find wouldn't validate what I told her because there wasn't much to learn.

Treshauna Lee Jones was twenty-eight years old and had been born and raised in Oliver Springs, Tennessee, where her father was a schoolteacher and her mother a homemaker. She had gone to The University of Tennessee and gotten her R.N. She worked as a surgical nurse in Richmond, Virginia, for two years. She had been seeing an intern there briefly until she awoke one morning in her bed with no knowledge of how she got there and it was obvious that she had been sexually attacked. She had reported him to the medical authorities and then had accepted a two-year grant to work at St. Nantes in the emergency room and there she had met me. She was five eight and weighed one hundred fifteen pounds and worked out every day. She had never seen a handgun until she met me and, under a two-week tutelage with Beecher McFalls, had become an expert. She and I were currently taking Tae Kwan Do. She had never questioned me about my penchant for security but had accepted it.

Now she had to know everything.

Chapter 8

I put my arms around her and she around me, each holding a Berretta in one hand.

"Before I tell you there are two things you should know. Number one is that fact that I do love you, you must believe that."

"I never doubted that for a minute, Daws, and you know that I love you."

"Yes, of that I am certain. The second thing is that my life is about to become extremely dangerous. I think that people are going to die and I could be one of them. I don't want you to go forward with me without knowing that. So, I am giving you the opportunity to walk away and stay alive."

"I don't ..."

"Wait, I am not done. If you decide to stay you are going to learn some very bad and surprising things about me. And once you know them, you can't leave alive."

She stared at me with the big brown eyes that never failed to start my blood boiling. "You mean ..."

"No, of course not. I could never harm you. But once you know everything about the past and what's in the future, there are people who will want to know and they won't be nice about how they learn the information. And once they have that information, you won't be needed any more and you will know too much about them."

"Who are you?"

"I won't say anything until I know that you are going to stay. And I don't want you to rush your decision."

"Daws, you don't have to wait. Wild horses could not tear me away from you. I have known from the start that there was something sinister ... no, not sinister ... but dark and possibly awful in your past.

"That doesn't bother me because, as you know, my past is not all that rosy. I am not leaving so let's get this dark cloud between us removed and get on with it."

"Are you ...?"

"Yes, I am. So do it."

"Okay, first let's put the weapons away. Then we'll get a pitcher of *Painkillers* and go out on the deck."

"But security ..."

"We'll try Beecher's new white noise projector. I sincerely doubt that anyone is listening today but in a day or so, who knows."

With the guns put away and *Painkillers* made, we retired to the deck under an umbrella and sat across the table from each other. I poured two glasses and handed her one. I started to drink and she said," Wait." She was lifting her glass toward mine to toast, "To the future whatever it may hold."

"The future." I said and we clinked glasses and took a deep draught. The coconut flavor filled my senses and I could, as usual, barely detect the rum.

Then I set the glass down and started.

"I am not Dawoh Mbayo, at least that is not the name I was born with. My name is Stuart Andrews and I am dead."

It all spilled out, the life story of my dead self. The fact that I was an investment advisor and money launderer for a group I knew nothing about until today and didn't know much more other than a name. The fact that I had been married. That my wife, her brother and a friend of her brother had tried to kill me by hitting me on the head with a beer bottle (Heineken to be exact) and then tried to drown me leaving my "dead" body floating in the Caribbean off St. Nantes while on a fishing excursion during a cruise. The fact that they had faked my reboarding of the cruise ship and then told the world I had committed suicide – actually the report was that I had disappeared and suicide was assumed – 500 miles away in the southern Caribbean. I didn't go into great depth about the approximately sixteen hours I had spent in the water before finally making shore on the small island you can see from the deck. I told her about the succor offered by this house that I had entered using a hidden key. Then about how I had retrieved my Sierra Leone passport and gone to Amsterdam to acquire some false identification. I told her about Quentin Baston and how Joaquin and I had faked his death and hidden him aboard the Zàkpa. I pulled no punches telling her how I had convinced Keith Mitchell, my brother-in-law Howard's friend, to write his confession and then to end his life. I felt no qualms about that and I had no guilt about the execution of Howard and my wife Elise. After all, they had tried to kill me. Then I told her about the trial, and Judge Michel Villar coming to the Zàkpa after the trial and telling me that he knew who I was and giving me the one piece of evidence that could have tied me to Keith's suicide, a picture of the harbor of Genivee. I basically skipped over the trip around the world with Joaquin and all its adventures.

She sat quietly listening until I finished.

"So this judge ..."

"Michel Villar, the man who was here."

"He is the money man for this group – Cercle des Frères?"

"Yes, but at that time I didn't know the name of that group."

"And the picture. Is that the one on the desk in the study?"

"Yes."

"Can I see it?"

"Of course, I'll go ..."

"No, you sit. I'll get it."

She was up in a flash and inside the house and back before I could pour us each another *Painkiller*. They were our thirds or fourths, I can't remember which.

She removed the back of the picture frame and took the picture out. She looked at the picture and I could see the writing on the back, put there with a computer printer at an Internet café at the airport in Memphis, Tennessee.

Four went out, three came back.

We know what happened!

Then she read the writing.

"I think the judge is right. I think this could have been trouble."

"Yes, it could have but that's water over the dam now."

She put the picture back in the frame and set it on the table.

"Okay, Daws, now tell me what happened today."

Chapter 9

"Someone or some group of people in this group Cercle des Frères believe that Michel Villar has access to money that I made while laundering their funds."

When Michel Villar sat at the bar telling me his story, I had begun to feel sorry for him.

"I don't know how they got on to it," Michel Villar had said. "After you ... Stuart Andrews ... died, I had gotten another person to handle our business. She isn't ..."

"She," I interjected. "She?"

He had smiled that beguiling sardonic smile of his. "Yes, she, but she was the best I could get and it took a while. She and I never met so don't get in a lather, as you Americans like to say.

"She has done well, not as good as you but then the markets aren't very good. She isn't keeping nearly as much as you did and neither was I because of the market. Somehow someone got suspicious. I have a feeling that someone has been in contact with her and has begun to put two and two together and gotten two – you and me. Excuse me, Stuart Andrews and me.

"So I was questioned and revealed nothing, but they know or think they know. Basically I have been given an ultimatum to return all the funds you have hidden. Their estimate is probably conservative at sixty million dollars but I am just guessing.

"Of course, I can't get any of it unless you give it to me ..."

"Which I won't. I earned it."

"I agree and I know that you won't give any of it back. I wouldn't either. But I have been given one month."

"And after one month?" I asked.

"Then I become immediately expendable. They will hire someone – probably already have hired someone – to make me nonexistent."

"You mean someone like The Facilitator?"

The Facilitator was a Russian whose real name was Fredek Gavrilovich Kondrashin. He was a Jack-of-All-Trades as far as the eradication business went. He played a small but basically irrelevant role in the part of my life I had just revealed to Tres. Howard and Elise had hired him to silence Quentin Baston, the fisherman who had taken Howard, Keith and I fishing that fateful day. Howard had given Quentin ten thousand dollars with a promise of ten thousand more in a year to keep silent but had decided for some reason to make the silence permanent. Fortunately I had gotten to Quentin first and The Facilitator's services weren't needed, but he had been paid anyway as Howard thought he had done the job. He was tied to Howard and Elise because she transferred money from one of my offshore accounts, the only one she knew about, to his account in payment for "services rendered." This was revealed during the trial held here on St. Nantes and helped convince the jury of nine of the conspiracy the three had wrought. At least seven of the nine determined that Howard and Elise were guilty and in a French court, a majority of six is all that is required.

"Not just someone like The Facilitator," Michel Villar had said. *"It will be The Facilitator. He is the only person that Cercle des Frères has used. At least to my knowledge. Not only was I the moneyman for the brotherhood but I was also the man who made the contracts. Unless someone else has been used and I have been circumvented, that is the person of choice."*

"Don't you find these two duties you perform for Cercle des Frères to be contradictory to your position as a judge?" I asked.

"Not at all. The two are completely different. The one is here on St. Nantes and the others, although originating here, have no impact here."

"Except in your bank account."

His sardonic smile was a bit crooked this time, as he had continued to imbibe. *"Well, actually the account isn't here, it's ..."*

"I don't want to know. So, if I understand, you have a month to live?"

"I really wish you wouldn't put it that way. Besides I was hoping that you ... we ... could come up with a plan to make the Cercle des Frères not have to resort to that."

"And that is how we left it," I said. "I understand that the Cercle des Frères probably won't be happy until they get the funds they believe to be theirs. They're going to keep looking until they find them and what that means is that they will find me."

"And me," Tres added, reaching her hand across the table to grasp mine and squeezing it tightly. "We are in this together, you and I, Daws. I stayed. Remember that.

"I know that you think that if I left, the Cercle des Frères would come after me to learn what I know about you. Of course, I wouldn't have known much ..."

"Except for the security provisions we have for…"

"…The House at the End of the Road," Tres continued. "I know. And once I had revealed them, I would be of no more use to them and thus of no more use.

"You know, I have never heard of these people … this Cercle des Frères. I know of the Italian Mafia, the American Mafia, the Russian Mafia, the Medellin Cartel, but the Cercle des Frères?"

"Not well known. Very quiet. Very low profile. At least until now."

"Do you think that if we made it known …"

"But we don't know anything about it. Just putting a name out wouldn't mean anything. But there may be a way to bring it out into the open. Getting the group involved in something that is noteworthy in a nefarious way might work."

"You mean something like the Judge's participation being revealed?"

"Yes, or something like the Judge being killed or perhaps something like me being killed."

"You, but why?"

"Let me rephrase that, something like Stuart Andrews being killed."

Chapter 10

I had realized when Michel Villar showed up on the doorstep of The House at the End of the Road that my life was never going to be the same again. I was never going to be able to live without fear of someone coming after me and trying to kill me. I also felt that I owed him something because, in fact, he had kept me out of the trial of my wife and brother-in-law. And he was right; I was complicit and had drawn Joaquin into it. Now also I had drawn Tres into it, although both had at one time been given the option of stepping away.

When I explained my idea to the judge the following week when he again stopped by after a doubles tennis session with his partner Guillaume Martineau, he was immediately receptive.

"Sounds workable," he had said. "The Facilitator likes to keep things simple. Killing me in a hospital will work especially with Tres there to watch things."

He smiled at her sitting across the war room table from him. I had decided that the most secure place in our home to talk strategy was in the war room, once a home theater. It was accessible from the foyer by a staircase that curved back toward the back of the house and then opened into the theater. We had torn out the seats, donating them to a local nursing home and throwing in the theater equipment as well as constructing a theater for them. All this was done anonymously or as anonymously as one can do in such a small country. The previous owner of the house had been a Hollywood person who had entertained his island friends and government officials with pre-release movies. More than that you don't need to know. His death had permitted me to acquire the home about six months after the trial.

"Even better," he mused smiling that sardonic smile of his, "I have talked to the Facilitator and he agreed to go along with whatever I planned."

"What!" Tres and I exclaimed together looking at each other. "You talked to the man who is going to kill you?"

"It's alright, " Michel Villar said. "I offered him twice what Cercle des Frères is going to pay him to make it look like he killed me. He agreed. All I have to do is let him know what our plan is."

"What do you mean, 'our plan'?" I screamed rising from my seat. "You told him about us?"

I was pacing the floor. Tres was ashen.

"No, I didn't. I told him that I was going to come up with a way that my death could be faked. No one will know. He certainly isn't going to tell Cercle des Frères because that would be signing his own death warrant. This was going to be his last service anyway. He has acquired the money he needs to live a quiet life and he is going to take the opportunity offered to make it even more comfortable."

"I don't know, Michel. I am not at all comfortable with this. You are putting the both of us in jeopardy."

"No more than you are already in by being associated with me. You are in the clear. No one knows about you, not even my closest friend."

"And who is she?" Tres asked, aware of his proclivity for the opposite sex.

"He is Guillaume Martineau."

"Your bailiff?" I said.

"Bailiff, doubles partner, and other things."

"This certainly complicates things, Michel. You should have talked to me ... us ... first."

He was silent and had gone into his church mode, elbows on the table, forearms up, fingers interlaced, fore fingers making a steeple and the top of the steeple against his chin – a familiar contemplative stance I remembered so well from the trial.

"You are probably correct, Daws ..."

"Damn straight, I am ..."

"But you are not the one who is going to die!" he said emphatically, bringing his palms down hard on the tabletop. "I am."

I walked to the table directly across from him and leaned forward hands palm down on the table getting myself as much in his face as I could.

"WRONG," I shouted. "With you gone, faked death or real, what do you think that Cercle des Frères is going to do? Give up the hunt? From what little I know based upon what you told me, there is money out there they think is theirs. They are going to tear the world apart looking. And if you could come up with me, they probably will, although it will take a while ... maybe."

"You're right," agreed Michel Villar. "But at least you have a head start. If I hadn't come to you, regardless of what happens to me, they would do the same thing, only you wouldn't be prepared. At least this way you can plan."

I had to agree with that logic, like it or not. They were going to come and I was prepared, somewhat, but I had a lot of planning to do. And I knew, that like Michel

Villar, Tres and I were going to die at the hands of Cercle des Frères.

Part II

Repos de Dieu Votre Âme, Michel

Chapter 11

The modified plan we came up with was simple … if it worked. Michel Villar had to cross the hill in the middle of the island whenever he played tennis, because the Genivee Racquet Club that he had founded was on the opposite side of the island. One stretch of the road was particularly windy with a steep drop off except at one point. There was still a drop off but it was not as steep or as high. He was to drive his car through an already weakened guardrail and would be taken to the emergency room. Tres would be on duty. There Michel would undergo treatment for his injuries and have to spend the night. We wanted The Facilitator to take advantage of this, a setting similar to those he had used many times, to inject a poison intravenously, this information provided by Michel. Often The Facilitator used nicotine if the victim smoked because it was expected to be in his blood and any search for poisons would come up short. Since The Facilitator was with us on this, he would use water, Michel would "die," and Tres would be the first medical person to reach him and would inject him with a drug that would put Michel into a deep coma simulating death. Michel would be hooked to a heart monitor that would be fooled and he would be pronounced dead, taken to a crematorium and burned – only it wouldn't be Michel that was burned. That was the plan.

It was supposed to go down three days later and all we had to do was wait.

It was a beautiful day and Michel Villar was happy, nervous and scared to death. His palms were sweaty as he drove his Porsche through the first of the turns of the windy road down the north side of St. Nantes. Thankfully there was no traffic or he would have had to abort. In his mind he ran through what he was supposed to do: Reach the start of the right hand turn and accelerate to forty-five miles per hour just before he hit the guard rail. That would be enough to break the corroded bolts that Tres and I had put in the barrier the night before. We had consulted with Beecher McFalls and he had run the scenario through one of his software packages and determined that the force was sufficient to brake through the barrier and retard the speed of the car so that it would not go flying over the edge but would basically just slide off and most likely end up a short distance in a wooded copse below. There was a possibility that the car might tumble but Beecher was certain that it would not. On that possibility we all crossed our fingers.

The turn was approaching and Michel Villar began his acceleration. He was so preoccupied that he failed to notice the pickup that had approached him from behind. As his car increased in speed there was a crashing jolt from behind and his vehicle seemed to pick up too much speed. He just had time for one look in his rearview mirror and the sight of the face behind the wheel of the pickup sent an electric shock through his system: Fredek Gavrilovich Kondrashin, The Facilitator.

The Porsche burst through the guardrail with a thunderous crash and went hurtling into the air and began to tumble. Its nose hit the ground just ten feet from the copse and crumpled. The airbag had failed to deploy upon impact with the barrier and Michel Villar screamed as the car smashed into the ground and continued its forward tumble careening into the copse with such impact that three tree trunks were splintered and two of the trees crashed over the car, virtually hiding it.

I saw all this from my vantage point hidden in the trees in the next turn as the pickup roared past so fast that I couldn't see who was at the wheel. It actually slid around the turn and then disappeared from sight. I rose to my feet and fought the urge to run to help Michel, but I knew that I couldn't be associated with this any more than I was going to be. I had the police emergency number already programmed into my phone and pressed the button.

"St. Nantes Urgence. Quel est le problème?"

I understood this to be "St. Nantes Emergency. What is the problem?"

"Il y a eu un accident sur Rue du Nord au marqueur kilomètre 15. Un pickup bleu foncé a forcé une Porsche noire par le biais de la glissière de sécurité, et il s'est écrasé dans les arbres. Une ambulance est nécessaire."

This in the best French that I could muster, but languages have never been my forte. I hoped that I had said, "There has been an accident on the Nord (North) Road at kilometer marker 15. A dark blue pickup has forced a black Porsche through the guardrail and it crashed into the trees. An ambulance is needed."

I terminated the conversation and then set off back up the hill where I had left the road half an hour before. It was part of a run that I had started as a routine two weeks before so that my presence would not be suspicious. I wanted to call Tres at the hospital but knew that I shouldn't because she would be upset. She would just have to deal with things until I got to the hospital that evening.

Chapter 12

The first to respond to the call for help was a rescue squad based at the hospital. The squad vehicle stopped near the hole in the guardrail. Even before it had stopped completely, the back doors had been swung open and a doctor jumped to the ground, carrying a black bag. He looked and saw the trees across the car and shouted to the two EMTs just opening their doors.

"Nous aurons besoin des scies à chaînes et probablement les mâchoires de survie (We'll need chainsaws and probably the Jaws of Life.)" Then he vaulted over the guardrail and started down the hill slipping and sliding. Close behind him came a nurse with a backpack. She wasn't quite as agile and sat on the hill and scooted her way down.

Reaching the car they could see that it lay on its roof, the engine compartment facing the hill and road. One of the trees blocked the driver's side window and the doctor dropped to the ground and shone a flashlight into the car. "Le pilote est un homme (The driver is a man.) Inconscient (Unconscious.) Il est suspendu par sa ceinture de sécurité (He is hanging by his seatbelt.). Le sac gonflable ne s'est pas déployé (The airbag did not deploy.) L'arbre bloque l'entrée (The tree is blocking entry.)"

At this point, the nurse arrived on the other side, closely followed by the two EMTs bearing a litter. The nurse crawled up to the passenger window.

"Je peux obtenir par le biais de ce côté. (I can get through from this side)," she said. She got the backpack off and took a Life Hammer from one of the pockets. Although difficult to get a good swing, she shattered the safety glass with her first attempt. Using her fist, she punched out the glass and carefully pulled herself into the car. Propping a flashlight so that she could see, she checked for a pulse first in Michel Villar's wrist and then his neck.

"Il est vivant. (He's alive)," she reported and then started a more detailed examination. "Il a des blessures du visage, rien de grave (He has facial wounds, none serious.) Semble que le volant sur sa poitrine (Looks as though the steering wheel impacted his chest.) Servious de possibles blessures (Possible serious injuries.) On dirait que le fémur droit est fracturé (Looks like the right femur is fractured, compound.) Il porte des shorts, faciles à voir (He is wearing shorts, easy to see.) Également possible gauche radius fracturé.. (Also possible left radius fractured.) Aucun saignement grave visible (No visible serious bleeding.)"

At this point the fire department's rescue squad arrived. The nurse crawled out from the car and two chainsaws made short work of the trees on both sides. The Jaws of Life pried the driver's side door open. A firemen disconnected the battery, rendering the airbags powerless if they weren't already. One of the EMTs crawled in through the passenger window and the other was at the driver's side. First they moved the seat back to get more room and then, with each getting a grip on Michel Villar, they cut the seatbelt. Michel's body dropped a bit but they held it and then moved him out onto the litter. The doctor checked his vitals, gave the okay and the two EMTs strapped him on.   While the rescue was being performed, two firemen were preparing to get the litter up the steep incline. A block and tackle with a long rope was fastened to the rear bumper of the ambulance that had been pulled so that the rear bumper fit in the opening caused by Michel Villar's car. One of the firemen went down the hill with the end of a rope with a hook that was fastened to the litter.   Then with the fireman combining forces with the two EMTs, the litter was carried, pushed and pulled up the hill as the other fireman, acting as a counterbalance, came down the hill with the other end of the rope. When the litter was safely up, the hook was detached and the block and tackle removed from the bumper. The litter was then placed into the ambulance and secured.   After the nurse and doctor climbed aboard, the EMTs closed the door, got in and started the drive for the hospital.

* * *

While this was happening, the dark blue pickup pulled into a small neighborhood garage. A small man no more than five foot five and one hundred ten pounds soaking wet closed the garage door behind the truck. The Facilitator got out and shoved a small black transmitter in front of the man's face. "Voir ceci (See this)," he shouted. "Il n'a pas fonctionné (It didn't work.)"

The little man shrugged.   "Parfois, ils le font (Sometimes they do.) Parfois ils ne sont pas (Sometimes they don't.)"

After Michel Villar's car had crashed, The Facilitator had activated the transmitter and pushed the button expecting an explosion that would definitely have finished the job but nothing happened.

"Peut-être vous n'a pas installé la bombe correctement (Perhaps you didn't install the bomb correctly)," the little man offered.

That was the wrong thing to say and definitely the wrong time to say it. The Facilitator was not in any mood to be admonished – truthfully, he never was in a mood to be admonished. He struck the little man across his face and he dropped to the floor unconscious, but fortunate (at least temporarily) to still be alive. Walking to a workbench in front of the truck, The Facilitator got a five-gallon plastic bucket and put it on the floor. Then he proceeded to peel off the dark blue static cling sheets revealing a beige pickup truck. The sheets and the transmitter he put into the bucket and then poured a liquid from a can into the bucket. Immediately the dissolving agent turned the static cling sheets into a liquid mass.

Using a floor jack, The Facilitator raised the driver's side front wheel of the pickup off the floor and placed a nail on the floor under the tire. Releasing the jack, the wheel settled onto the nail and the tire went flat. Raising the front wheel once more into the air, The Facilitator removed the lug nuts and lay the tire on the floor near the pickup. Then he slid the body of the little man under the front of the pickup, put a work light under beside him, and added a socket wrench. Once again he released the jack and the pickup settled to the floor, crushing the life from the little man. It hadn't really mattered that the little man had admonished The Facilitator because this had been the plan all along. Adding some greasy rags and oil to the five-gallon pail, The Facilitator lit one of the rags and left the garage. He got into a two-tone blue Smart Car outside and drove away never looking back.

The afternoon shift at the St. Nantes emergency room is ordinarily quiet that time of year, but Tres was not surprised to hear the announcement of an incoming victim from an automobile crash on Rue du Nord in the middle of the afternoon. She started to smile to herself until she heard that the victim had possible life-threatening injuries. Unless something had gone drastically wrong, there was no way that the crash could have caused severe injuries to Michel.

She was on the receiving dock waiting when the ambulance backed in. Its doors swung open and a gurney was pushed out, with the EMT holding a glucose drip bottle and the doctor walking beside the gurney. The amount of blood stunned her. Michel's face was covered in it and there were bandages everywhere.

"Fractured left radius and clavicle, broken right femur – protruding, several cracked ribs, and possible internal bleedings. He's stable but needs immediate care," reported the doctor.

"Take him to examination two," Tres said and followed after them, joined by two duty doctors.

The EMT and ambulance doctor got him onto the bed and left leaving their paper work at the reception desk. The two doctors set to work and confirmed what the ambulance doctor had said. "We need to get his leg fixed and then we can get an MRI to check on internal injuries."

Chapter 13

It was six hours before Michel Villar was stabilized and in his room. He had lost his spleen. Tres had called me as soon as she could and I was at the hospital just as he was admitted to a private room in the intensive care section. I could not enter the room but Tres could and had done everything that needed to and could be done in accordance with our plan.

"I just hope that The Facilitator is on our side. In Michel's condition he won't be able to do anything to stop him if he's not."

"Don't worry, Daws," Tres assured me. "I have everything set. The Facilitator is a creature of habit and everything will be fine. All we can do is watch via the closed circuit camera I installed. There is an empty room just down the hall."

Five minutes later we were ensconced in the room and had the laptop set up. With help from McFalls, we had tapped into the hospital's security cameras and were watching the entrances to the floor. It was two hours later that The Facilitator appeared. He came from a stairwell and was wearing a doctor's coat, glasses, and carrying a clipboard. Even with the goatee – we guessed it was bogus – we recognized him from the grainy pictures that Michel had provided us. Even if it wasn't him, we were not taking any chances.

Tres left the room carrying our specially prepared glucose bag. A few steps and she was at the door of Michel's room. Nobody at the desk just one room away questioned her right to be there since she was wearing her nurse's uniform. As she opened the door, I watched The Facilitator pause looking at his clipboard, turning a page. It was just a few short, but for me long, minutes before Tres came out of the room and closed the door. She walked away from The Facilitator and entered another room a few doors down. Just another nurse with many patients' needs to attend. The Facilitator immediately resumed his path to Michel's door and entered.

I switched cameras to the one we had installed earlier. The Facilitator, if it really was he, looked at the clipboard at the bottom of the bed and then walked to the side of the bed. Bending over, he appeared to be looking at Michel's wristband. Obviously he was making certain. Then he studied Michel's face, gaunt and pale because of the trauma. Then he walked around the bed to the other side and looked at Michel's neck. I knew what he was looking for, a small birthmark shaped like Italy with a mole almost where Sicily would be. Apparently satisfied, he returned to the other side of the bed by the intravenous line, removing a syringe from his pocket as he did so.

He bent close to Michel's ear as he removed the needle's protective cover. He appeared to be whispering something to Michel but I couldn't hear although obviously Michel did. Eyes wide open, his head snapped over to look at The Facilitator as he straightened up and took the intravenous line in his hand. Michel's head was shaking furiously as the needle was inserted into the injection port and the plunger was pushed. The Facilitator put the cover back on the needle, put the needle in his pocket and stepped back to stand beside the hinge side of the door.

Michel stared at him then appeared to be reaching to remove the intravenous line when his body was shaken by wild spasms. His upper body jerked partially upright and then fell back. As it did the cardiac monitor flat lined and a beeping was heard in the hallway. "Code de Bleu" someone shouted and moments later the door was swung open as Tres entered pushing the triage cart in front of her. Closely behind her was another nurse and as she entered, The Facilitator exited the room. I changed to split screen so that I could watch Michel's room and the hallway and I watched as The Facilitator retraced his steps to the stairwell, opened the door and disappeared.

Back in Michel's room, I saw the other nurse checking for a pulse as a doctor or intern, not that it mattered, entered the room. He saw the flat lined cardiac monitor, the nurse shaking her head, and reached for the paddles of the defibrillator but Tres said. "No, he has a DNR (Do Not Resuscitate) order." The doctor replaced the paddles on the cart, put his stethoscope on and listened to Michel's chest, then took his wrist to check for a pulse. He dropped the hand, shook his head, looked at the clock on the wall and said, "Moment de la mort, 21:17."

He signed a form and then he turned and left as he had other duties to attend. The other nurse started removing the intravenous line.

Tres said, "I'll do that, I am a friend and it is the least I could do."

The other nurse nodded and left the room pushing the triage cart. As the door closed behind her, Tres pulled a syringe from her pocket, and quickly injected its contents into intravenous line not far from the needle. She glanced up in the direction of the Blu-ray camera, hopelessness obvious in her eyes, and then turned her attention to Michel. She watched closely for a few minutes, and then felt his wrist and turned to the camera, smiling broadly.

She turned back to Michel, removed the intravenous line from his arm, and then bent over whispering to him. Then she covered him with the sheet and sat down to wait for the gurney squad, a look of grief on her face. It was mere minutes before the removal squad appeared and lifted Michel Villar's "corpse" onto the gurney and pushed it out the door and down the hall with Tres closely behind. Just before she left the room, she looked up at the Blu-ray camera smiling broadly as she reached up. Her hand covered the lens and the screen went black. I turned my computer off, closed it, put it into a cloth tote bag and left the room.

Chapter 14

I exited the hospital by using a staircase and a fire door whose alarm had been deactivated earlier. I knew that Tres would activate it before she left. Then I walked through the parking lot and turned onto the fronting street and hurried to my car parked a block away. We felt that The Facilitator would be watching to see the body removed and would probably trail it to the mortuary. My hope was that he wouldn't notice an apparent employee— I was wearing scrubs—walking away from the hospital but not at the end of a shift. Halfway to the car, I stepped into the shadows of a building and waited, but there was no one following me—or at least no one I could detect.

I opened the trunk and put the computer in it. Closing the trunk, I pulled from my pocket my cellphone, which had begun ringing.

"Mr. Em-bay-o ...,"the voice hesitated.

"Yes, this is he," I replied.

"This is St. Nantes Memorial Hospital. I am sorry to be the bearer of bad news but your friend Michel Villar has just died. Our instructions were to notify you."

I paused dramatically.

"Yes, thank you. I ..."

"We have called the mortuary as instructed and they will come to pick up his body. You were supposed to meet them and accompany the body."

"Yes, where will they get the body?"

"On the loading dock next to the Emergency Entrance. It will be about half an hour."

"Thank you. Is there anything else?"

"No. We are sorry for your loss."

"Thank you."

I terminated the call and punched in the number for Michel's lawyer Huard Jubert, who had been prosecuting attorney at the trial. He answered on the second ring.

"This is Dawoh Mbayo. I am on my way to the hospital. Michel Villar just coded and has been pronounced dead. I am proceeding with his cremation as directed in his will."

There was silence on the other end of the phone and then a sigh.

"I am sorry to hear that. Michel and I were good friends. I have heard about the accident and hoped it wasn't too bad. The hospital wouldn't tell me of course."

"I will notify Guillaume Martineau and make arrangements for the disposal of the ashes in the morning."

"Very well and thank you."

Michel's will had been set up only a month ago and in time some might find that convenient. It specified that he was to be cremated immediately and his ashes spread on the Caribbean where he loved to sail. I was responsible for both the cremation and – in conjunction with his good friend, bailiff, and tennis doubles partner Guillaume Martineau – the spreading of the ashes at dawn the next morning. In the will he termed it as "the dawn of a new day and a new life." Most people would accept that as his Christian belief in the resurrection but I knew better. Before I called Guillaume Martineau, I quickly stripped off the scrubs and put on slacks, white shirt, and black blazer. A pre-tied tie quickly followed and I pulled it tight although I left the collar unbuttoned so I could breathe – I can't stand tight things around my neck. Hadn't been able to ever since my "murderers" had been hung.

Guillaume Martineau answered the phone immediately.

"This is Daws," I said simply.

"Michel," he said simply, "is he ..."

"I am afraid that he didn't make it. I don't know the details. I have just had a call from the hospital and am on my way. As his will indicates, I will accompany his remains to the mortuary and oversee the cremation. Dawn is at 5:42 tomorrow so we should probably meet at the dock at 5:00."

"Which dock?"

"I think that main one. I will call a fisherman friend and arrange for it unless he has a client" – I knew he didn't other than me – "and he will meet us there."

"Okay. God this is just awful. So unexpected! I knew when he was late today something was wrong. He is never late. After half an hour I called the gendarmes and then the hospital, but of course they wouldn't tell me anything."

"I know, we were supposed to dine together this evening and his office called me. My friend works at the hospital and kept me informed of his condition but not about his death."

At this point my phone informed me that "my friend" was calling me.

"She's calling me right now. If I find out anything, I'll call back."

"Thank you, Daws," and the connection was broken.

"Hello," I said.

"Daws, its just awful. Michel died twenty minutes ago."

It was all ad lib but there was a governing directive.

"I heard. The hospital called me and I am on my way," I glanced at the time and estimated, "should be there in about five minutes. What happened?"

"We don't know. His heart went into some heavy fibrillations and just quit. He had a DNR so there wasn't anything we could do. According to our directions, his body is to go to the mortuary immediately for cremation."

"Yes, I am on my way. I have to call Quentin to set pickup time in the morning. Are you okay?"

"Yes, of course. I was there. It was awful. I don't think I like DNRs."

"But that was his request."

"I know but still, as a nurse …"

"I understand. Almost there, need to ring off. See you at home."

"Of course, chère."

I got into the car and started the engine just for background noise and dialed Quentin. I had called him earlier in the day, so he was aware that he would be needed but we kept it strictly business.

"Michel Villar died about thirty minutes ago, so we will need you in the morning at the main dock about 5:00. That would give us a good thirty minutes to get far enough out."

"Yes, dat be true. I will be there for you."

"There will be two of us."

"Dat is no problem. See you in the morning."

As we were talking I saw the mortuary's hearse pass me and enter the parking lot. I ended the call and followed the hearse, finding a place about three rows from the emergency room door. I could see the loading dock but nothing on it. The hearse backed up to the dock – obviously this was old hat – and stopped. The driver got out and walked to the steps, mounting the dock and walking to the rear doors of the hearse. He opened the doors and pulled out his gurney. By this point, I was climbing up the steps.

He noticed me.

"Mr. Em ..."

"Yes," I said. "Just call me Mr. Daws."

I knew that because of the nature of the business, Daws would not be acceptable.

"Sometimes I cannot pronounce the name either."

He smiled and we shook hands.

"I'm Vincent," he said by way of introduction.

Then he punched the bell by the door. Very quickly the door opened and Tres stood there.

"He's in here," she said. "Should I ..."

"No need, we ...," and he nodded indicating me, "can handle it."

We wheeled the mortuary's gurney into the large receiving room where the hospital's gurney sat. On top of it in a blue body bag were the remains of my friend. I hoped they weren't just remains. We placed the mortuary's gurney beside it and locked the wheels. Taking the bag at what I assumed were Michel's shoulders and Vincent his feet, we moved the body onto the gurney. Vincent fastened the straps, unlocked the wheels, and we guided the gurney out the door.

"Wait."

We stopped and turned to face Tres.

"You need to sign the release form."

"Of course," Vincent said. "I forgot."

Tres handed him a clipboard and pen. Vincent looked at the form, signed it and handed it back to her. She tore out the third (pink) copy and handed it to Vincent.

"Thank you," Tres said, smiled at each of us, entered the hospital and closed the door behind her with a solid thunk.

Vincent was obviously an old hand and we got the gurney into the hearse and secured it with no problems. Doors closed and latched, we left the loading dock. We drove slowly out of the parking lot and turned left, going back the way he had come. Based on information received later, in a dark corner of the lot behind us, a two-tone blue Smart Car started its engine, turned on its lights, and started following us. The driver was so big that he was exceedingly uncomfortable, but the pickup he had driven earlier in the day was permanently inoperative.

Chapter 15

It was a ten-minute drive to the mortuary and crematorium located on the far side of the harbor from the dock where cruise ship tenders land. It was next to the freight docks that made it convenient for any coffin headed overseas by water, although nowadays most bodies taken off the island left by air. The building had been a small warehouse, converted forty years ago to its present use. Around the site was a wire fence covered with vines to prevent the curious from gawking. The gate into the complex was closed and locked, again to prevent the curious from access when Vincent, the only full time employee (owner, funeral director, embalmer and cremator), was not on the premises.

Vincent got out and unlocked the gate, swinging it open. The hearse was driven through and I got out and locked the gate. There was a box by the gate with a sign saying that if one wanted admittance after hours, which it certainly was, one should press the buzzer. Vincent had explained that if he were not on the premises, his cell phone would ring. The hearse had been parked under a porte-cochere and Vincent had the back doors open by the time I got there. We pulled the gurney out and the wheels automatically dropped down and locked. We wheeled the gurney into what I learned was a storage area and prep room and Vincent locked the wheels.

"My instructions are that you are to put the body into the crematory casket. It is on that gurney" and he indicated one, shabby and obviously well used. On it sat a cardboard box as big as a coffin. He obviously noticed my surprise.

"It is a shame to burn an expensive coffin and why waste wood? These are all made from recycled material."

"That seems reasonable," I said.

"It is not standard protocol to have this done, so I am hiring you as an assistant for the evening. I will pay you what I would anyone else – in cash – more to ease my conscience than anything else."

"My friend had a phobia about anyone touching his body, even in death. He rarely – on verge of death – went to the doctor."

This was fact and helped us plan this particular part of Michel's "death."

"Ahh so," he said in a Charlie Chan manner, smiling at me. "Always a little levity when possible. I shall prepare the retort while you handle the preparations here. I will be gone about twenty minutes. Holler if you need me."

Not waiting for an answer, he turned and went through a door in the back wall. No sooner had the door closed behind him with a distinct thud, than I unzipped the top of the body bag. Michel was staring at me, eyes wild with apparent fear.

"Don't say anything," I said. "We are in the mortuary. Are you okay?"

He shook his head violently, then stopped and nodded but the eyes remained wildly alert.

"This is the difficult part. We have to get you to the zodiac and get your replacement in here. Stay still."

I started to zip the bag closed and he shook his head vehemently.

"Right. Just stay calm."

Leaving him I went to the door we had entered just minutes before and opened it. Looking out I saw nothing other than blackness. There were no lights on in the porte-cochere. I was trying to decide how to prop the door open, since I was certain that it locked automatically when I heard a sound. Looking to my left, I saw a bulky form moving toward me. In moments, the smiling face of Joaquin Gagalac appeared in the light filtering through the opening behind me. I could see that he was struggling with a body bag slung over his shoulder.

I opened the door wide and he struggled past me, and started to let the body in the bag go.

"No," I whispered loudly and grabbed at the bag. Together we eased the bag to the floor and Joaquin bent over, hands on his knees, breathing heavily.

"On second thought," he said, "The answer is no. I don't want any part of it."

He looked up at me and smiled, "But it's too late now."

I had contacted him as soon as the plan had come together, asking him to clear at least a month of any other obligations aboard the Banyuhay (Tagalog for "metamorphosis" as he and his wife Jovelyn had renamed the Zàkpa). I had been surprised when I heard the name and its meaning because Quentin Baston had named his new boat Renaissance, a strange name for a fishing vessel. They had joined willingly, no questions asked. Joaquin had been my crew during the time I lived aboard the yacht when I had brought Elise and Howard to Justice and then we had gone around the world. He had reunited with Jovelyn in the Philippines; she had joined our crew and they eventually married. I had given them the yacht with the proviso that if I ever needed it, it would be at my disposal. I had never thought I would collect.

Leaving him to catch his breath, I retrieved the gurney with the retort box, and together we lifted his body bag into it. As we sealed the box, I looked at him questioningly.

"He was a derelict on St. Martin, died a week ago and we claimed him as a long lost cousin. No one questioned us as it saved them money. He has been on ice since then."

I knew he meant it. Together we walked over to the gurney where Michel lay in his body bag. I looked at him, his eyes were closed.

"Michel," I whispered and the eyes flashed open. "We are going to have to move you now. It may hurt but we will be as careful as possible."

Glancing at my watch I noticed that there were twelve minutes remaining of Vincent's twenty.

"Quickly, let's get this gurney out to the gate."

With Joaquin's help, we got the gurney out the door and into blackness toward the harbor. Within twenty feet we came to a fence.

"We had to cut the padlock," Joaquin said. "It was the only way. We made scratches on the door we just came through to make it look like someone attempted to break in. The zodiac is about fifteen feet away."

We each grabbed Michel, I the shoulders and he the feet and as carefully as we could carried Michel to the zodiac, which was docked alongside a wharf but several feet down. We lowered his body onto the wharf, and I climbed into the boat. I got my arms under his knees and shoulders and as quickly as possible lowered him into the zodiac and onto the stretcher Joaquin and Jovelyn had improvised.

"What do I use to tie him on?" I asked Joaquin.

"Bungee cords," he answered. "It's all I had. I'll do it, you get back."

I took a minute to open the body bag where it had collapsed over Michel's face. I could just see the whites of his eyes flitting side to side wildly.

"You'll be safe soon," I said. "Just hang on."

And to Joaquin, "Do you think the two of you can handle him?"

"We have to, don't we," Joaquin said. "Now go."

I climbed up to the wharf and gave him a hand getting down into the zodiac.

"I'll wait here for Jovelyn. She is watching someone in a Smart Car who followed you."

"Probably the man who tried to kill Michel."

Chapter 16

With that I turned and ran to the gate, closed it, and pushed the gurney to the back of the hearse. No sooner had I gotten there and opened the doors than the door to the mortuary opened and Vincent came out.

"There you are!"

"Yes, sorry, I thought I would try to put the gurney back in the hearse. You made it look so easy."

"It is when you know how."

And it was as he proceeded to show me.

"Now, if he is ready, let's get him into the retort."

Together we wheeled the gurney through the door he had exited earlier. We were in a small patio with high walls on both sides; in front of us was a brick wall with several gauges and wheels. In the center was a large metal door with what appeared to be a peephole. Vincent slid two bolts that apparently locked the door and then reaching up unhooked something and, grabbing a chain I hadn't noticed, began pulling it and raised the obviously heavy metal door, revealing an opening. I could feel a wave of heat that wafted out as the door opened.

"Is it on?" I questioned instinctively stepping back.

"No, I lit the afterburner to heat the air in the chimney."

"Why?" I asked querulously.

"To consume any unburned matter from the last time." I winced at the thought. "It helps reduce emissions and that is important nowadays. This is an old retort that my father constructed, but we still have to conform to modern requirements."

"How hot does it get?"

"In the chimney, you mean?   430 degree Celsius, which is over 800 degrees Fahrenheit. That's what I was doing for the twenty minutes you had to say good-bye."

He paused as though he wanted to add "or whatever." But he didn't.

With the door raised above the opening, we maneuvered the gurney forward until it reached the brick wall. The height was a perfect match with the bottom of the retort's door opening. Reaching into the opening, he pulled out a rack and fastening it to the front of the gurney. Together we slid the cardboard coffin onto the rack and I realized that under the cardboard coffin were rollers. It required a bit of effort to get the coffin onto the rack. Then the rack was unhooked, the gurney slid back, and Vincent pushed the rack and its burden into the darkness of the retort. He threw the two bolts and then turned one of the knobs above and to the left of the door. From inside came a loud whoosh as the gas ignited. He moved to the door and opened a small peephole. Looking inside he nodded satisfactorily and turned his head to me, looking over his shoulder.

"Want to say a last good-bye?"

"No thanks. How long does it take?"

"Your friend will be ready for the final stage of his journey in approximately three hours."

"Well, I think I'll get a nap then."

"You could, but you have to stay awake and be certain that the retort functions perfectly."

"Me," I squeaked. I wanted no part of this.

"Yes, remember you are my employee. Part of the bargain. Please come here."

He motioned to the gauges and wheels to the left of the door. The gauges were temperature gauges, one marked Chiminée and the other Chambre à gaz. Vincent pointed to the one marked Chambre à gaz.

"You watch this until the temperature reaches 875 – it's Celsius – which is over 1600 degrees Fahrenheit. At that time the body will continue to consume itself."

I grimaced. Vincent noticed but said nothing.

"Then you turn this wheel," he indicated the one he had turned to bring about that initial whoosh, "counterclockwise. That will shut off the gas."

"That's it?"

"No, watch the gauge. When the temperature falls below 875 you have to turn the gas on again. At this point it will remain on until everything that can be consumed is consumed."

"And that will be when?"

"Three hours from now."

"And where will you be?"

"In my office, attending to other matters. I have a viewing tomorrow afternoon. If you need me, just open the door to the prep room and call."

He pointed into the darkness to the left of the door.

"There is a chair over there you can use. Questions?"

I shook my head no; he looked through the peephole once again, and left.

Thus was my introduction to the mortuary business. I decided early on in the evening to find another line of work.

Outside the mortuary, a block down the street, the behemoth in the Smart Car made a call. When the call was answered, he said, "Assholes to ashes, dust to dust. It is done."

"You're certain."

"As certain as I talk to you. At this moment I am watching the asshole go up in smoke."

Silence on the other end. Then "Our business is over. I have just authorized transfer of the final payment."

"It's been a pleasure." The big man paused. "But you know what? I would have done it for nothing if you had asked. I hated that man."

He started the Smart Car and headed for his hotel where he would arrange for the earliest possible flight out of this tropical hell and back to his beloved Russia, where a man could get a decent vodka, borscht, vodka, pelmeni, vodka, and piroshkies.

Chapter 17

Several minutes after the tail lights had disappeared, the darkness at the top of a palm tree across the street from the mortuary's gate seemed to separate. A dark apparently human form materialized below the top of the tree and made its way agilely down the tree to the ground. Jovelyn, dressed in black from head to toe, looked warily around but all was still. Then she quickly crossed the street, and unlocked the mortuary's gate. Opening it slightly, she slipped through, closed and locked it. Quickly and silently she made her way past the hearse and to the back gate. Through it, she moved quickly along the seawall to the wharf. Stopping at the edge of the wharf, she whistled softly. Hearing an answering whistle, she walked quickly out on the wharf and then lowered herself into the zodiac where Joaquin sat waiting, in the center seat, facing Michel's stretcher across the back since that was the only place it would fit. Jovelyn undid the painter holding the zodiac to the wharf and slid onto the seat beside her husband who handed her an oar. Both fitted oars into the oarlocks; Joaquin pushed them away from the wharf and they began to row. It would take them half an hour to reach their yacht – a trip that would have been made in ten minutes if they could have used the motor but the stretcher prevented that. It was only after they were safely away from the wharf that they risked speaking.

"What happened?" Joaquin asked.

"After the hearse pulled in, a blue Smart Car came down the street, passed, and turned around and parked about fifty meters away. The driver was a big man and he kept the car running and the air conditioning on. He sat there over half an hour until there was smoke from the retort's chimney. It didn't last long but he must have been satisfied because he left soon after that. And I know why the chimney of the retort is so tall – it's the smell."

"Yes, I understand that the smell of a human burning is not pleasant."

"If I had stayed up in that tree much longer I would have gagged. Any word from my mother?"

"Yes," Joaquin paused in his rowing and Jovelyn did also. "She caught the plane and will arrive in St. Martin tomorrow evening. She is bringing as many medical supplies as she can, but we will need to talk to Mrs. Joseph in the morning and find out if we need to do anything special."

He then told her about giving Daws (whom they knew as Joseph) the body and getting Michel onto the zodiac. Both up to date on the happenings, they went back to the rowing, staying close to the island in the harbor until they could make straight for their anchorage. Reaching the Banyuhay, they tied the zodiac with both bow and stern lines. Jovelyn climbed aboard while Joaquin loosened the bungee cords holding the stretcher to the zodiac. Opening the flap of the body bag, he whispered to Michel, "We are at our yacht. We will get you below and out of this bag as quickly and as painlessly as we can."

It wasn't easy, but with Jovelyn pulling and Joaquin lifting they managed to get the stretcher onto the yacht and then below to the master cabin. Placing the stretcher on the bed, they undid the straps holding the body bag and unzipped the bag, then moved Michel onto the bed as smoothly as possible. His eyes were alert and questioning.

"We are friends of Joseph. You are on our yacht – it was his yacht."

"Zàkpa," croaked Michel Villar .

"Yes," Joaquin said. "We will care for you. Just rest for now."

They brought out the monitoring equipment they had purchased and been trained on and attached the leads to Michel. Jovelyn set up an IV drip and attached it to Michel via the entry still in his arm. By then Michel had fallen asleep.

The two stole quietly from the room and went to theirs where they stripped off their dark clothing and put on their standard gear. They were frequent visitors to the port and were friends with the customs agents and had been cleared for an early morning departure. They secured the zodiac in its place and raised anchor. With Joaquin at the helm of the flying bridge and Jovelyn acting as nurse, the Banyuhay (nee Zàkpa) slid silently out of the harbor bearing Michel Villar out of harm's way – hopefully.

Chapter 18

A wise man once said or wrote, I don't remember which, "It is always darkest just before dawn." Or something like that. I am not a scholar and don't know if anyone knows who said it first or if he was a wise man, but as I stood on the wharf in the St. Nantes' harbor at 4:45 a.m. I could certainly agree. He (or she not to be sexist) could have been standing where I was. Maybe it wasn't darkest but it certainly was the quietest. There was no wind, little wave motion and I could hear no waves lapping. There were streetlights on, a few scattered ones along the wharf area just for safety's sake I guess, but there was no one else around.

In my hands, I had a cloth bag containing a cardboard box with the purported cremains of Michel Villar. I had stood my watch faithfully, watching the temperature and making all the necessary adjustments. At the end of the three hours I had shouted for Vincent but he had not come. I shouted a second time with the same response and was heading across the prep room to find him when he appeared. I could see from the condition of his clothing that his preparations for tomorrow's – make that today's – viewing included, and may have been entirely composed of, a conference with Morpheus.

He looked into the chamber via the peephole and declared the cremation completed, turned off the gas and headed back to his office.

"What now?" I had asked.

"We have a one hour cooling and then we will gather the cremains."

"Cremains?" I said querulously.

"Yes," he turned. "The remains of a body after cremation. I don't know who came up with the term but it is what people say although I find it distasteful."

"I agree."

After the one hour cool down which I spent again cooling my heels, Vincent opened the door. Inside I could see a skeleton.

"I thought it would be ash," I said.

"It is," Vincent said and used a long handle shovel like a fireplace tool, to poke the "skeleton" which collapsed into ashes. These cremains were swept into the square opening in the middle of the chamber's floor through which gas had been introduced. Walking around to the right side, Vincent opened a small door and pulled out a long tray containing the cremains that looked for all the world like the ashes from a fireplace. He poked around in them looking for any metal (artificial hips, etc.) and found none, thankfully as Michel Villar had none. Then the ashes were put into the cardboard box (no sense in buying an urn for a burial at sea, Michel had opined and it was his funeral). I called a cab and thanked Vincent for his services as he closed the gate behind me. The cab had brought me here.

As I stood waiting, I heard two sounds – first, the engine of a boat and then a car's engine which grew louder quicker. There was a squeak of brakes followed by the sound of a car door shutting, a chirp as the locks were set, and then footsteps coming in my direction.

"Uh, Daws," the voice said and I turned to face Guillaume Martineau, face-to-face for the first time.

He was a big man, probably six feet one and two hundred forty, having put on some weight in the last year. My first impression was that of Herman Munster and I thought that if he were, he wouldn't have been agile enough to partner with Michel Villar and win all those island doubles championships. To add to the Frankenstein likeness, he had red hair and grey-green eyes that seem to glow like a cat's in the faint light of one of the wharf's lights. I stuck my hand out.

"Yes, I am Daws. A pleasure to meet you."

He stood staring at me, not offering his hand in return.

"I don't know who you are or how you managed to weasel yourself into Michel's good graces but ..."

"Hold on there," I said, raising the proffered hand like a policeman stopping traffic. "If anyone did any weaseling, it was Michel. I didn't know him until about two months ago."

He started to protest.

"Right, right. I was at the trial of the brother-in-law and sister of that American. Can't remember his name ..."

"Stuart Andrews."

"Yes, I guess so. But I didn't know Michel. I was just an observer. A couple of months ago he came to me for financial advice."

"But he needed no advice ..."

"Not to make money but to keep it – no, to be honest – to hide it. He was worried that someone was after him and his money and he thought he might have to flee. He said he couldn't – wouldn't – trust anyone who had been around him for a while. He said he was sorry and knew that you would take it the wrong way, but what he was going to do might be seen by some as illegal and he didn't want to get anyone involved – especially you. You were his best friend.

"He had this feeling that something bad was going to happen, and that is why he conceived his new will. You know that he didn't like strangers touching him in any way."

"Aphephobia, I think. It came on in the last couple of years," Guillaume said and I could see a great sadness in his eyes. "Lately, he hasn't even wanted to shake hands."

This was true. It was a phobia of Michel's for which he couldn't trace an origin and we had decided to accentuate it.

"But not with you," I confided.

"No, there was nothing like that. Only a little distance that seems to have grown recently."

"I understand."

Behind me I could hear a boat's motor being cut to idle and then a gentle thump as it came in contact with the wharf. I turned and saw Quentin's fishing boat alongside the wharf; he was forward making a line fast to a divot.

"Looks like our ride is here. We have about a forty-five minute ride to get beyond the twelve-mile limit to avoid any legal problems. Let's get aboard and continue our talk."

We walked side by side to the Renaissance where Quentin greeted us.

"Good morning, Monsieur Daws," he said, teeth of a broad smile gleaming in the dim light. I had hired him a month before for a fishing excursion and he hadn't known who I was until he had arrived at the wharf to pick up Tres and me. As with Joaquin and Jovelyn, he had only known me as Joseph and I had to acquaint him with my new name. We had a great morning fishing, hooking and landing six fish, which was a great difference from the previous two times I have been fishing with him aboard Mahi Mahi, his former boat that we had to destroy to keep him alive. In fact, possibly only a few hours ahead of The Facilitator, whom my brother-in-law Howard had hired to eliminate the only other witness to my drowning. Well, not the only other witness – there was Keith Mitchell who turned out to be the weak link and whose deathbed confession led to the conviction of Howard and Elise, my wife.

"Good morning, Quentin," I said. "This is Guillaume Martineau, who will be accompanying us today."

"Morning, Monsieur Martineau. It is a beautiful day and there will be a beautiful sunrise. I zink it will be a proper sendoff for you friend," he said, crossing himself.

Chapter 19

Guillaume Martineau and I sat on the stern as Quentin took the Renaissance out of the harbor of St. Nantes heading for the open international waters of the Caribbean. For a few minutes we were quiet, then I began.

"I don't know a lot about the problems that Michel had. He was secretive pretty much on that. He had the feeling that someone was after him – wanted him dead. He didn't know whom or why – at least that is what he told me. He said he might have to disappear and wanted to know that his money would be safe.

"I worked in the financial market and had, for myself, squirreled away some money."

Guillaume Martineau looked at me questioningly, "Squirreled?"

"Hidden, like a squirrel … hmm, no squirrels … animals who collected foodstuffs and hide them for a time when food is scare. Or like a miser who buries his money in a jar in his backyard."

"Oh, I see," said Guillaume Martineau. "But how did …"

"I don't know how he knew he actually was in trouble or if whether he just suspected he was in trouble. I helped him hide some of his money…"

"Then it's not hidden," Guillaume Martineau said, "if you know where it is."

"No, what I mean is that I taught him how to do it and I guess he did it. At least he told me he did."

"But why the cremation so quickly and why you?"

"The cremation so quickly was because of his phobia – the thought of a mortician embalming him was something he abhorred. So he set up the cremation and asked me to assist because he didn't want you to have that as a last memory of him. And believe me, it is something you wouldn't want to have done. I am sorry that I had to do it. I don't know how anyone can be a mortician – even a funeral director dealing with dead people all the time."

"It was that bad ...?"

"I thought it was. Just be thankful that your last vision of him is alive."

"But he is there," Guillaume Martineau indicated the bag I held.

"No, he's not."

Guillaume Martineau looked at me not understanding what I meant.

"What Michel Villar was is not in this box. In this box are the ashes of a vehicle that was home to a human's essence, soul, or whatever you want to call it. When that body ceased to function, the essence – whatever it is – ceased to exist, at least in that vehicle. That essence is ..." and I waved my free arm at the horizon already starting to be tinged with the colors of a new morning.

For a moment Guillaume Martineau was silent and then he said, "May I?" and reached for the cloth bag. I gave it to him and he sat holding it during the rest of our trip.

Some twenty minutes later, Quentin slowed the Renaissance until it sat gently rocking in the small swells of the Caribbean. There was no landfall to be seen, at least not without considerable effort and a good pair of binoculars. Guillaume Martineau opened the bag, reached in and pulled the box out.

He and I stood up and he turned to the stern opening the lid of the box. He looked at me and I nodded. For a brief moment, he looked at the contents of the box and then holding it out, he turned the box over and the ashes poured out and into the Caribbean. I saw tears steaming down his face and he made no effort to staunch them.

" Adieu, Michel," he said. "Repos de Dieu votre âme." (God rest your soul.) And dropped the box and the lid into the water. Then he turned and sat down on the gunnel his face in his hands and he wept. I felt sorry for him; I wished that I could tell him but I couldn't. Michel said not to trust anyone and other than a very few, I didn't. I nodded to Quentin who eased the throttle forward and started the Renaissance on its way back to St. Nantes.

It was at this point that the irony of it all hit me and I saw the message I had written on the back of a picture of the island's harbor:

Four went out, three came back.

We know what happened!

Part III

The Inquisition of St. George

Chapter 20

He was undoubtedly the biggest man I had ever seen. He filled the doorway almost from top to bottom and easily from side to side, and that was with me looking at him from inside and him standing outside. At first I thought him to be a mortician or funeral director from the manner in which he was dressed, complete with the starched white shirt and somber tie that I thought was black with red caskets on it. I guess that is why I thought he was a funeral director, but then the caskets appeared to morph into drops of blood and I realized that whosoever and whatsoever he was it certainly was associated with death and, I thought morbidly, it was most likely mine.

That thought surged from deep within the recesses of my brain when I noticed the bulge under his right coat pocket – he was definitely carrying and I wasn't. *Why not?* I thought. *I always did when I answered the door.* Tres had yelled at me that a car was approaching – I was in the backyard puttering with some flowers I was trying to grow – blood red roses, a new variety I had read about. I had raced up the steps to the deck and into the house. She was standing behind the bar where one of our gun safes was with a drink in her hand, and here it was only ten in the morning. It was probably water but there was a lime in it. Also strange. I hadn't stopped but had just gone straight for the door. A definite death wish.

Now I faced Mister Pork Pie, a name I gave him because of the completely incongruous hat he wore. I had seen it before but where ... where? My mind raced, running through histories, scanning, searching like a Google search when someone types in "pork pie hat" and hits enter. Bear Bryant? That was it, the famous checkered pork pie hat. No, no, it was a houndstooth hat. Then who had a pork pie hat?

It was hot outside already but it almost always is in the middle of the summer on St. Nantes. It would get hotter later in the day, which is why I was outside gardening. Better in the cool of the morning than the heat of the afternoon.

He was hot. I could see the sweat drops beginning to form on his brow, just under the brim of his hat. Soupy Sales – that was it! Soupy Sales wore a pork pie hat didn't he? I don't know! I am too young. He definitely was not Soupy Sales because he was black. Not Soupy Sales – he was white. Mr. Pork Pie Hat was black as the night sky with no stars out. I stupidly just stared at him, transfixed by the drop of sweat that was starting to run down the bridge of his nose, having already made its way from the hat down his forehead and between his eyebrow. How could the drop have made it between his eyebrow?

Then he opened his mouth and I jerked back a bit as though the words I expected to hear were going to blast me. But he didn't speak – he just smiled. A gleaming white and black smile. Not completely white and black because the front two top teeth were gold. On either side of them was black as there were no other top teeth but there were teeth on the bottom, gleaming white teeth, impeccably white. But only two top teeth.

Then he moved – well, he didn't move, his hands did. His right had been hanging straight down at his side, just like his left hand. That one I could see but the right one was hidden until he moved it, blocked from my view by the size of the door. Not the size of the door or even the doorway, but his size. Have I said he was huge? He was easily two Roosevelt Griers.

His hand moved slowly upward and toward me until it stopped about eighteen inches from my face, while his left had moved up outstretched toward my left until it was in line with my navel, thumb up waiting to be shaken. In his right hand and directly in front of my eyes was a black leather case, one half held in his clenched fingers and the other half dangling down displaying a gold shield like a police badge because that is what it was. On it was the outline of St. Nantes complete with Guerre Isle over which was written in raised letters *Prefecture of St. Nantes* and under it three numbers: 666.

And then he spoke. "Do I have the honor of addressing Mr. Andrews? Mr. Stuart Andrews?"

Chapter 21

It was always the same. Night after night for the past three weeks.

"Do I have the honor of addressing Mr. Andrews? Mr. Stuart Andrews?"

And I would wake up and find myself sitting up in bed, sweat cascading down my face. Usually Tres was sitting up beside me – the first night she had been terrified, just as I had been but then she knew, we both knew, that it was only a dream.

No, a nightmare. A nightmare based on fact. Inspector St. George wasn't that big but he was big, and he was black – like a native islander – and he did wear a ridiculous pork pie hat even on the hottest of days and insisted on wearing starched white shirts with a somber tie. When he first appeared on my doorstep the tie was dark with red skulls. The realization had sent chills up and down my spine. Tres had called me to the door and I had been in the front yard weeding a bed of cacti and other indigenous plants. She had been behind the bar but the drink in her left hand was water with lemon and my Berretta was in her right. Hers was lying on the bar just in front of her. She handed me the pistol.

"Just in case," I said.

"As always," was her reply. "And maybe even more so now."

Through the peephole in the front door I could see the street but there was nothing there. Unexpectedly there was a knock on the door. I looked through the door's peephole and saw nothing. Not wanting to appear anxious or even expectant, I waited. After what I thought was too long, there was another rap at the door. This one a little more persistent I thought. Once again I peeped. This time I saw something. A gold badge with the outline of St. Nantes complete with Guerre Isle over which was written in raised letters *Prefecture of St. Nantes* and under it two numbers: 66. I opened the door.

Standing there was the biggest man I had ever seen – in person. He was easily six feet six and weighed in excess of three hundred pounds, but none of it was fat; by that I mean that he seemed to have the body of an athlete. I wanted to make some smart comment about the badge but didn't.

"Yes," I said displaying my empty hands having tucked the Berretta into the waistband of my pants in the small of my back, with the safety off – just in case.

Then he smiled and the whiteness of his teeth was dazzling against his dark face, except for the two gold teeth in front. He had the rest of his upper teeth, at least from what I could see.

"Mr. Em-BAY-oh? Mr. Day-woo Em-BAY-oh? Please excuse my mispronunciation. I am unfamiliar with Sierra Leone."

"I understand," I said trying to smile. "I am used to it."

I didn't even bother to correct him.

"What can I do for you, officer? Sorry, I don't know your rank."

"Lieutenant, Detective Lieutenant St. George."

"I haven't seen you around before," I said truthfully.

"I just arrived today," he said. "From St. Martin. May I come in?"

I was startled by his forwardness.

"Uh," I stammered. "What is this about?"

"The death of a friend."

"A friend of whom," I said, " I don't …"

"If you would be so kind to invite me in out of this heat, I would be happy to explain."

He paused expectantly.

"Or, we could have this conversation at Fort Rideau."

My decision was forced by this since Fort Rideau on Guerre Island housed the island's gendarmes. I stepped back and extended my hand indicating the way to the great room.

"May I take your hat," I said as he doffed the pork pie just before entering the dark coolness of the foyer.

"Thanks, but I will keep it."

I closed the door behind him and followed him into the great room. He walked straight to the glass wall and looked out at the expanse of Caribbean. I glanced to my right and saw Tres, still standing behind the bar that she was wiping with a damp rag.

"Can I offer you a glass of water, Detective," I said as I leaned over the bar to kiss her while sliding my pistol into her hand that then disappeared behind the bar. No sense being uncomfortable.

"That is most kind," he said as he turned and moved toward the sitting area. "Why don't you ask Miss Jones to do the honors and you come and sit with me."

He sat in one of the armchairs and swiveled it to face the other, as though being in his own home and me the guest.

I nodded at Tres and she smiled, a questioning look on her face, and started preparing two glasses of water. I walked around the sofa and sat in the other chair that I turned to face St. George as I passed behind it.

"Now what is it I can do for you, Detec... Lieutenant?" I asked.

"Nothing to be worried about, Mr. Mbayo."

Tres set down a crystal tray bearing three glass of water on the coffee table and handed St. John a glass of water that he took in his left hand, holding the pork pie in his right. Tres picked up the other two glasses and moved toward me extending one glass.

"How well did you know Judge Michel Villar?" St. George asked.

The glass of water Tres was bringing me hitting the floor and shattering, spewing water and glass everywhere, punctuated the question.

Chapter 22

For a few seconds you could have heard a pin drop –
actually I heard water dripping from somewhere and, for a
brief moment, an ice cube skittering across the blue tile
floor.   Tres just stood there looking astonished and
frightened.   Then she laughed, setting her glass on the
table as she bent over to start picking up the glass and ice
cubes.

"I'm a klutz," she said semi-apologetically.   "I guess
the glass was slippery from the perspiration."

St. George looked at his glass, the outside of which
was completely dry and then at Tres's, which had not a
hint of water showing.   A quizzical look crossed his face
and then a wry smile, reminiscent of Michel Villar's.

"Strange, he said, "my glass ..."

"Oh," said Tres straightening up and looking at hers
and his as she started for the bar.   "Yours and mine are a
synthetic – they won't break.   But Daws won't drink out
of anything but glass."

"That's right," I said.   "A funny habit of mine."

St. George looked at his glass and then at Tres.   He
held his up and dropped it.   The air was punctuated with a
loud THONK as the glass hit the floor volcanically
spewing water and ice and rebounding several inches into
the air.   Then it thonked quietly back on the tiles, fell on
its side and rolled across the floor toward Tres, who was
returning from the bar with towels, a dust pan and brush.

"This is another fine mess you've gotten us into,
Ollie," she said in one of her famous non-impressions.

She set the towels on the table and started sweeping ice cubes and glass fragments into the dustpan.

"I believe it is 'another nice mess,' " St. George said, "if one wants to be truly accurate. The title of the film was *Another Fine Mess* but Stan always said 'another nice mess.' "

Tres stopped her sweeping and she and I both started disbelievingly at St. George.

"I am a bit of a Laurel and Hardy connoisseur," he explained. "I have all their films and watch one almost every night. I just can't get enough."

"Then why the pork pie and not a bowler?" I asked.

"Because I look stupid in a bowler."

Tres looked as though she wanted to say something but didn't.

"I know," St. George said for her, "I don't look good in a pork pie either, and it is a bit ridiculous in this climate, but I like it."

While Tres was cleaning up, I picked up St. George's glass, went to the bar and replenished it, got myself a drink in a glass glass, returned just as Tres was finishing, handed St. George his drink, and resumed my seat. I had considered getting my armament but decided against it. I still had no idea where we were headed. Tres gathered the towels in one hand, dustpan in the other.

"I'll leave you two," she said and started for the bar, passing behind St. George.

"I'd really like you to stay," he said.

Tres's steps stuttered but didn't stop.

"Certainly," she said and she went behind the bar. There was clinking and clattering as the ice and glass were deposited into the wastebasket. She put the towels into the hamper, the dustpan and brush back on the hook and made herself a drink. Returning she took a seat on the couch near me and was about to set her drink on the table when she saw her other drink near St. George.

She smiled at me and then, looking at St. George, said, "I am really thirsty," and took a huge swallow of its contents, almost draining the glass. Then she reached and picked up her original glass.

St. George smiled that wry smile. "I seem to have that effect on some people."

Turning to me he continued, "Now about Judge Michel Villar."

The distraction provided by Tres's slip had given me a few minutes to think about the possibilities but I still decided to play dumb.

"You mean the Judge who was killed in an automobile accident recently?"

"Actually, he died as a result of the accident. At least that is what I am told." St. George took a drink of water. "But yes, that judge."

"First, are you recording this conversation?"

St. George looked at me momentarily stunned. For a few moments at least I had the upper hand.

"Well, I ..."

"Because if you are, then this conversation is over and, I guess at least according to the television, we can continue this at the station."

I had seen the flashing blue light on the console beneath the flat panel television in front of the sitting area. I was constantly sweeping the place for bugs of any kind. Yes, I was that paranoid.

St. George reached into his left coat pocket and the flashing blue light became dark.

"Not any longer."

"Good, now what are you looking for?"

"Were you friends with Michel Villar?"

"Why do you ask?"

"Answer my ..."

"Why do you ask?"

St. George sat quietly for a moment.

"There are questions about his death."

"But he died from injuries in the accident, didn't he?"

I asked this looking at Tres.

She looked at me and then at St. George.

"You know I was there when he coded?"

St. George smiled wryly at her.

"He had a DNR and a request for immediate cremation and his ashes spread at sea. This was done."

"How do you know?"

"Because I was there and stopped the crash team from reviving him. Then I sat with him until the mortuary hearse arrived. I watched him put into the hearse."

"Did you go with the hearse to the crematory?"

"No," I said. "I did."

Chapter 23

St. George looked at me.

"You?"

I nodded.

"Why?"

"Because he asked me to."

This was a fact. He had become paranoid about possibly dying and having the disposal of his "husk" – his word – held up by legalities.

"Why you?"

"I don't really know. Maybe because I barely knew him and he felt more comfortable with a stranger doing it rather than burdening a friend."

"Right. How long had you known him?"

"Less than two months. I don't remember exactly." I looked at Tres. "Do you? The day he came seeking help?"

"No, not exactly. Oh," she said looking at St. George, "I remember when he showed up on the door step but I don't remember the date."

St. George thought a moment, then said, "No, I don't believe you were there."

"Yes, I was." Tres looked at me for reassurance. "I saw him coming … heard him and …"

"I know all about your security setup," St. George said. "Well, not all about it but I know what you have and know that you would have been alerted to a visitor just as you were alerted to my arrival."

He looked at me.

"Tres wasn't there that first time, was she?"

I looked at him not comprehending.

"A year ago. When he came to the Zàkpa, wasn't it?"

Once I picked myself off the floor, I sat dumbfounded. How had he known? He wasn't even at the trial. I would have seen him – a man of his size is difficult to hide.

"The Zàkpa?" queried Tres.

"Yes," St. George said. "His yacht."

Tres looked at me.

"It wasn't mine," I managed to get out. "It belonged to a friend."

"A South African friend?" St. George asked, the edges of his probe sharpened and beginning to color with blood.

I nodded dumbly totally mystified.

"How?"

"Oh, it's in the reports. There were questions about his scurrilous behavior and an investigation had been ongoing for several months, even before that trial."

"What exactly …, " I managed.

"That is not germane to this conversation."

"Well, if he was under investigation then and I am now …"

"You are not under investigation … at least not yet." St. George smiled wryly at me. "What is under investigation is the death of Michel Villar." He paused poignantly. "And your involvement. Now back to my question. How long have you known Michel Villar?"

I sank back in my seat, my entire lives beginning to unravel before me.

"That last day of the trial. He came to the yacht as we were preparing to leave."

"What did he want?"

"He wanted to know why I was there reporting on it to a newspaper."

"You were a reporter?"

"Only out of convenience. I happened to be in the Caribbean and was asked to attend the trial and send reports."

"Why?"

"I don't know. Friends knew where I was and must have told the editor of the paper."

"Why would people in Sierra Leone be interested in that trial?"

"I asked the editor that and was told that it had become an international curiosity. Then he asked since I was there, would I attend and send some reports?"

"And you did?"

"Yes, I had just sent the last one when the judge showed up. He asked the same questions you have and I gave him the same answers."

"And did he know you as Dawoh Mbayo or Josef Viljoen?"

Chapter 24

Things had gotten out of hand. St. George knew too much. How much more he knew, I had no idea, but if I didn't get this inquisition stopped, it would lead him to the truth.

"I don't know if he ever knew about Josef Viljoen. He knew me as Dawoh Mbayo." I was trying to stay ahead but not succeeding very well. What was he after and how did he know all this?

"Who is Josef Viljoen?" Tres asked. She really didn't know.

"Someone who never existed," St. George said smugly as though he had known where this was going and where it would end.

"That's not true," I said. "I was Josef Viljoen for most of my life."

Both of them stared at me.

"Please explain," St. George said. I could tell that I had him, at least for a moment.

"Africa is a land of retributions, a land of tribal rights, of racial cleansings. My family was a victim of such things. I would have been dead long ago if it were not for the foresight of my father and friends that he had.

"We were not native to Sierra Leone – my father moved the family there when extermination in our homeland seemed inevitable."

"And where was that?" St. George asked. He obviously didn't know. But then, neither did I.

"That is not important … and don't bother asking because I won't tell you. I won't even tell you my real name because my life would surely be forfeit, even now."

That was no lie.

I continued. "We thought we were safe in Sierra Leone, but my father never stopped worrying. When the inevitable exterminators started to close in once again, he worked his magic for my sister and me. We were both taken at night – given by our parents to people whom we didn't know. My sister went with one group and I with another. I don't know where she went, I'll never know and she – if she still lives – knows nothing and will never know more of me.

"I was taken to England, given a different name and raised to manhood, never knowing what had happened to the rest of my family. It was only a few years ago that I was told the truth. I should have stopped then – just continued my comfortable and safe life – but I couldn't. I had to know more. My parents – or foster parents if you must – knew nothing of my background. That was intentional. All they knew was that later the same night that we were taken away, my family members who remained behind were burned to death in our home. As far as we know – as far as I know – our enemies thought that my sister and I were in the house.

"I have tried to find more. I spent six months in Sierra Leone but to no avail. I could find nothing – no trace – and I had the advantage of knowing who I was and what to look for but there was nothing. My handlers – for want of a better word – were (perhaps are) very good and there was no trace.

"I used the identity I had been given of Josef Viljoen for several years but when I felt that it had served its purpose, when I felt that I was really safe in my truer identity, Josef disappeared."

I noticed St. George ready to interject something.

"Oh, there are traces for the last months that Josef existed, things that I could not erase because I didn't and still don't have that ability. At that point, at my own insistence, I was on my own. My handlers agreed with my decision because it was important to know if I had survival instincts. I wanted to live free, so to speak, without the bodyguards who were around me although unseen most of my life.

"Oh, I still have my security, I still value my isolation but my life – and the existence of Dawoh Mbayo begins only a year or so ago."

Again St. George started to inject something but I wouldn't let him.

"Oh, yes, the identity was created longer ago than that, but that was because we, I, wanted to know if there would be any interest. Once I, we, felt there wasn't, I was permitted to go on my own."

St. George sat passively, thinking. Did he believe? Tres did, I could tell by the wetness of her eyes. She is a sucker for a sad story.

Chapter 25

"So Josef surfaced in Amsterdam and lived for just a few months?" St. George asked.

"Oh, no, he was around before that but you won't find him. There are traces of me also around that time but just to see if there was interest. Josef took over while we waited but once we were certain that there was no interest, we put Josef to bed so to speak."

St. George was quiet.

"So if I look ..."

"You will find nothing. Look, St. George, you wanted answers. I didn't want to give them to you but I know people like you. You will keep looking – and I can't stop you – but you are wasting your time. My handlers are that good."

"But the CIA, MI5, Direction Centrale de la Police Judiciaire, ..."

"Are not even in the same league and I can't tell you what that is, because I don't know. Even government organizations in Sierra Leone know nothing of me other than I exist."

I hadn't been able to come up with anything and that was just as well.

"Well, still ..."

"What?"

"Why did Michel Villar come to you two months ago on ..." and he gave the day of the week and the date. At least he knew.

"Money."

"Money?" St. George sounded perplexed.

"Yes, money. Or rather ways to hide money. I am well off financially – some with family money which was hidden away and the rest of my own."

"How ...," St. George stammered.

I thought I had him on the ropes and wanted a knockout but couldn't come up with the sucker punch.

"Did I make my money? I am afraid that I will have to pass on that. Leave it to say that Michel knew I could make money and hide it. How he found out I don't know. Why he was looking, I don't know and I guess never will. Our relationship was brief and one sided – his side. He wanted information from me and offered me nothing except my privacy and security. At this time in my life ..." and I smiled at Tres who smiled back mystified but understanding "... those are very, very important to me."

St. George sat silently, although his fingers were drumming on the coffee table top.

I didn't know if anything I said could be verified or disputed in anyway. It would take a lot of digging to get to the bottom of the hole that I had dug for myself. Regardless, as Collin Raye said in song, "*Well, that's my story and I'm sticking to it.*"

"If it was just money," St. George asked, "why were you the one to accompany him to the crematory and to the burial at sea?"

He was no slouch, he knew a lot, and I was wondering if it was from the same source as Michel Villar's knowledge.

"He was a bit paranoid, had a phobia about people touching him. Aphephobia I believe it is called. It had gotten worse during the last couple of years. You can ask his best friend Guillaume Martineau."

"I have."

He had done his homework.

"He felt that someone was out to get him. Why I don't know, but that is what he told me. He didn't trust anyone completely, not even Guillaume."

"But he trusted you?"

"I guess. You'll have to ask … Sorry, I keep forgetting he's dead. He was making a new will and he asked me to be there when he was cremated and when his ashes were spread at sea just to be certain that his body wasn't violated in any way."

"But his ashes are just that."

"Not if you believe in voodoo and witchcraft."

"He didn't believe, did he?"

"I don't think so – he never said for certain but I sort of got that impression. So my job – at his request because I certainly wouldn't have volunteered especially now that I have been through it – was to insure that the sanctity of his body was not violated."

"And Vincent, the mortician?"

"Never touched him, actually never saw him."

"Then you are the only one …"

"No," Tres interrupted. "I did. I helped put him into the body bag and accompanied it to the hearse where Daws and Vincent took over."

"That's very convenient, isn't it," mused St. George. "You being there and all?"

Chapter 26

"He came in on my regular shift and I volunteered to stay with him after his surgery."

"Why?"

"For the same reason that Daws was with his body. He had a fear of people touching him. He had to have the surgery or he would have died …"

"But he did …"

"Yes, he did. But without it … oh, what does it matter? It's what happened."

She stood up, tears streaming down her face. "I liked him. He was a nice man and he was all alone."

She turned and walked to the bar.

St. George looked at me as if to say "I'm sorry", but I don't believe he was. I was getting tired of his digging and where it might get him.

"Now, if you have nothing further, Inspector St. George, we value our privacy."

"So you don't …"

"No, we don't."

St. George started to stand and then sat back down.

"Very well, but let me tell you a couple of things that we have found strange about the judge's death."

"Strange?" I thought thinking about the bolts we had replaced.

"Yes, actually these things make it look more like murder rather than an accident."

"Murder!" Tres said. "But he didn't die in the accident."

"That is true," St. George said, "But he did die – supposedly – as a result of the accident."

Tres started to say something but kept her mouth shut.

"And what are these strange things?" I queried.

"His air bag had been disconnected quite expertly so that no alarm was given."

Well, that explained the seriousness of his injuries.

"Also there was a bomb attached to his gas tank."

"A bomb!" we both exclaimed.

"Yes, it was small but would have made a great explosion and undoubtedly he would have been killed. It was remotely controlled but a tree had landed it on and rendered it inert. I suppose that the judge was fortunate in this. At least for a little while."

"That's awful," Tres said. "Who would want to ..."

St. George sat there waiting for her to finish but she turned away.

I stood and walked toward the door. Behind me I heard the cushion sucking air back into it as St. George stood.

"Thank you for your time, Miss Jones."

Tres said nothing but I suspect that 1) she nodded or 2) stared at him noncommittally. If I had to, I would have voted for the second. By the time I reached the door, I could hear St. George's footfalls on the foyer tiles – smaller room, more of an echo and Tres was barefoot. I opened the door and stood aside. St. George brushed past me and paused on the threshold. He turned to look at me.

"If I need to talk to you ..."

"I'll be here unless I'm not."

He stared at me contemplatively, nodded, donned his pork pie hat at a rakish angle, and walked toward his car

across the yard of sand and local flora. There were no
windows on the back of the house and I didn't care what
the neighbors saw. My only gardening interests, which
were minor, were in the front of the house, the part that
faced the Caribbean. It's waterfront property, not …
never mind.

St. George got into this car which was too small for
him but anything other than a Suburban or Expedition
would have been too small for him. He sat there
momentarily, started the car, looked toward the house,
and then drove off.

"Glad he's gone," Tres said, startling me as I had not
heard her approach, never did if she was barefoot.

"Now what's all that about, Josef?"

I turned to her and she stepped back into the coolness
of the foyer and out of the light of the sun. I closed the
door and wrapped my arms around her, her lips finding
mine hungrily. After a wonderful eternity, she rested her
head on my chest.

"I don't think I could have been with him another
minute."

"You were wonderful. You gave just the right
appearance of shock and disbelief."

"I was shocked with disbelief. Where did that all
come from?"

I laughed.

"Honestly, I don't know. I had to do something and
for some time I have known it, so I have done some
research and thinking."

"Can he check?"

"Certainly but he won't find anything as there is
nothing to find. Hopefully it will keep him off the correct
path but I don't know for how long. As I told you,

Michel found out so other people can if they know where to look, I guess."

"So we are safe?"

"For now."

The dream didn't start that night but it did the following one.

* * *

The next morning we were sitting out on the deck enjoying a last cup of coffee.

"Whose side is he on?" Tres asked.

"Who?" I said although I knew.

"St. George. Is he a good guy or a bad guy?"

"Who are the good guys?"

"Us and Beecher, Joaquin, Jovelyn, Quentin and his family…"

"And the bad guys?"

"The Facilitator, Cercle des Frères …"

"I noticed there is an exception – Michel Villar," I interjected.

"Yes, he's gray. I am thinking there are those that are not just black and white, good or bad; there are some who don't fit."

"Like Michel. So you are certain he is telling the truth?"

"No, I think he is telling the truth – some of it but not all of it. He is a secretive person. I can tell he is not telling the whole truth."

"Maybe just what we need to know? Or is it more just what he wants us to know."

"Both."

There was some silence between us.

"And where does St. George belong?" I asked.

"I don't know. Is he after Michel or is he after you?"

"Could he just be seeking the truth?"

"Certainly. But for whom? For the authorities or for Cercle des Frères? Good or bad?"

"There could be someone else. Like the French government. If Michel was, and I definitely believe he was, hiding money, then he didn't pay taxes on it and maybe the government was after him for the taxes."

"Like you."

"Me – Daws Mbayo? I have done nothing wrong!"

"As Michel said, 'that is debatable.' Legally you could be a murderer."

"Okay – so there are some gray areas as you said. I guess I need to talk to Michel."

"On the phone?"

"No, face to face."

"Where is he?"

"Don't know for certain other than he is on the Banyuhay. I'll call Joaquin and we'll set something up."

Chapter 27

Three days later that I found myself sitting in a zodiac in the Caribbean watching Quentin and the Renaissance heading away, fishing lines trailing behind as Quentin went in search of fish to sell. We left early in the morning before much of Genivee was astir so that no one would see us. Using a GPS and coordinates Joaquin had given us over the phone, we located the zodiac that Joaquin had prepared and dropped. In calm seas it had been relatively easy. The painter, supported on an oar, had a loop tied in the end and we simply had to snag it with a boat hook and pull it alongside so I could get it. It may seem ridiculous but if we were being watched on radar the zodiac couldn't be seen unless the radar was very close. Of course there are planes – but that would make me overly paranoid.

I didn't like sitting here because it took me back to the episode that had started me on my current path – the fishing excursion with my no-good brother-in-law Howard and his equally no-good friend Keith. A "friendly" bop on the head with a beer bottle and I was in the Caribbean, lucky to be alive. Sixteen hours later I came ashore on a small island near The House at The End of the Road. The rest is history, but that doesn't make me any happier about being out there in a small rubber raft with no one in sight other than Quentin's Renaissance just a speck in the distance.

I had time sitting there to think about things, especially what went wrong with the "accident." The main thing, of course, was the idiotic move by Michel Villar telling The Facilitator about the plan. That was an effort to keep him from being killed but it backfired, of course, and almost did get him killed. Save for that tree falling on the gas tank bomb, Michel Villar's estate could have saved the cost of the cremation because the car fire would pretty much have done the job. He wouldn't have cared and it would have, quite possibly, made my life a lot simpler. And I might not have made the acquaintance of St. George. And I wouldn't be sitting in this raft either. And I wouldn't ... no, I still would be worried about Cercle des Frères

For all my worries, I was only in the water about fifteen minutes before Joaquin cruised by in the Banyuhay and picked me up. As I climbed aboard, I noticed an apparent stranger sitting in a chair sunning himself. The individual was bald (not completely but obviously had shaved his head rather than have a bald spot on top) and sported a Van Dyke type mustache and goatee. He was dressed in a white tank top and blue bathing suit and was holding a cup of coffee in his right hand. His right leg was still in a cast but his left arm was wrapped in an ace bandage.

"I trust that's Michel Villar behind those Foster Grants."

Michel raised his coffee mug in mock salute.

"Give that man a cup of coffee. It's quite good by the way."

"Glad to see you're up and around," I said settling myself in another chair and accepting the cup of coffee offered by Jovelyn.

"Yes, I have made good progress – still a little sore from the bruising but other than that all is well."

Douglas Ewan Cameron

"Good. The baldness surprises me."

"Vanity got the better of me when I started losing my hair. I thought about one of the places that transplants hair and decided against it and went the Rogaine route. Works as long as you keep it up, but I decided even before the accident that I would stop and take on the bald look. Besides, I can do it myself and not have to go to a barber. When needed, I will use contacts to change the color of my eyes. We are just about ready to take pictures for my new ID."

"Which is what?"

Michel looked at me and smiled his trademark sardonic smile.

"You honestly don't expect me to tell you. When I disappear it will be as completely as possible."

"You already have disappeared – you're dead, don't you know."

"Ah, yes, and my ashes spread upon the azure Caribbean waters. Guillaume seemed genuinely upset with my death?"

"As far as I could tell. He was actually in tears after spreading the ashes. He could be one hell of an actor but I don't think so."

"Yes, I don't think acting is a strong suit. I could always tell when he was lying."

"Yes, I don't think he is a problem."

"But someone else is?"

"Yes. Detective Jacque St. George."

Michel looked at me quizzically. "Who?"

Chapter 28

I looked at him a bit bewildered.

"St. George," I stammered. "Detective Lieutenant St. George, from St. Martin."

"Oh," and Michel laughed. "Saint Georges. He must have Anglicized it for you. He is from French Guinea. Don't think that is his original name. He grew up in Saint-Georges, a commune on the Oyapock River, which forms the border with Brazil. In fact, right across the river is the Brazilian town of Oiapoque. Actually he didn't grow up in the town but near the town."

Then he turned deadly serious. "Has he been to see you?"

"You could say that. Tres and I spent an uncomfortable hour or so with him four days ago."

"What did he want?"

"You."

I have never seen anyone move as fast from the sitting down to standing despite the cast on his leg.

"Me," incredulously, shaking his head.

"He knows all about you and me."

"You... and me?"

"Yes, from the first time we met on my yacht after the trial."

"Way back then?"

"Yes."

He just stood there shaking his head.

"Michel."

No change.

"MICHEL."

He snapped out of it.

"What?"

"That's my question or it could be why? What were you doing then and why were people looking at you?"

"Cercle des Frères?"

"Or the gendarmes! Were you using your position for profit?"

He looked at me questioningly, almost sneering. "I've told you I was skimming."

"That's not what I meant."

It took a minute, too much sun I guess, and then the light came on. "No, never! That's not even funny. I never abused my judge's position. Never."

"Not even to get in someone's pants?"

Historically Michel had two problems: his mouth and the zipper on his fly. The latter costing him his marriage.

"That's not the same."

"It's not?"

He started pacing – of course he couldn't pace very far.

"No – I didn't take bribes or kickbacks. I was fair and square."

"But you knew about me ..."

"Yes, but that wouldn't have mattered. Here attempted murder is the same as murder. They still would have swung."

He wasn't joking there, because the death penalty on St. Nantes is enforced by the gallows.

"You never ..."

"No absolutely not."

"So whoever is looking at you, St. George in particular, is doing it for ..."

"The Brothers – yes, it has to be and that means only one thing."

"I don't think so."

"Yes, it does." He stared at me without the slightest trace of conscience or remorse. "St. George must die."

I stared at him.

"Not by my hand."

"Then someone else. You have contacts."

"If St. George dies, then all hell will break lose around me. He has to keep records."

"Of course he keeps records."

"Well, I am not going to kill him."

"Then he'll kill you."

"Why?"

"Because you know something he wants and if you won't tell him, you might as well be dead."

"Then call The Facilitator."

It was his turn to stare at me.

"I can't. I'm dead."

"But your new persona can."

"No. No. I can't risk it."

"Why not?"

"Because of what he said that night in the hospital."

I had been wondering about that, remember that The Facilitator had leaned over and whispered something to Michel. I remembered the panicked look in his eyes and how his head shook wildly.

"What did he say?"

"He said that he was sorry but that someone wanted me dead more than I wanted me alive."

"What's that mean?"

"It means that whoever wanted me dead paid him more than I did."

Half an hour later I once again found myself in the zodiac, this time doomed to sleep with the fishes. The zodiac, not I.

Michel had been adamant in putting St. George off the case permanently but, as I told him, we needed no more attention than we were already getting. If St. George disappeared at the very least there would be an investigation and that would lead them back to me and maybe further. Maybe, and this was what shut him up, to the Banyuhay.

Then it was a consultation with Joaquin. Beecher McFalls was already on the way with his small sailing yacht. They would make rendezvous and entrust Michel to Beecher's care. I didn't like doing that because it revealed another source but I didn't think there was any choice. True, Michel knew about Beecher but had not, at least to my knowledge, seen him or knew where his establishment was. Beecher would have the boat sitting in the water, faking need of help. Joaquin would miraculously appear, fix the problem and be on his way, leaving Michel behind. Once Michel was off the Banyuhay, it would be sanitized as well as it could be, hopefully removing all trace of Michel's existence on it. Then they would take Jovelyn's mother to a plane and sit by and wait.

We had taken passport pictures of Michel and I would get them and other necessary information to Beecher who would then have a passport and other documentation made and offloaded to Michel and he would be on his own – at least temporarily.

Part IV

Tres Cher

Chapter 29

"Now it's time to pay, bitch."

That was all Tres heard before the anesthetic on the cloth covering her nose and mouth took effect. It was a Wednesday night several weeks after Michel Villar had died and she had worked a double shift in the hospital because it was the height of the flu season, at least on St. Nantes. A third of the nursing staff was either off with it or taking advantage of being able to be sick and not be checked on.

At 01:00 she left the hospital, having just called me, and was putting her phone away when someone surprised her with an arm around her throat and the cloth over her face. Her cell phone dropped to the pavement where it slithered under a car, unnoticed and out of reach. The cell phone was found about forty-five minutes later, its inherent GPS tracking device of no use in finding her.

It takes about twenty minutes at that time of day to reach The House at the End of the Road from the hospital despite it basically being at the other end of the island. At 01:30 I began to get worried and so I called her. There was no answer and the call switched over to voice mail. I left a message and called again with the same effect but this time I left no message. Now overly concerned, I was heading for the basement and our new, yet untested, tracking equipment when my phone rang. Caller ID said it was her phone.

"Tres, you had me scared silly."

"Sorry, mate, this isn't Tres. I guess this is her cell but it was under my car in the 'ospital parking lot. I heard it ringing as I was getting in my car. It was a bloody effort getting at it, I'll say that."

"Who is this?"

"Uh, James will do, mate."

"Who are you?"

"Not important really, but I was visiting me mum in the 'ospital and heading home.

"Sort of late for visiting hours."

"Well, yes, but she isn't doing too well after ... again not your business."

"Right, can you see a red Toyota Camry around anywhere?"

"Yes, right behind mine." He read off the license number.

"Anyone in it?"

"Sorry, mate, not a soul. Bonnet's cold so it's been here a while."

"Okay. I appreciate it. Could you do me one favor?"

"Sure as long as it don't take long, I'm bushed."

"Put the phone on top of the driver's front wheel of the red Camry."

"Will do, mate."

"And, James..."

"Yes."

"Thanks."

"You're welcome. Hope you find her quick."

"I will ..." but he was already gone.

During the conversation I had continued moving down to our combat center as it was certainly becoming. After Michel Villar's accident, we had made some significant changes in the property, not directly because of the accident but because of the consequences. One of the other changes we had made was tracking chips inserted under the skin in each of us – just in case – and now this was a case. I hadn't expected Tres to be a target but she was with me and that made her vulnerable. The possibility of Quentin's family being involved flashed into my window of concern but I dismissed it. They were peripheral and shouldn't be a problem, but there were Joaquin and Jovelyn and, of course, Michel Villar.

I flipped the switch on the tracker and the screen jumped into life. One blip in the center – me – and another fainter blip – Tres – moving away from the island. I blinked – moving away from the island! I checked again. Moving away but slowly. That meant not in a plane. In a boat! Whoever had her was leaving the island in a boat.

Chapter 30

Fifteen minutes later I stood on the wharf in downtown Genivee carrying a duffel, watching as a red cigarette boat eased alongside, Quentin at the helm. He waved and grabbed the duffel I handed to him as I shouted, "It's heavy." He grimaced slightly at the weight and set it on the deck as I virtually leapt into the boat.

Once I knew that Tres was in a boat I made three phone calls. The first was to Quentin who must have been awake because he answered the phone on first ring. "Qui," he said.

"I need a fast boat at the wharf and I need it fast. Someone has kidnapped Tres."

"Fifteen minutes, Josef." The line went dead.

My next call was to Beecher McFalls, who answered on second ring. "Someone has kidnapped Tres and has her in a boat heading toward St. Martin," I said.

"I'll be airborne in fifteen." The line went dead after he gave me quick weapons instructions.

The third call was to Joaquin. It was five rings before he picked up.

"This is Josef. Someone has kidnapped Tres and has her in a boat heading for St. Martin. Where are you?"

"St. Barth's. I can be underway in twenty minutes."

"I'll call in thirty," I said.

"Hit it," I shouted to Quentin, wanting the big vessel to go from stop to flying immediately. But of course that couldn't happen except maybe in a movie. We were in a commercial harbor and despite it being just after 02:00, we couldn't just open the throttle. Violation of harbor rules is not condoned and the consequences are high – financially high. I could afford the cost but we couldn't afford the time. Quentin turned the boat around and accelerated to the maximum speed without drawing attention. I reached for the throttle to go faster but he pushed my hand away and pointed to a sign "No Wake Zone." I was frustrated but there was nothing I could do.

"Whose boat is it?" I shouted above the throaty rumble of the engines.

"Et iz my friend Jean. Which way do we go?"

In my anxiety to get moving I had forgotten to check the mobile tracking device I was carrying in my backpack. Removing the pack I took out the tracker and looked at it before Quentin snatched it from me and looked at it. Then he swung the wheel and steadied on a course toward the blip that was Tres.

"Et iz about eight miles ahead of us," Quentin shouted.

"How long to catch it?"

"Not long," Quentin said as we passed the harbor limits and he pushed the throttle to full bore.

I was not prepared for this and found myself sitting down and sliding the short distance to the stern and slamming into the bench seating. The bow came up and hung there for a moment before it dropped and the sleek vessel leapt forward becoming a red rocket. The heavy thud, thud, thud of the hull bouncing off the waves quickly settled into a thip, thip, thip as the vessel literally flew across the water. Knowing there was nothing I could do, I opened the duffel and started getting the weaponry ready.

I am not the most proficient weapons person—basically distaining them—but my life had become so complicated lately that they were a necessity. All this just because of a simple fishing expedition – oh, and fifteen million dollars. Don't want to forget that.

Beecher's instructions had kept it simple for me: what I was carrying was a M-4 carbine with a sniper scope and laser and M203 grenade launcher. I hoped I wouldn't have to use either – especially the latter. But if I needed to stop the boat, that is what I would use. I was counting on Beecher and his weapons proficiency to do the stopping for me if that was necessary. I also had brought two pairs of night vision glasses although the scope had laser capability. I put one on, stood, and handed the other to Quentin.

"What iz zis?" he asked holding them up in front so he could see them while also trying to see ahead and watch the tracer screen.

"Night vision glasses."

"Ah, I have heard of zese," and he tried to fit them on his head one handed. The boat was bouncing so much he was having trouble keeping it straight with just the one hand, so I got them on for him.

"I'll tell you how to use them when we need them. How far away is the other boat?"

"Four miles," was his answer and then "What? Look like zey have stopped."

Chapter 31

"Stopped?"

"Yes, zey are dead in ze water."

Looking at the screen, I could see that our vessel was quickly eating up the distance between us.

"Cut the lights and throttle back. I need to call Beecher."

He answered immediately.

"Where are you?"

"Circling above them at least a mile out. They shouldn't hear me. They've gone dead in the water, but navigation lights are still on as well as a spotlight or something. That'll kill his night vision."

"How many are they? What kind of boat?"

"A jet boat, and just two people. The guy is dressed in black pants, long-sleeved black shirt, black baseball cap on backwards."

A jet boat meant no prop and thus negated the use of the grenade launcher to blow the prop, but right now that wasn't needed.

"Where's Tres?"

"Sitting or lying port side bench in the cockpit's rear. Looks like a Yamaha SX210. Got a deck on the back. Her hands are behind her and her feet appear to be taped together. Wrists probably also."

"What's the guy doing?"

"You really want to know?"

"Yes," impatiently.

"Chumming the water."

That meant sharks!

"He is going to throw her to the sharks," I said. "That will leave no evidence. We've got to get there fast."

"Hold on, partner," Beecher said. "Usually takes a while to get sharks. You go roaring in and you'll spoil the surprise, which may be all we have on our side if they are Cercle des Frères."

After the Michel Villar dying episode, I had hid nothing about that aspect of my life from Beecher.

"Cut your lights, cut your speed so you'll get there in about ten minutes. Use the night vision goggles until you get close. Getting into the bright light of the searchlight makes them useless. When you get about a hundred yards away, cut your engine and glide in. I'll tell you which side. He won't see or hear you until you get close."

"Then what?"

"He'll be preoccupied with you. Based on how he is doing things, he's not a professional. Like now he is talking to her and pointing at the water. She's shaking her head violently, probably yelling at him."

"I zink I may know zis fellow," Quentin injected.

"What," I said knowing that he had heard only my end of the conversation.

"Yes, two days ago I take a fellow fishing deep sea. He said he wanted to catch a shark so I takes him to where he iz now. He has a GPS and he marks it."

"Who is he?"

"Ez name iz Richard Burton, I zink. Like ze actor."

"Richard Barton," I said.

"Yes, zat iz it."

Richard Barton was the intern who had raped her. She had turned him in to the medical authorities and left the country. It was painfully obvious that he had come after her.

Chapter 32

"There's another one," Richard said excitedly, pointing in the water. "That makes two. There'll be more."

"You can't be serious," Tres screamed at him.

"Deadly serious, Ms. Jones."

"But why?"

"Now you can't be serious," Richard took another handful of fish guts from the bucket and threw them in the water. "Why? You ruined my life. All I ever wanted to do was be a doctor. You lied to the Board and they canned me. I can't ever become a doctor in the States. Now I have to go to some third world country, maybe even change my name. My parents were embarrassed. My father's a prominent doctor in Milwaukee."

"Lied to the Board? You raped me, you bastard. I ruined your life? What about mine?"

"What about you, cunt? You prick teaser. Just like all of you – you're just one of those nappy-headed hos. Getting the most from men without giving anything back."

"But we only had two dates? What did you expect?"

"Actually there were three."

"You're counting having coffee in the cafeteria as a date? That third one was when you drugged and raped me?"

"It wasn't rape. You wanted it."

"How did you make that brilliant decision?"

"You went out with me!"

"So?"

"When a black pussy goes out with a white man for the third time, she wants him."

"Where did you ..."

"Three ...," Richard shouted pointing. He grabbed the searchlight he had placed on the gunnel and raised it, pointing at the water.

"I need a better place for this," he said half to himself. "I've got to see what's happening and have my hands free."

He put the light down and opened a cloth bag, removing a roll of duct tape that he then used it to fasten the light to the starboard strut of the Bimini cover of the Yamaha jet boat. It took a little maneuvering to get it adjusted the way he wanted it. He clapped his hands in glee.

"Won't be long now, bitch," he sneered at Tres, getting as close to her as he could since she was half lying on the bench seat. He sneered at her, laughing, spittle spray covering her face. "Bet you want to give it to me now to save your miserable life."

"I wouldn't give it to you to save the world, you son of a bitch." She struggled helplessly against her bonds. "HELP!"

"Forget it, bitch. We're in the middle of the Caribbean over fifteen miles from land. No one will hear you. Hey," excited he peered into the water. "There's another – that makes four. Is that enough or do you want a six-pack? Yeah, a six-pack of Land Shark! Only these are water sharks, the real deal. A couple of hammerheads for certain, maybe a great white. Daaaa Dum, Daaaa Dum."

"You bastard. Just wait until Daws ..."

"That black son of a bitch you're living with? I don't worry about him. He's a dweeb. Just another fucking brainless jungle monkey … ." Then he laughed. "Wonder if they'll think about that when they pick up the pieces." Richard stared upward, intent, listening. "What's that?"

Tres could hear it faintly – a motor. Daws? Richard searched the sky and ocean for lights but saw nothing. Then, making the final decision, he reached into his pocket and withdrew his knife. Turning to her, he opened it. She shrank back as much as she could, confined as she was, trying to burrow into the seat.

"Don't worry about it, bitch. I'm not going to cut you – at least not yet. I might though if you don't behave. Bet the sharks would like that – but it would be too quick. I don't want it quick – I never want it quick."

Leaning down he cut the duct tape holding her ankles together. Grabbing her arm, he yanked her to her feet and started moving between the seats to the rear platform. Then he caught movement out of the corner of his eye. He spun toward the starboard side, straining to see but not losing his grip on her arm.

"What's that? Who's there?"

Chapter 33

Following Beecher's directions, we had come up on the starboard side of the jet boat, getting as close as we could before cutting the engine. I had positioned myself on the port side of our boat, getting as steady a position for the rifle as I could. I liked to think I'm a decent shot although I only had about two weeks of target practice, intense target practice. But I wasn't certain how good a shot I could make in a boat rocking in the waves, shooting at someone on another boat also rocking in the waves, especially if Tres were anywhere close. I wished I were one of those Navy Seals aboard the U.S.S. Bainbridge that had shot the Somali pirates and rescued Captain Phillips.

As the cigarette boat glided closer, I could see Richard bending over Tres. Then he stood up, yanked her up by her arm, and started moving her toward the rear of the jet boat. The red dot of the laser sniper scope was wavering all over the place as I tried to keep it on him. Then he knew we were there.

"What's that? Who's there?" he shouted as our boat glided to a stop about a hundred feet away and settling down, gently rocking on the waves.

"Daws," Tres screamed and Richard slapped her and dragged her out onto the rear deck of the jet boat.

"Are you all right?" I yelled, trying to steady the rifle but not succeeding as the red dot flicked around uncontrollably. I should have been concentrating on the shot but then – I am not a Seal.

"Yes, ..."

"Shut up, bitch," Richard screamed at her and then turned toward us. "How did you find us?"

"Not important, Richard," I said. "Let her go."

For a moment Richard stood dumbfounded, then "Or what?"

Then he noticed the wavering red dot. He took another step closer to the stern, Tres struggling with him at every move.

"Give it up, dweeb," he shouted. "Shoot me, you black bastard, and this bitch goes in with me."

Then he stooped down picking up the bucket of offal chum and threw it into the water between the boats. The bucket sank immediately releasing the fish guts and there was a thrashing of the water as the enticed sharks sensed more food.

"Ha, we got a six pack. Time to go swimming, bitch."

He turned and started to grasp her with both hands. I stood up, dropping the rifle, listening to the voice in my head.

"Tres – Français," I shouted. "Une."

In the darkness behind them, I could see motion – my job was distraction and I started waving my hands.

"Deux."

Richard released one of his hands on Tres and swung around to face me.

"What are you doing, you black bastard?" Richard shouted.

"Trois," I shouted at the same instant that Beecher fired the engine of his Helio Courier. He couldn't have been more than twenty feet from the port side of jet boat and ten feet in the air at that instant. At the sudden roar, Richard turned toward it and then instinctively stepped backwards hitting the gunnel and starting to fall, dragging Tres with him.

I didn't see any more as Quentin and I ducked below the gunnel so as to not be hit by the Courier as it flashed over the cigarette boat, one of its wheels hitting the top of the gunnel and rocking the boat violently. Quentin and I jumped to our feet immediately looking toward the jet boat but just saw blackness – the searchlight was out. Quickly I put on the night vision goggles and the world turn green. The jet boat sat rocking in the prop wash of the Courier, the water between the two boats a jumble of black, green and white.

"Tres," I screamed and leapt for the gunnel.

As fast as I was, Quentin was faster and his grip was strong as he dragged me from the gunnel and down into the cockpit.

"Man," he said, "Zere be sharks zere."

"But Tres," I screamed fighting against his grasp.

"Zen zere be no Daws either. Ze sharks are big."

Struggling, I pushed him off me and stood up looking for Tres but seeing nothing in the water but images of sharks and bloody bodies.

"Daws!"

That scream stopped me and I searched the frothy sea trying to see. But I just saw water and black shapes moving quickly just below the surface.

"Daws," came the scream again and I looked at the jet boat.

Tres was standing up in the cockpit, arms still bound behind her.

Chapter 34

Fifteen minutes later, Tres was safely in the cigarette boat and the jet boat had been sanitized as best we could without eliminating signs that Richard would have made. The seat on which Tres had been seated had been wiped clean, hopefully, of her fingerprints. If she had left any falling over the seats, they would have to stay – a totally sanitized boat would raise too many questions and we weren't prepared to burn and sink it. The Bimini cover struts had been damaged as the Courier passed over. We had removed the cover and struts to be deep sixed far away from where the mayhem had taken place. We also had the cloth bag and the duct tape but we left his hat and the keys in the boat. There are numerous instances of people mysteriously disappearing overboard from boats in the Caribbean and this would just be another. After all, he was a novice boater and going out alone at night is never a good idea.

There was no identification of any type in the bag, but we were taking no chances.

I had talked to Beecher, the voice in my head via a Bluetooth earbud, as soon as all was secure.

"That was close," I said. "You could have knocked Tres into the water as well."

"Didn't knock him into the water," Beecher said. "He jumped, or fell, before I crossed the side. She was already falling out of the way – she kicked the son of a bitch and he let her go. Only problem was hitting the Bimini cover."

"And our boat."

"Had to bounce off something to get airborne," Beecher retorted. "Any damage?"

"Nothing major, we'll get it fixed. We'll give the guy some story if he asks."

"We were bombarded by a pelican using coconuts," Beecher offered.

"Don't think that will fly."

"Probably not, but I have to. Got a charter in the morning."

"Glad everything worked out. And thanks."

"Glad to do it. Plan B usually doesn't fail."

"Plan B? What was Plan A?"

"You were to drill the son of a bitch between the eyes. But I discarded that immediately because you couldn't have hit the boat the way it was rocking much less if there were no waves."

* * *

One of the many things that Tres and I had done under the tutelage of Beecher McFalls was to set up certain codes. One of them was to get out of the way in time of danger. It was always counting in different languages: in some languages we only counted to two, some to four, French was three. I had listened to him in my Bluetooth earbud as he glided in toward the port side of the jet boat.

"Only got one chance, Daws. Got to make it good. Can't use the night vision goggles because of the searchlight. Using that as a guide. Okay, tell Tres on three, starting ... now!"

It worked; just like in the movies, only it had almost cost Tres her life. It was only by pure reflex that she had kicked out as Richard started falling backwards. She didn't know what was happening only that she had to get down and away. The impetus of his fall or jump had dragged her forward and into the framework of the Bimini cover. She had kicked at almost that same instant and the force of the kick and the momentum stoppage caused by her slamming into the framework had done the job. As she had tumbled into the seat, she had pushed upward and tumbled over and onto the floor. She remembered his scream of horror as he fell back and she wasn't certain if it was because of the plane or the sharks. She was certain that there had been only the one cry.

Quentin was amped.

"Zis was great fun. I like ze new Josef. Can we do some more?"

I knew he was kidding and figure that, like me, he had been scared shitless, but I understood the adrenalin rush. I was glad that he had a clear enough head to stop me from jumping to a certain death. His friend Jean, who Quentin admitted used the boat from time to time for nefarious purposes, declined to ask for an explanation, had the boat fixed by someone who also didn't ask questions and sent Quentin the bill, which I paid also without asking questions.

The ride back to Genivee was quick with only a stop to drop the Bimini cover into the water well away from the jet boat. We took care to slice the cover enough so it wouldn't hold air and even then it sank slowly. Hopefully it will never turn up, but if it does, who can say where it came from. I had called Joaquin who was barely out of port and heading our way telling him all was well and he could go back.

We were alongside the dock in Genivee well before dawn. We stood there for a moment watching the cigarette boat leave the dock and head for its anchorage.

"It's happened again," I said staring across the harbor at nothing.

"What has?" Tres asked.

"Four went out – although two at a time."

"Three came back," Tres added. Then looking at me, "We know what happened."

Then we walked to my car, duffel in one hand, one of Tres' hands clasped in the other, neither of us saying a word. There wasn't any need. We were home in less than fifteen minutes, duffel and backpack dropped in the foyer, security system activated and a trail of clothing showing the way to our bed. We didn't get to sleep for almost an hour and then slept deeply.

Chapter 35

"Fish on," I shouted at the same time that Quentin was moving toward the rod. Always the first to notice but then that was his business. It was the fourth fish of the morning and although it was not the thing we wanted to do after only a few hours of sleep, it was something that we had to do. We could have deep sixed the boat that Barton had used but didn't want another missing boat because that could have possibly come back to haunt us. We felt, during the discussion on the way back, that what we were doing would present the fewest problems. We were going to find the empty boat, passing it once thinking that maybe someone was sleeping and then return to it on the way in and investigate – unless another person had found it first. We would have Tres go aboard to give a reason for her fingerprints to be there. Fortunately this was her day off, so we wouldn't need to worry about the hospital.

It had been a beautiful morning of fishing, but we were both exhausted after the frantic night before and just a few hours of sleep.

"Let's make this our last fish, okay," I said as Quentin gave me the rod.

"I second that," Tres said sleepily from where she sat dozing, sitting against the side of the boat. She had handled one fish but then had given up. I had handled the other three. We hadn't said a word about the night before. As agreed, our conversation was about the day and its events. We wanted to answer honestly – or as honestly as we could – when we were questioned by the gendarmes and we were fairly certain that we would be questioned. We had passed the boat and wondered about it.

"What's that boat doing there?" I had asked Quentin.

"Maybe someone ez diving," he had answered.

"But wouldn't there be a diver's buoy?" Tres had asked. We had coached her in this as we discussed options the previous night.

"Yes, zere should be," Quentin had answered, "if ze person diving knows to do zat and wants to be safe."

"And legal," I added. "There is probably a fine."

"Only if you get caught," laughed Quentin.

Then we were past it, getting ready to put the lines out.

After I had gotten the last fish in, we had headed back to port, tired but happy. I was thinking how fortunate we had been that Quentin hadn't had a charter today. Cancelling it would have been bad in that we would have had to let someone else find the boat. That would have possibly caused more problems.

The reef where the boat was anchored was in international waters, so the St. Nantes gendarmes really had no authority there but would have over the missing person. Or at least they would try.

"That boat's still there," Tres said on schedule.

"We had better take a look," Quentin said slowing the Renaissance and pulling alongside. I grabbed the jet boat's gunnel to hold us steady.

"Don't see any sign of anyone," I said. Then I turned to Quentin and adlibbed, "Do we have salvage rights?"

He smiled. "I zink so."

"Well, I have always wanted a jet boat."

"Let me check things," Tres said and climbed into the jet boat, slipping (intentionally) and falling onto the cushion where she had lain.

"There are keys here in the ignition. And there's a cap," she said reaching for it.

"Don't touch it," I warned. "The gendarmes may be interested. Are there any signs someone is diving?"

"No sign of dive gear. Everything's dry so if someone is diving, it's been a while."

"Let me call it in," Quentin said.

He used his radio to notify the boat's rental agent using a fob on the keys.

It was an hour before the first boat showed up. This was another jet boat from the rental agency bearing two men, one to drive it back. Five minutes later a gendarme boat showed up carrying four men. Two were divers who quickly were over the side; a third went into the anchored jet boat and did a cursory examination. Everyone waited half an hour until the two divers surfaced.

"Aucun signe d'une personne," one of the divers said. "Vie du poisson apparemment normale."

"Sauf," put in the second diver, "pour un couple de requins à traîner, et cette." And he threw a black piece of cloth into the gendarme boat.

We looked at Quentin quizzically.

"Zey say zere is no sign of anyone. Za reef is normal except for sharks and zat piece of clothe." This last word he pronounced with a short o.

The gendarme in the jet boat said something to the men from the rental agency and began to pull up the anchor. The other jet boat turned around, went a short distance, and then the helmsman hit the throttle and it was gone in a relative flash. While the anchor was being retrieved, we gave our identity cards to the gendarme in the other boat. He made note of names and addresses, said that someone would be around to interview us, and started back to Genivee closely followed by the jet boat.

Quentin started his boat and followed slowly, letting them move away as they picked up speed.

"That went well," I said.

"Maybe too well," Tres said. "I don't like it."

"You never like et when ze gendarme are here," Quentin said.

Chapter 36

"Quentin Baston?"

Quentin looked up from his boat anchored at the wharf. He was cleaning it after the fishing excursion and "discovery" of the empty jet boat. He always scoured it clean, all gear cleaned and precisely stored so there would be no problems the next time he used them. He had taken time to go home and eat lunch. He had also showered to try to rid himself of the stench of the affair but, like Lady Macbeth, the spot was indelible.

What he saw was what I had prepared him for – Detective Jacque St. George. Prepared as he was, the size of the man unnerved him. But even before seeing him, he knew who it was since his name was pronounced as a French speaker would say it.

"I am sorry, it is too late today for fishing. Maybe tomorrow. I have nobody scheduled."

"I am not looking to go fishing," St. George said as he displayed his shield. "I have some questions for you."

"About what?"

"About that boat you say you found this morning."

"I did find a boat. But I was not alone. I had two customers with me."

"Yes, I know. Dawoh Mbayo, people call him Daws, and his friend Treshauna Lee Jones, people call her Tres or at least her friends do."

"Yes, they were with me. They have fished with me before, but you must know that. We went fishing again this morning and found the boat."

"Why did you go to that place?"

"Why not? The ocean is big and fishing is good near that reef."

"But there are other good spots."

"Yes, that is true, but they wanted a different spot than before and I had good luck in that area a couple of days ago."

"With whom?"

"Three Canadians. They caught ..."

"Immaterial," St. George waved him off. "Any other time there recently."

"Yes, day before yesterday."

"Was that a charter also?"

"Yes, a single man. His name was Richard Burton, like the American movie star. You know, he was married to Elizabeth Taylor. She was Cleo..."

He stopped when St. George waved his hand at him.

"Yes, yes. Immaterial. This Richard Barton, what ..."

"Burton," Quentin corrected, knowing full well that St. George was correct. "Like the actor."

"No, it's Barton. But Burton, Barton, Borton. Immaterial. Did you take him fishing?"

"Well, I thought we were going fishing. That is what he hired me to do. But he wanted to see sharks. I had to come back to the port and get some chum."

"So that is unusual?"

"Chum? No, if you want sharks..."

"No, that people want to see sharks."

"Yes ... no. I mean I have had people before, but they wanted to catch sharks. That is not easy to do. I always say that it is better to fish for barracuda ..."

Again St. George waved him off. "Immaterial. So this Burton …," he glowered at Quentin. "This Barton, he wanted to see sharks?"

"Yes, he wanted to know how to attract them," Quentin was having fun.

"Why?"

"I don't know. That is what he wanted and that is what I gave him. He paid me well. As much as …"

"Immaterial. So you took him to the reef and threw chum in the water and sharks came."

"Yes, a couple. I told him that maybe at night there would be many more."

"Immaterial … no, maybe it is not," St. George mused. "Did this interest him?"

"What?" Quentin asked, playing the dunce role to the best of his ability.

"More sharks at night."

"He didn't say."

"What happened then?"

"I brought him back to Genevieve."

"And this morning?"

"I took Daws and Tres fishing."

St. George looked surprised.

"Daws and Tres?"

"Yes, that is what they told me to call them."

"Okay, so this morning …"

And Quentin told him the story as we had scripted it up to the arrival of the rental company's boat and the gendarme craft.

"So after they took the boat, what did you do?"

"I took them back to the harbor where I had picked them up."

"And …"

"I came back here, tied my boat up, went ..."

"Immaterial," St. George said. "I may have more questions. Where do I find you?"

"I think that a detective like you knows how to find a simple fisherman like me," Quentin said trying desperately not to laugh.

St. George glowered at him, turned, and started away.

"Detective St. George."

St. George stopped and turned around taking a step back toward the boat.

"I didn't say I was a detective."

Quentin smiled at him. "I did some detecting. Shield, plain clothes, not a gendarme uniform. Detective."

"Yes, yes. Immaterial. What did you want?"

"When I dropped Burton," and he smiled at St. George, "at the wharf, he asked me where to buy chum."

St. George turned to go again.

"And he marked the reef on a GPS."

He told me this over the phone immediately after St. George left.

Chapter 37

St. George was standing on the back porch, just a concrete pad, nothing fancy, when I opened the door twenty minutes after he left Quentin. I had been expecting him ever since we got home. We had gone immediately to bed and I had been awoken by the alarm announcing that someone was nearing the house. It had taken me several minutes to wake up and dress, but I knew whom it was and didn't rush. I had listened to the message that Quentin left since I took time to start a pot of iced tea, decaf of course. I was holding a glass of tea in my hand when I opened the door. Of course, my other hand hidden behind the door was holding my Berretta Nano. When I saw that he was unarmed, at least his hands were empty, I slipped the pistol into one of the large pocket of my cargo pant shorts.

"Detective St. George. What a pleasant surprise."

"Not really," he said and smiled that broad smile. "You knew I was coming."

Nothing surprises me anymore. If it had been me I would have suspected that Quentin would call.

"The motion sensors and all," St. George added.

Maybe he didn't suspect that Quentin had called, so I responded accordingly.

"And to what do I owe the pleasure?"

"Hopefully it is 'to what do we owe the pleasure?' " The "we" emphasized.

"Of course it is." Tres voice startled me. I hadn't known she was up. I turned and she smiled at me. I noticed that she was holding two glasses of iced tea, each adorned with a slice of lemon and a sprig of mint. "Please, come in, Detective."

Opening the door wide, I stepped back and St. George entered, accepting the glass of tea from Tres and then following her into the great room.

"It is such a nice afternoon, let's sit on the deck if that is okay with you," she said, crossing to the slider and opening it.

"Of course," St. George said, "Anywhere is fine with me."

Too condescending, I thought. Passing the bar, I considered putting the gun away but decided against it. On the deck we took chairs around the glass table and I opened the umbrella.

"This is delicious," St. George said, and I noticed that his glass was half empty. "Just the right amount of sweetener."

I looked at Tres and she smiled at me. How had she known he wanted sweetener, neither of us use it?

"So," I said. "What is this all about? Oh, I'll bet it's the boat we found this morning."

St. George smiled. "Yes. How astute of you."

"Well, the officer who took our information said that it was very likely that someone would be around. And here you are. However, I would think that this is below your level."

"Ordinarily I would agree. However, this is a special case with ties directly to you," this last directed at Tres.

"Me?" she said. "Why me?"

"Richard Barton."

"What does that pervert have to do with this?" She was livid, face red, shaking.

"It was his boat – a rental, he did not own it." St. George was watching her carefully.

"He's here? On St. Nantes?"

"That is debatable," St. George said. "What do you know of him?"

"First," Tres said. "What do you know of him? Obviously something otherwise you wouldn't be here."

"He had your picture in his room."

"My picture?"

"Yes, well, a digital image of you. On his camera."

"He took a picture of me? Here? On St. Nantes?"

"Yes, actually many pictures. Or are they digital images? Immaterial."

"Where?"

"In his room."

"I was never in his room."

"No, I mean the pictures were in his room. That's where we found the camera.

"Well, if I had been in his room, he would be dead," Tres stated vehemently.

"Most likely he is," St. George said with a smirk. "No one has seen him since early last night."

"Good riddance."

"Why would he be interested in you?"

Tres looked at him and then at me. Then she sighed.

"I thought this was all behind me. I thought I would never see or hear about that bastard again. This is really dredging up bad memories."

St. George said nothing and waited for her to continue. Tres shrugged in acquiescence and continued, "I was a nurse in a hospital and he was an intern. We had coffee in the cafeteria and he asked me out. We went to a movie. Then after a week he asked me out again. He said for drinks but he drugged me. Used Rohypnol – a roofie. I woke up in my room. Don't know how he got me there, but he had raped me."

St. George's face didn't change expression.

"And what did you do?"

"I reported him to the hospital's medical governing board. They took away his license to practice and they helped me get the position here. I thought I would never see … or hear about him again."

"See?" said St. George.

"I never saw him. Until today I hadn't heard his name and I don't want to, ever again."

"So what do you think happened?" I asked St. George.

"We know that he rented the jet boat yesterday morning and took it out. Oh, yes, two days ago he had a fishing guide take him out to show him where to find sharks and how to chum them."

"Was that Quentin?" Tres asked.

St. George looked at her questioningly. "How did you know that?"

"I didn't but he is the only fishing guide I know. At least on St. Nantes."

She looked at me and shrugged.

"I thought the same thing," I said. "Are there other guides?"

"Yes, a few. But … immaterial."

"So he took the boat out yesterday morning. He was gone for several hours. Not that unusual of course. When he came back he gassed the boat. Again, not that unusual. Then he purchased chum in the late afternoon. He went out sometime during the night – at least that is what we believe. We only know that because the boat was not there this morning. Again not unusual and, of course, since he had rented the boat for a few days – a week actually – it was not unexpected. The bed in his room was not slept in last night. We talked to the maid. There wasn't much in the boat. Of course, there were your fingerprints on the gunnel and several places on the boat," this to Tres.

"Yes, we told the gendarme that I had gotten in the boat to see if there was any clue as to who owned the boat."

"Yes, but that doesn't explain the prints on the seat."

"I'm a klutz," Tres said. "But you know that from before."

St. George looked at her uncomprehendingly.

"You remember. Your first visit here when I dropped the glass of water."

"Oh, yes," agreed St. George. "But immaterial."

Tres nodded in agreement. "Anyway I slipped getting into the boat and went sprawling on the back seat."

St. George was silent.

"And how was the boat held while this was going on?" This to me.

" I used a boat hook to pull us close and then just held onto it while Tres went aboard."

"Why didn't you go aboard?" St. George asked.

"Tres didn't have the strength to hold us in the waves."

"What about Quentin?"

"Did you ask him?"

"No, I thought I'd ask you."

"Well, he was busy with our boat doing something and we thought the fewer extraneous fingerprints, the better. Just in case there was a crime."

St. George was silent.

"I suppose," he finally said and drained his glass.

"What happened to Barton? I hope he's dead," Tres said.

"We don't know what happened. We suspect or suppose that he went to the reef to chum for sharks. Something happened and he fell in."

"Daa Dum," I said.

"What?" St. George didn't get it.

"Daa Dum, from the movie *Jaws.*"

"Ahh, I don't know that movie."

"Everyone knows that movie," Tres injected.

"I don't," St. George shrugged.

"Just Laurel and Hardy," I added.

"Yes," Tres said. "This is another nice mess you've gotten us into, Ollie."

St. George smiled.

Chapter 38

"I'll have another," Tres said holding her glass out to me.

"That's your third," I said pouring us each a refill.

"And your fourth," Tres said, "but who's counting."

After St. George left, I had mixed a pitcher of *Painkillers* and thawed some cooked shrimp in the microwave. Tres had thrown together a cocktail sauce and we had been on the deck watching the sun go down. The western sky was a brilliant patchwork of red, orange, yellow and purple.

"Isn't there something about a red sky at night that foretells good fortune," Tres said. It was the first words that either of us had spoken in the hour since St. George departed with a tip of his hat to Tres. He had never taken it off.

"Yes," the mention of this taking me back to my time at sea, trying to survive after being dumped by Howard:

Red sky at night,
Sailor's delight.
Red sky at morning,
Sailor take warning.

"But there is more than red," I said. "Don't know what that means. Does it have to be all red or does red mean there is no water in the clouds. I don't know. But why?"

"I would just like to think that the sky tonight means that our problems are over."

As the door closed on the departing form of St. George, we had grabbed for each other and held tight for a long time, her head buried in my chest and mine in her hair. Then I had lifted her face, kissed her and let her go. I had turned and headed for the kitchen and she had followed.

"If wishes were horses, then beggars would ride," I said, the quote from the recesses of my memory.

"What?"

"Or 'If wishes were fishes, the seas would be full,' " I mused.

"Oh. I know it's fanciful but things are going from bad to worse."

"All because of me," I said. "I'm sorry."

"It's not just because of you. Richard Barton wasn't because of you. That bastard was because of me. I brought that on."

"Yes, and I brought the rest."

She was quiet for a minute. "Actually, Michel Villar brought it on. If he hadn't come …"

"But he did," I said. "And you know what?"

She looked at me questioningly.

"If Michel hadn't come, if he hadn't asked for our help, I wouldn't have been able to save you," and I lifted my left arm where the chip was implanted.

Reflexively she looked at her arm.

"Oh," she said.

"Yes," I said.

"Daa Dum," she said.

Both of us were quiet for several minutes, watching the sun go down below the horizon and the colors begin to dissipate.

"Can't we just run away and hide?" Tres asked.

"Not from these guys. They know everything about us – at least everything about Josef Viljoen and Dawoh Mbayo. If they find out about Stuart Andrews, we won't stand a chance."

"What now?" she asked.

"We beat the bastards," I said.

"How?"

"We kill them all."

Chapter 39

I became acquainted with Beecher McFalls while Joaquin and I were preparing for our run from Nassau to St. Nantes where I would confront Quentin Baston for his part in my "murder." We needed explosives (complete with directions) on how to blow up his boat and a passport for him to use while he was in hiding. After all, a dead man can't use his own passport.

"I know just the man," Joaquin had said.

"Who?" I had asked surprised at his knowing someone so nefarious.

"Beecher McFalls. He lives on St. Martin. He is a former spook and deals in munitions and airplanes."

"How did you get to know him?"

"Like you, he wanted a yacht and came here to buy it. I spent time with him getting to know his boat."

"So how did the munitions bit come to light?"

"He was interested in knowing where he might be able to hide things like explosives and guns. Together we came up with some ideas. I don't know whether he ever did it, but at least he knew how."

"Why would he help us?"

"Money. Just like everyone else, he likes money."

But that wasn't the real reason that he finally helped us.

Beecher grew up on a farm in Iowa and started hunting at a young age, mostly birds on his father's farm, but he turned to deer in his teens. His father insisted that he learn everything about his weapons and instructed

Beecher on how the guns came apart. That got to be a game with Beecher and he practiced endlessly with the weapons he had until he could fieldstrip a weapon and put it back together blindfolded. He learned to fly because his father had a Sopwith Camel he had reconditioned and loved to fly. Beecher was a natural and longed to be a military pilot, but a congenital heart problem put the damper on that. He was well on the way, having received an appointment to the U.S. Naval Academy. Everything went well for his four years at Annapolis until a physical prior to graduation picked up on the problem, which had never caused him any difficulties. His senior advisor felt that he could still be of service to the country and arranged for him to have an interview with the C.I.A.

The interviewer asked him if he had any special abilities that might be of interest to the company.

"Do you have a weapon I could use?" was Beecher's answer.

"What kind of weapon?" was the interviewer's response.

"Pistol, rifle, automatic – your choice."

The interviewer made a phone call and within a few minutes, a pistol was brought into the room. The interviewer checked it to be certain that it wasn't loaded and then handed it to Beecher, who took it without looking at it and put it on the table in front of himself. With his eyes looking straight at the interviewer, Beecher fieldstripped the weapon. Still without looking at it, he reassembled it.

"Interesting," the interviewer commented, "but we can all …"

He stopped in amazement as in that length of time the fully assembled pistol had been fieldstripped once again.

"How did you do that?" the interviewer asked, accepting the pistol Beecher had reassembled faster than he had fieldstripped it.

"I just know weapons," Beecher said.

It took two more weapons and a gathering group of extremely interested onlookers before he was offered employment. Naturally he obtained a position in ordinance and quickly learned everything that anyone knew and then some. When he had left the Company, it was natural that he move into a business dealing with weapons. He wasn't a gunrunner but would provide weapons and ordinance when there was a case that he felt justified it. He met us in Las Galeras, our final stop before that long and almost deadly run to St. Nantes. He had flown in and joined us on board the Zàkpa.

"Joaquin has told me of your needs and I have what you have requested. However, I do have one final request."

"More money?" I said jokingly, because I could tell from his face that was not the answer.

"No. I agreed to provide the materials because Joaquin told me that this matter involved revenge. I agreed provided you could convince me that it is just."

I looked at Joaquin and Beecher must have caught a look of mistrust rather than surprise.

"Don't be mad at him," Beecher said. "I told him not to tell you because I wanted to hear it from you unprepared."

"There is nothing to prepare," I said, having already prepared my story when I asked Joaquin to join me in my quest.

"I had a good friend, Stuart Andrews. We had grown up together and remained close after going our separate ways out of school. We were in daily email contact, keeping each other informed of our goings on. He was on a cruise, a second honeymoon he told me. He had been working too hard, devoting too much time to his business, and his marriage was suffering."

"What was his business?"

"Investments."

"Was he any good?"

I had to laugh. "Very good."

"Okay, go on."

"The first stop on the cruise was St. Nantes. He had arranged for a local guide to take him fishing while the ship was in port. He was to be accompanied by his brother-in-law and someone his brother-in-law said he had met on the boat. I learned that last fact in the email he sent me, the morning the ship anchored in St. Nantes.

"I never heard from him again. Three days later there was a report that he had committed suicide by jumping overboard from the ship between St. Georges, Grenada, and Aruba. His wife claimed he had been despondent over money matters, but I know for a fact that he wasn't. He was in good spirits and knew that he could weather the financial storm with minimum losses for his clients. He even went so far to tell me that he might even augment the returns for some of his clients who were retired and counting on their investments to supplement their pensions."

"So what has this fisherman got to do with it?" Beecher asked, obviously intrigued.

"I believe, rightly or wrongly, that something happened on that excursion. Stuart was very excited and promised me pictures and full details upon his return. I never heard from him."

"So what is your plan?"

"I have already arranged for him to take me fishing. I plan to ask him what happened that day. If something did, and as I suspect, he had no part in it until it had taken place, I will find out why he didn't report it."

"Until what had taken place?" Beecher had pounced immediately.

"I think that Stuart was killed and his body sunk in the Caribbean Sea. I don't know how, but that is the only thing that makes sense to me."

"And you think that this guide ..."

"Quentin Baston."

"This Quentin Baston was not party to this murder?"

"No. Stuart was the one who made the arrangements. His brother-in-law was invited, more at his wife's insistence..."

"Stuart's wife."

"Yes, Howard, the brother-in-law, isn't married. At least he wasn't then."

"What about that other fellow?"

"I don't know. I hope that Quentin can tell me."

"Why would Quentin keep quiet?"

"He has a family. A wife and two small children. I think that Howard used them to keep him quiet."

Chapter 40

Beecher mused for a minute.

"Yes, that's plausible. But if I were this brother-in-law – Howard?"

I nodded.

"I wouldn't count on that being effective for very long. Quentin could tell the gendarmes and go into witness protection or whatever they call it in France."

"Or," I added, "Howard could arrange for someone to rub him out."

Beecher nodded. "That's the most likely, I think."

"Okay. So you get Quentin to talk. What if he says nothing happened? That they fished, caught some or not, he took them back, got his money and never saw them again."

"Then he and I fish and he takes me back, gets paid and I leave to try to find what happened after St. Nantes." However, I knew that would not be an option.

"What if he was part of the plan, despite you thinking otherwise?"

"Then I will kill him."

"With what?"

I pulled my Berretta Nano from its pocket holster.

"He'll be armed too. Or at least I would be."

"I'll take my chances."

"And if he is being forced to remain quiet?"

"Then I will convince him that I will keep his family safe. We will blow up his boat and hide him somewhere until Stuart's killers are brought to justice."

"Can you?

"Can I what?"

"Keep his family safe."

"I'll have to."

"How?"

"I don't know."

That was true. I hadn't planned that far. I suddenly realized that I should have but I hadn't.

"I guess that I will need to hire some mercenaries."

"Unreliable and too obvious. You need locals. Island people."

"I don't know any."

"I do."

And thus we became a team. He provided the security for Quentin's family while he was in hiding, coordinated their flight from St. Nantes to his refuge on Barbados, and continued the protection until my "killers" had been hung. When I had returned to St. Nantes, I had contacted him and gone through a three-week training course on the use of weapons and electronics. That had been reinforced after Tres had become part of my life and she had gone through the course also.

Now I needed his expertise in something that I couldn't do. On the way home from our "fishing expedition," when we had "discovered" Richard Barton's jet boat, we had gone to the hospital to get her car. I had gotten out, retrieved her cell phone from on top of the tire (never did get to thank that bloke properly) and was about to open her car door – the key just inches away from the lock – when she yelled at me.

"Stop. Don't move."

I had frozen as one is playing the childhood game of Red Light – Green Light.

"Back away."

And I had until I reached my car. I turned and looked at her.

"What?" I asked.

"Something Richard said. He said they would find you in pieces or something like that."

I spun and looked at her car. Of course, he would have known what car she drove. He had to be waiting near it in order to blindside her.

"You think he planted a bomb?"

She shrugged.

"Does he know how?"

"He could have learned," Tres answered. "Just like you and I."

That was when I had called Beecher and why he and I were in the parking lot at 02:00. He had flown his plane in and I had picked him up. He put on coveralls, a light on a strap on his head. Several different tools went into the pockets of the coveralls along with a tester of some sort, a roll of black electrical tape and some test leads (pieces of wire with alligator clips on both ends.) With another flashlight in his hand, he lay on the ground near the front end and started inching his way under the car. He was about halfway in when I heard a muffled whistle. I moved closer (I was watching for anyone who might find our project interesting, but it was between shifts and visiting hours.)

"What?" I hissed.

"Pipe bomb. Fairly sophisticated wiring. There's a transponder also."

"Remote detonation?"

"Doubt it. You could have come to get this vehicle while he was at sea with Tres."

That was true and if I hadn't known where she was, I probably would have.

"So what's it for?"

"Gas tank is my bet," Beecher said as he scootched his way out. Getting up, he moved to the rear of the car, and once again slid partway under.

"Yep, same thing here."

"Can you ..."

"That's why I'm here."

It took him about ten minutes to remove that device and then he turned to the one attached to the engine.

"He could have used the car's battery for power," he said from underneath the car. "But he had his own battery supply. This is hooked up to the ignition. Turn the key and boom."

Removing that bomb took him fifteen minutes. As he was changing out of his overalls, I said, "I can't thank you enough. Last night and now today."

He laughed as he folded the coveralls and stuck them into his bag.

"I left the bombs in your trunk. I don't want to risk taking them back and running into the gendarmes. You can add them to your collection."

"Thanks, again."

"It's not over till it's over," he said.

And I added, "And the fat lady has sung."

Part V

Goodbye to The House at the End of the Road

Chapter 41

"Someone's here, Daws," Tres voice came over the intercom.

"I know."

"I don't mean visitors – or at least not friendly visitors; they're coming up from the water's edge."

"Yes, both sides," I said.

It was two days later and we had been expecting it ever since St. George first visited us – more exactly, ever since I had been with Michel Villar and found out about St. George. We had spent the time since then, except of course for the period when Tres was abducted, in preparation. And we were ready – we hoped. The night before Tres's abduction, Beecher had arrived via zodiac on the beach with our final armament and we had spent most of the night installing it. All of it was custom made by Beecher.

"I've called Beecher and the plane is on its way. It will circle until we call it."

"When's sundown?" Tres asked, entering the war room that would soon live up to its name.

"About thirty-seven minutes."

She moved to my side and stared at the six television screens, each covering eighty degrees with a ten-degree overlap on each side. A red cursor was blinking on all except the one covering the back of the house. "Why aren't they covering the road?"

"Too obvious," I said. "I am certain that they have a couple of cars out of sight."

"How many are there?"

"Twenty or twenty-five, I can't be certain."

Her hand tightened on my shoulder.

"There's no way to beat that many."

"No, they have vastly superior forces. We can hold them at bay for a while, but they'll breach a window or a wall and it'll be all over but the shouting."

"When do you think it will start?"

I stood up and turned to face her.

"Any time but I suspect just about sundown. The twilight will give them better cover. We might not get out of this, Tres. I wish that you hadn't stayed but that's water over the dam …"

"Or under the bridge. I'm glad I stayed. I would rather be here than anywhere else."

"Really?"

"No, but you're here and that is where I will be – at your side."

"Well, you can't be, at least not yet. You have some things to do upstairs."

She stood on tiptoes and kissed me lightly on the lips and then turned and hurried away but not before I had applied a light tap on her fine tight ass. She turned her head and smiled at me.

"Don't leave without me," was her parting remark.

"Never," I said and settled myself in front of the monitors.

"This is another fine mess you gotten us into, Ollie," came Tres' voice over the intercom.

I pressed the intercom button.

"That's 'nice mess,' Stan."

"Shove it, St. George."

While Tres was about her business upstairs, I was about mine. Distracting and slowing down the invaders. After another fifteen minutes, I still wasn't certain how many there were, as several kept moving. About fifteen of them had dug in – not dug in but had selected positions and set up their weapons. If all went well, ten or twelve of them will have selected booby-trapped positions. Six months ago, even before we knew something was going to happen, Beecher and I had walked the property and selected the spots where invaders would opt to take cover. There were surprises waiting for them. We had installed a number of Vietnam-type traps. In Nam the Viet Cong had built camouflaged pits with bamboo spikes, for example. Only our spikes weren't bamboo and they weren't in pits. Also the traps weren't active until I made them so. For example, there was one guy lying behind what he probably thought was a safe bush with rocks in front. Actually he was on top of a number of tubes that contained spikes that would shoot upward about six inches above the ground and then sink back, hopefully leaving no trace. Hopefully a silent killer. I had been watching via wireless television cameras scattered all over the property, many hidden on the walls of the house. My yard was like the killing ground in *The Hunger Games* and I was the Game Master.

I zoomed in one of the wireless TV cameras and watched as the guy, confident in his chosen spot, sighted in his weapon. I flipped open the lid on a covered switch and pressed the previously covered button. His body jerked and then went still, head dropping onto the ground. One down, too many to go. The spikes were metal and thin – the proverbial Italian stiletto. They were powered by compressed air when triggered and then retracted by springs. I only had to get one spike in because they were all poisoned. I checked the other positions and only one of the people was at all properly positioned. I didn't want to miss and have him alert the rest so I settled in to watch. Sooner or later they would make their move.

Chapter 42

It was almost exactly sundown when it started. Beecher had assured me that he was just a phone call away. I watched through the infrared sensors what was starting to unfold. One man was moving crablike to each of his comrades, pausing briefly and then moving on. As he passed, each of the men put on their night vision goggles. He was getting close to the one man I had stilettoed. I watched carefully as he stopped by him. He reached out and grabbed the man's shoulder and rolled him over. He said something and immediately the majority of the men on that side jumped to their feet. I pressed a button and two AK47's dropped down from the eaves on either corner of the house and opened fire. A couple of the infiltrators were hit and went down but then they all went down and those that could opened fire on the house. It was a short fusillade and then the commander regained control.

I switched my attention to the other side of the house where there had been similar movement. Everyone now was deeply dug in but just to keep them down, I let the AK-47s on that side of the house give a short burst. There was an answered barrage but it was brief. I noticed one of the men pulling back and followed him with one of the Hunger Games cameras. He was heading back toward where they had beached, probably to pick up some different equipment. As he passed one of my traps, I activated it and a Bouncing Betty popped up and did its job. He would not trouble me any longer. Again that provoked a barrage. The outside of the house was going to need a lot of work when this was over.

I activated flares above each of the sides just to see what would happen and they did as expected, digging deeper into the earth. Based on their new positions, I activated two more of the poison spike traps and got both men. Four down for certain and still too many to go. Just to keep the rest honest, I let the AK-47s send another greeting and, naturally received an answer in return.

"How's it going up there?" I asked Tres.

"Noisy," she said.

"Are you ready?"

"As I can be."

"Any damage?"

"Well, duh! Not where I am, but the ends of the house are a mess."

"To be expected."

"Not much action from the front though."

"No, they knew we could see them better there. I think our cameras and traps surprised them on the sides though. They're afraid to make a move right now."

"How many are down?"

"Four for certain. Maybe five. Although there could be several out of commission because of the 47 fire. Many ducked for cover and I don't know how many were hit."

"Not enough of the bastards …"

Her critique was interrupted by a buzzing from the backside motion detector unit.

"What's happening?" Tres asked.

"Someone's coming down the road. Too far away to see anything."

"On foot?"

"Don't think so."

I zoomed in with a small joystick.

"No, it's a car, no lights, coming slowly."

I watched the car approaching the house. As the picture became clearer, I could see that there was a white flag on a pole, held out of the passenger window.

"Looks like a truce. They're waving a white flag."

"Giving up," Tres sounded hopeful.

"Don't think so," I said. "More like 'Ve haf you surrounded. Gif up or die.' "

"And our reply?"

"From the Battle of the Bulge."

"Oh, doing a little Anthony McAuliffe impersonation, are we?"

"Nuts," I said smiling, "you guessed it."

"So are you going to blow that car away?"

"No, I think I'll listen like any rational person would."

The car continued its advance and pulled up about thirty feet from the back door. It sat there for several minutes. I tried to get a good look at who was in there but couldn't. I decided to go upstairs and see what was what. As I raced upstairs whoever was in the car had gotten out and had come to the door. A rather uncivil person though as he chose to pound on the door rather than ring the bell. I reached into my pocket, pulled out my prop, and then slowly opened the door.

Chapter 43

It was St. George. Why wasn't I surprised? I opened the door enough so that he could see me but no one else could. I held up my left hand so he could see it.

"What's that?" he asked.

"Dead Man's switch. I let go and the entire place explodes."

"I guess you are not going to invite me in."

"Is this an official visit?"

"Officially I am not here. I flew to St. Martin last evening to visit my sick mother."

I stared at him.

"Your mother's dead."

"I'm sorry to hear that."

"Has been for four years."

He shrugged but didn't look the least amazed.

"You know a lot about me."

My palm holding the switch was beginning to sweat – nerves.

"More than you might think."

An eyebrow – make that, his eyebrow – rose above his right eye.

I was getting tired of this.

"What is it that you and your friends – brothers – want?"

The other end of the eyebrow twitched.

"Brothers?"

"Yes, Cercle des Frères or whatever."

"You know a lot."

"Yes, Michel Villar was most informative."

"Yes, he would have been. So you can be of help."

"How exactly?"

"Tell me where his money is."

"His money?"

"Yes, and while we're at it, yours."

"That's a high price for a life."

"I didn't say anything about a life – actually two lives."

I sensed that Tres had moved up behind me.

"There is one at either corner covering him," she whispered to me. "I'm armed."

My attention returned to St. George whom I sensed was growing as impatient as I was.

"His money is gone."

"Where?"

"He didn't tell me."

That was the truth.

"And yours?"

"It's mine."

"For a little while. I am growing tired of this trivial banter," St. George shifted his feet.

"Life is not trivial," I said.

"No, I agree, ..."

"So to keep yours, leave and take your hoodlums with you."

"I will leave," St. George said, "For now. You have ..." and he looked at his watch. "...twenty-two minutes. Open the door before that and I will come and you can tell me."

"After twenty-two minutes?"

He shrugged.

"Even with a white flag?"

"Not even with a white flag."

I closed the door. Through the peephole I could see him shrug, salute me in a non-honoring manner and leave.

We spent the next twenty plus minutes getting the finishing touches on our surprise package for the Brothers and then my cellphone rang. Not too many people have the number and the caller ID said the caller was blocked but I knew who it was.

"Time's up?" I said.

"No," responded St. George, "still ticking but not much time left. Just over a minute."

"Well," I said, "I guess we had better get moving."

"Do you want to tell me anything?"

"Yes, I do."

There was silence on the other end.

"You'll be in hell before I will," and I cut the connection.

The time on the cellphone told me that the twenty-two minutes had elapsed, so I went to the door and opened it, being certain not to expose myself. A hail of bullets thudded into the door immediately. I turned to Tres.

"I guess they're serious. Time to get out of here."

I called Beecher who answered immediately.

"Show time," I said.

"Five minutes," he said.

Chapter 44

He was off by thirty seconds because the Helio Courier appeared ten feet above the ground about one hundred yards up the road from the house in four and a half minutes. It must have been a surprise because there was nothing from the Brothers until the Courier was almost at the house and then there was a fusillade of bullets about the same moment that the Courier dropped smoke bombs. There was an unexpected answering hail from both wing-mounted Saws forcing the enemy to seek cover as the Courier pulled up to get over the house. As good a pilot as Beecher was, he apparently misjudged his climb and the front wheels bounced off the roof near its apex. The small plane appeared to stall about fifty feet above the house and then made a slow one-eighty, seeming to swivel in place, and then started retracing its path even to the bouncing off the roof. Guns ablaze, it glided back to settle just twenty feet from the house, difficult to see because of the covering smoke.

Its right door and the back door of the house opened simultaneously and one figure emerged and started running for the plane followed shortly by a slightly taller figure. The figures appeared jerky in the dim light and smoke that seemed to completely obscure them at times. About halfway to the plane, the first figure appeared to stumble and knees touched the ground as bullets seemed to hit all around it. The second, upon reaching the first, picked up and carried the fallen comrade to the plane, both disappearing in a new burst of smoke just as they reached it. No sooner were they aboard than the Courier, engine revving the entire time, literally leapt into the air, turning to its right and heading back over the house and toward the sea and its covering darkness.

On the little rocky island just offshore, a group of men, apparently alerted by the plane's arrival, were ready. One of them raised a Stinger missile launcher to his shoulder and sighted the plane as it appeared over the embankment. The missile's tracking sensors started beeping indicating that its passive homing seeker was locked in, the trigger was pushed and the missile leapt out of its tube. Almost simultaneously as though the Courier's pilot knew the missile had been fired, the little plane turned left and up, straining to get altitude. However, with the short distance and the Stinger's deadly effectiveness, it was for naught. The smoke trail lengthened as the missile gobbled the short distance between its launch site and the small plane. There was a thunderous explosion and a huge fireball as the extra fuel tanks and ammunition aboard the Courier exploded. The fireball seemed to hang in the air for a minute and then, with flaming debris falling toward the Caribbean, started its death spiral into the sea.

Half a mile away, St. George watched the fireball until it disappeared behind the house.

"Guess you were wrong, Daws," he smirked, motioning to the two cars behind him, he headed toward The House at the End of the Road. One of the cars followed and the other pulled across the road blocking it and started its blue and white flashers.

Chapter 45

The back door stood open and fifteen men were on either side – eight right, seven left – flattened against the wall as St. George drove up. Getting out of his car, he motioned to the apparent leader of the men who hastened to his side.

"There will be booby traps, so be careful. Clear the first floor and wait before going to the steps from the foyer to their so-called 'war room' and hurry. Someone has certainly heard the explosion if not everything else and the authorities will be here soon. I don't know how long my man can stall them."

"Right," said the man who turned and gave a signal that sent the fourteen men into the house that soon resounded with shouts of "clear."

St. George and his man walked into the house. Men appeared from the front of the house and both side hallways.

"All clear, sir," they agreed, "except for the stairs leading down."

One of the men stepped forward holding a plastic device in his hand.

"Found this on the floor over there," he said pointing.

St. George accepted the object, a cylindrical tube with a red plunger-style button at one end. He looked at it, bouncing it slightly in his hand.

"It is nothing," he said. "An empty tube with a button on one end. This was his Dead Man's threat. How childish."

He held the tube in his hand as Daws had and pressed the button.

The house erupted in an explosive fireball bursting walls outward and the roof upward. The three cars parked out front were enveloped in the fireball and devastated with parts from the house. Debris and glass from the front windows was thrown seaward enveloping the group of men who had made their way from the beach and were approaching the house. Energy expended, the fireball collapsed upon itself, exposing shattered walls burning, as were the cars and some of the bodies.

It took only ten minutes for the first of the island's emergency forces to arrive. Within thirty minutes there were four fire trucks and as many emergency vehicles, but there was nothing that could be done by any of them. Hoses were used to spray water into the fire, but it was obvious that nothing could be saved. The one occupant of the second car who had not followed St. George inside was a charred husk as was one man who had apparently been standing outside near St. George's car. Five other husks were found in the front yard. Unknown to the island's emergency contingent, only two men had survived and had made their way to the shoreline where they had gotten into a small boat and fled to rendezvous with their mother ship.

Four hours after the explosion, the fires were out and a cursory examination had been made of the remains. A number of incinerated bodies had been found in what remained of the house. The heat and potential danger the ruins offered in the darkness prudently permitted the withdrawal of forces until daylight when cooling would permit better examination of the site. Two men were left to keep a watch in case there was any flare up of the fire.

The two made half-hourly circuits of the area for the first two hours and then settled in for the remainder of the night, watchful yet not totally vigilant. Possibly because of their neglect, they continued to live. If they had been more alert, they would have noticed a zodiac docking on the shore and two figures stealthily making their way up the hill to the front of the house. One of them spoke into a communicator, received an answer, and the two used pry bars to pull away some of the debris reveling a small door in a concrete wall. Three quick raps, a pause and then three more were immediately answered by the door starting to move. The pry bars quickly helped getting the door open enough for fingers to grasp and pull as it was pushed from inside. Soon there was room enough and two figures emerged from the ruins. The door was closed and then the four quickly retreated to the zodiac, which headed out to sea powered by a silent electric motor. When they were about a quarter mile offshore, the zodiac stopped and the four looked back toward land. One of them pulled a small device from a pocket and pressed a small switch. A red light appeared, flickered, and turned to green. Then a button was pressed and an explosion and second fireball rocked the ruins and shocked the negligent watchers into wakefulness as the zodiac continued on into the sea's darkness.

Chapter 46

So much of one's lot in life you have no control over but it is the essence of what you are or will become. For example, I'm black, well half black – my mother was from Sierra Leone and my father was Irish. I was raised in a good environment that enabled me to grow up well educated and obtain a college degree from Cornell. However, I just as easily could have had a broken home and not gone to college, maybe even have gone back to Sierra Leone. But that didn't happen. Much of the mess I was in now was of my own making. Admittedly I was forced into this life by my wife and her brother who had tried to kill me. But I didn't have to help Michel Villar. That was my own choice as was Tres' decision to stay with me. Looking back on it, I don't know why I decided to help Michel – maybe because he knew I wasn't dead during the murder trial and kept silent, thus enabling me to stay alive.

It hadn't been easy to do what I knew had to be done, but there was no other way because, with St. George on our trail, we had to die by our own hands or be killed by his. However our planning started long before we met St. George. Once Michel Villar had made his appearance and we had "allied" with him, I knew that we had better plan ahead – far ahead. Thus one weekend about three weeks after the alliance was formed, Tres and I had flown to St. Martin for a weekend with Beecher. He had come up with the plane idea, complete with smoke and we knew that he could remotely – none of us was actually in the plane – land it within a hundred feet of the house. So we made a movie of Tres and me – just silhouettes – against white background, filmed with strobes for the flickering although the smoke would help with that. The original film was a dash of a hundred feet. Sophisticated projection equipment with a laser distance finder started the film at the proper spot once the plane had landed. Beecher was flying the plane from St. Martin in the comfort of his office and had loaded it with fuel and explosives so there was little, if anything, left once the Stinger hit it. We hadn't known there would be a Stinger but we knew there would be something. Anyhow we needed to rig the explosion because we had to die with no chance of remains being found for identification.

The house had been loaded with explosives a few weekends later with Beecher landing at night and the three of us carrying the munitions to the house and spending the weekend getting them located. The first explosion was shaped charges directed outward and not down, because we were in the war room until the plane exploded and then had secreted ourselves in what once was the film safe. It was strong enough to withstand the explosion that had annihilated St. George and his Brothers. We knew the fire would burn for a while and had confidence that the island's emergency forces would get it under control and wait until it had cooled before a complete investigation. Nothing on the island moves quickly anyway.

We had been watching the invasion of the house via TV and actually cheered, albeit silently, when St. George was given the Bluetooth dead man's button. He thought it was fake because it was so light, but all it needed was some small electronics and a hearing aid battery. St.

George was not going to take a chance with his own life – at least not knowingly. May he burn in hell.

One of our worries was that everyone might be killed and then no one would know that we had died in the plane explosion. However, we felt there would be watchers from a safe distance and so that worry was mitigated somewhat.

We sat in dim light provided by batteries because running a generator would cause noise we didn't want. With the explosion and fire, all contact to the outside was lost – there was no cellphone contact. We would have to wait for our rescuers to come. If they didn't, then we would have to get out ourselves or die. We did have some tools and drastic measures inside including a small shaped charge to blow a hole in the outside wall, but that was a last resort.

"Daws, what's it like to die?"

Tres' question came several hours after the explosions and fire.

"Easy, I've done it twice."

"No, really."

"I don't know. There are people who have and then come back…"

"I'm not talking about Jesus."

"I'm not either. You know stories of people seeing light at the end of a tunnel and then being brought back by CPR or something."

"Yes, but they weren't dead then, were they?"

"No, body function ceased but they still lived."

"So, what do you think?"

"Well, I guess it's like going to sleep and not waking up. I know that sounds stupid but it is that easy, I think.

The act or cause may be painful, bullet, car accident, etc., but the dying itself isn't."

"And after?"

I was silent. I reached over and squeezed her hand.

"I am not ready to find out."

It was opportune at that time there came three raps on the outside wall, soon followed by three more. We unbolted the door and started to push it but the explosions had bent it. We had a pry bar for just such an emergency and start prying the door open, a fraction of an inch at a time. Soon there was enough space for a pry bar to be inserted into the crack from the outside and the door began to move faster. When the opening was large enough Tres went out first into the welcoming arms of Joaquin and Jovelyn. I followed and the four of us moved stealthily across the front yard down the slope and into the zodiac. I was the last one in and pushed the zodiac away from the shore. Joaquin started the motor and we moved out into the Caribbean. At a distance of about a quarter mile from shore, Joaquin stopped the zodiac and we all turned to look back. You couldn't see the house because of the blackness of the night. I pulled a small black box from my pocket, flipped a cover open and pressed a button. A green light came on. I felt Tres' hand grab mine and squeeze. At this point, I had no choice but to press the detonation button. There were flashes of light from shore quickly followed by sounds of explosions and soon flames illuminated the devastation that had once been my salvation. In time more emergency vehicles would arrive but there would be little to do. The biggest blast had been from our hidey-hole to forever eliminate any trace that we had been there and managed to get out. I dropped the controller into the sea and Joaquin started the zodiac and, using his GPS to guide him, took us out to where the Banyuhay (nee Zàkpa) waited. I couldn't help it when tears welled up in my eyes. I quickly dried them with the back of my hand but not so quickly that Tres didn't notice.

Chapter 47

We stopped about a hundred yards from the Banyuhay, which sat quietly on the calm Caribbean. Joaquin pulled a small laser from his pocket, pointed at the Banyuhay and pressed it three times. It was about twenty seconds before an answering two flashes came. Jovelyn had put on a pair of night vision goggles and looked at the yacht. Then she took them off and gave them to me.

"Look and tell me what you see," she said in a whisper.

I put them on and looked at the yacht.

"I see a man – Quentin – standing on the open deck at the back," I whispered in return taking her hint.

"What else?"

I strained trying to see.

"I'm not certain what you mean."

"What about the ensign."

I looked at the flag on its pole at the stern of the Banyuhay.

"It's there."

"Describe it."

I looked trying to see what she wanted me to see. Everything was shades of green and black.

"It's hanging loosely because there is no wind. I can make out the white triangle that should have the star in it."

"Where's the blue stripe."

"Hard to tell."

"Is the top stripe lighter or darker than the bottom?"

"Lighter."

"Yes. When we left we put it like that, upside down. A sign of war. When we signaled him that we were coming, he was supposed to change it if all was well."

"Obviously it's not," I said.

"There's trouble on the Banyuhay," Jovelyn said as she removed her shoes. She spoke rapidly to Joaquin in Tagalog and then slipped over the side.

"She will hitch a ride with us to the yacht. While we go to the stern, she will swim to the front and climb up the bowline. We should have some problems getting out to give her time. One of you can act wounded. Best if you do, Josef. Tres can stay out of the way and they may think she is Jovelyn. They may not know how many people we picked up."

Starting the motor, Joaquin guided the zodiac so that it came at an angle, more from the front in an effort to give Jovelyn a shorter swim. The zodiac rocked ever so slightly when she let go. Joaquin pulled the zodiac alongside the landing platform. Tres was in front, I was in the middle and Joaquin at the rear with the tiller. Keeping her head down, Tres grabbed a line and Joaquin did also to hold the zodiac steady. I was bent over in the zodiac, not wanting whoever was aboard to see that I was wearing night vision goggles.

"I need a hand, Quentin," I said. "I hurt my leg coming down the slope. May have broken it."

I held my left hand up as Quentin stepped to the edge of the docking platform in front of me, effectively blocking the view of anyone aboard. I knew that whoever it was would make themselves visible quickly. As Quentin grabbed my left hand, I jerked it sharply and pulled him over my head and into the water. Almost simultaneously Tres and Joaquin pushed themselves backwards off the zodiac and I threw myself forward onto the docking platform, the Beretta in my right hand seeking a target that it quickly found. A man also wearing night vision goggles and brandishing an automatic weapon of some kind stepped through the slider from the living space. He hadn't expected me to be low and so I had the momentary advantage and put four quick shots into his chest before he could fire. The burst knocked him backwards and he crashed into someone behind him, his gun erupting upward as he tried to kill some stars.

I could see forms getting up off the deck and then a fuselage of shots over me and some ricocheting off the deck on either side of them. There were two quick flashes and accompanying reports from further back in the cabin and the two forms dropped to the deck. There was silence and no movement from inside. Then I could see motion, someone coming into the cabin from the bow holding a pistol. I could tell it was Jovelyn. She bent over the two forms and I heard two more shots and I knew those were headshots, making certain that they were dead.

"All clear," Jovelyn said coming out onto the deck.

I got up and the two of us helped Tres, Quentin, and Joaquin up on the landing platform.

Quentin was laughing. "Ets a good zing I can swim, Josef. But I was expecting what you did. I was going to dive in taking you with me anyway."

A noise from inside made us all turn, my pistol and Jovelyn's at the ready. Once again a crackle and then a noise. Jovelyn and I entered the cabin cautiously, Tres and Joaquin close behind but Quentin hung back. There was that crackle again and Jovelyn reached down and removed a walkie-talkie from one man's belt. She held it up,

"Hans. Wat gebeurt er?"

"What language is that?" Jovelyn asked.

"Have no idea but I know what it means," I said.

"What?" everyone else said.

"There is another boat out here with more Brothers on it."

"Zat is right," Quentin said have entered the cabin. "Zey came in a zodiac. Et is on ze port side of dis ship. Zeir other ship, et must be close."

Simultaneously Joaquin moved to the cabin bridge and turned on the radar. It took a minute but the screen was illuminated and revealed a blip about half a mile away.

"Quickly! We have to get underway before he gets away," I shouted heading for the flying bridge. "There can be no witnesses."

Chapter 48

By the time I got to the flying bridge, the Banyuhay's engines were already on. I turned on the radar and pushed the throttle to slow. The Banyuhay started moving forward slowly and I turned the wheel to port in the direction of the blip. I could see nothing on the surface of the water and knew that the Brothers' mother ship – as I thought of it at the time – was lying dark and silent just as we had been. I also knew that with the Caribbean calm, it would be easy for the people aboard the Brothers' mother ship to hear our engines start. They had heard the gunshots but those were louder and unexpected. If I had been one of the Brothers I would have been listening for engines. I was certain they had their radar on and would see us moving. Admittedly it could be their men having taken control of the Banyuhay and capturing the returning party heading to rendezvous with them. But certainly they would have informed the Brothers' mother ship of that.

Just as I had anticipated, the Brothers' mother ship was underway heading to port away from us. I shoved the throttle to maximum and the Banyuhay surged forward. I had no idea how fast the Brothers' mother ship was, but I was determined to catch her. Just about the time the Banyuhay flattened out, I felt a presence beside me and heard two clicks. I turned to see Jovelyn and Joaquin. Jovelyn was holding a long tube that I thought was a bazooka.

"What's that?" I shouted turning back to look ahead, one eye on the radar.

"LAWS rocket with a laser sight. We have to get within 150 meters for this to be accurate. We've only got one."

"Where ..."

"Beecher thought it might come in handy."

Thank God for Beecher, I thought.

Momentarily at least we were gaining on the Brothers' mother ship having had the slight advantage of being underway before it was. After five minutes the gap had steadied. Unless something happened there was no way we were going to get close enough. Suddenly there were flashes ahead and a second, but faster, moving blip had appeared on the screen. Quickly the Brothers' mother ship veered to starboard and as it did, the distance closed. Just as suddenly as it had appeared the second blip disappeared.

Joaquin had moved in front of the radar. For a couple of minutes, the Brothers' mother ship continued to starboard and I adjusted our course to intercept. The distance was closing but then the Brothers' mother ship started turning to port. Soon the second blip reappeared on its port side and in the distance we saw flashes. Just as quickly the second blip disappeared and the Brother's mother ship once again veered to starboard and once again the distance closed.

Joaquin and I looked at each other and simultaneously said, "Beecher McFalls."

For ten minutes this process continued and with the third volley from Beecher's plane, we heard the sounds of gunfire. Ever so slowly it seemed to me, the distance between the two ships closed.

"One hundred seventy-five yards," I shouted at Jovelyn just as Beecher's plane made another pass. This time there was a louder explosion and we could see that a fire had been started. That helped us keep our course straight for the Brothers' mother ship.

"One fifty," I shouted to Jovelyn. "One forty. One thirty. One ..."

My countdown was interrupted by a loud BANG and a trail of red streaked toward the Brothers' mother ship. There was a great flash of red and yellow followed almost instantaneously by the sound of an explosion, and I cut power while simultaneously turning to port. The missile had started a fire and as it increased in intensity, we could see the black outline of another ship. We had just about come to a stop when there was a second explosion from the Brothers' mother ship and we all ducked reflexively. When I looked again there were several small fires on the water's surface but nothing else. Joaquin turned on the ship's spotlight as I gave power to the propellers and turned toward the place where the Brothers' mother ship had been. On the radar screen there was nothing. Then in the distance we saw red and green lights appearing about three feet apart with that distance increasing rapidly as Beecher McFall's plane came toward us. Just before he passed above the Banyuhay, he waggled the wings as evidenced by the movement of the lights and then he was gone.

We crisscrossed the area several times looking for any sign of survivors but found none. Quentin and Tres had searched the bodies of our welcoming party and found no identification of any kind. We decided that it was best if we dumped the bodies there rather than run the risk of being stopped and boarded, despite the fact that we couldn't think of who would stop us. The "Why" could be obvious. Satisfied that we had done the best we could, we left the area running with no lights for half an hour. During that time at various places we dumped the weaponry that we had used so that bullets couldn't be linked.

"I thought I put about four bullets in that one guy," I said to Jovelyn. "Yet I could see that there were two inside afterward and then you put them down."

"They were wearing Kevlar vests. I got them with head shots."

"But then you shot them again."

"Can't be too certain," she replied.

It was two days before anything was said in the news about what happened. Everyone agreed there were explosions – the number varied between one and five. Officially it was drug related. Supposedly we were making Crystal Meth and that was the cause of the first explosion. The cause of the second was uncertain but possibly related to gun smuggling. Some rumors said that the blast occurred during a police raid lead by Detective St. George since his car was found out front but there was no sign of his body. The few bodies found were beyond recognition and the few that produced DNA had not matched any known individuals (this fact was several weeks in the coming). People reported seeing and/or hearing an airplane and a small explosion shortly before a larger explosion. There was no report of an explosion at sea and no reports of a missing yacht in the area. Within a few weeks, everything died down – or so we hoped.

Part VI

The Facilitator Retired

Chapter 49

When Fredek Gavrilovich Kondrashin (d.b.a. the Facilitator) had finally retired, having made a killing in eliminating Michel Villar by being paid by two separate sources – including Villar himself – he left Moscow and moved to York, England. He had never made a kill in England and felt that gave him a safety edge because the police there had no reason to want to find him. He had travelled extensively in England on several occasions, either on the way to a job or returning, looking for a place to buy and had fallen in love with York's quaintness. That and he had developed a fondness for Yorkshire pudding.

The place he selected was second from the left in a row of six brick three-story townhouses. He didn't want the end unit because of the additional window space that provided more opportunity to anyone who might come looking for him. He had carefully scoped out the neighbors and felt no threat from those on either side of him. He had installed a security system of his own design, not monitored by anyone. Arriving home after his usual morning walk to a nearby coffee house where he drank a chocolate latte and read two papers bringing two others home with him, he used a handheld unit to see if there had been any breaches and, of course, there hadn't been.

He turned the system off, opened the door and entered the house, activating the system that was only external because of his cat Sasha. He hadn't planned on having a pet, but Sasha had appeared on his rear doorstep two weeks after he moved in. He had opened the door to take out the trash and Sasha had walked in and made herself at home. Who was he to argue with that? He hung his jacket up and entered his living room, stopping short at the sight of Sasha sleeping in his favorite chair. It wasn't the fact that Sasha was in the chair – she often was. It was the fact that she was curled up contentedly on someone's lap – someone who was dead. His amazement was what would ultimately cost him his life. It delayed his reaching for the pistol that he had in his belt in the small of his back.

"Hello, Fredek," Michel Villar said. "Unless you want to die now, I suggest you leave your gun where it is."

Fredek stopped just before he pulled his Glock. He had been watching the look on Michel Villar face and knew that he would never make it. Also he had seen another figure standing to the left with a pistol aimed at him and knew that he couldn't get them both. He released his grip on the Glock.

"My hand is empty, Michel," he started to say but all he got out was "My hand ..." when unexpectedly he fell backwards, hitting the floor with a thud. Sasha didn't ever stir.

* * *

Fredek Gavrilovich Kondrashin had been careful in selecting his house, even investigating the residences on either side of him. He didn't want any surprises. The townhouse on the inside of the block was owned by a ninety-three-year-old spinster, Agatha Crawford Spenser. She was an old maid and preferred it that way. Her parents had married only because her mother was pregnant with her and that only because she had been experimenting – that one time had gone wrong. The only thing her parents had in common was the sex they shared, which wasn't that often. Other than that, their relationship was stoic except for the occasional rhubarbs that any marriage, particularly one without love, has. Her father spent several hours of each evening at the corner pub, sitting in a corner, drinking his ale with an occasional gin thrown in if it had been a particularly hard day. If anyone had asked him (and they didn't) which were the hard days, he would have said, "Any day yew spend more 'an eight hours with thet battle axe I married is a 'ard day."

Fortunately her father had died when she was twenty. Unfortunately her mother died when she was twenty-four. Fortunately her mother left her the townhouse. She immediately got rid of everything that had been her parents and set about refurnishing it to her likes. She had done all right as a secretary for a solicitor and had put enough away to live a comfortable retirement that she had been enjoying for eighteen years. Her routine was easy to observe. Every day about ten o'clock, she would appear on her front stoop, always dressed in dark clothes as though in mourning. She always had a small hand cart with two wheels, much like a piece of modern carry-on luggage although the container was basically just a bag. Of course, it was black also.

She would turn right from the bottom of the stairs and pass by Fredek's place and that of Lissel and Monica Davies. At the corner she would turn left and walk two blocks to a small grocery where she would do her shopping for the day. Everything was fresh in her daily diet except for an occasional tin of beans, a litre of milk, or a loaf of bread, each of which lasted several days. As the years had progressed her posture had suffered with the onset of scoliosis and arthritis. Now her gait was more of a shuffle. She looked at the pavement as she walked, never right nor left. At the corners she turned her head to look for oncoming traffic. Often a gentleman would offer to assist her in crossing the street. Lately she had been accepting the offers.

Chapter 50

If anyone had been watching Agatha the day before Fredek encountered the ghost from his past, they would have noticed that her shopping cart appeared to be heavier than usual when she pulled it down the stairs. It would have been apparent that it wasn't empty. That day it was serving as a suitcase and she was being especially furtive about it although trying desperately hard not to show it. A week before she had met a nice gentleman, French she thought and would relate later, who had offered her a financial proposition. He had approached her as she exited the green grocers. She had almost shied away because of his pronounced limp as she detested handicapped people.

"Excuse me, Madame," he said with a doff of his bowler. "My name is Miles Bjornberg. I am a businessman in need of a place to hold a couple of secret meetings during the next week or ten days. I have been scouting the area and noticed you leaving your house. It would be perfect for what I want."

Agatha Spenser had listened patiently to his entreaty. Listening was a virtue and she was a good listener – a necessity in her employment. She shook her head and started to turn away.

"I would be willing to pay."

This caused her to pause.

"Quite handsomely," he added.

She turned back.

"How much?" she asked.

"Ten thousand euros."

The amount was so unexpected, she almost fell from shock but managed to stay upright.

"Are you alright?" Miles Bjornberg asked.

She nodded. *He's mad,* she thought but she needed the money. She had, despite what she told people, outlived her finances and had been pinching pennies for over a year. This was something that Fredek's investigation hadn't revealed but, truth be told, if he had known it he wouldn't have cared. All he cared about was the fact that she was an old biddy who lived alone and didn't have any friends.

"All I need is your living room and the loo, of course. Maybe the kitchen for water and to keep some snacks. I will get a cleaner in when I am done. Clean the whole place top to bottom."

It needed that, she knew.

"I know you would need a place to stay while I am using your house. I am prepared to send you to Edinburgh ..."

"Scotland?" she said turning her head to look at him. She had never left York. Not even been to London.

"Yes. I have a reservation in a wonderful hotel and a ticket to the Tattoo."

"Really?" she queried tremulously, not believing her ears.

"Yes."

"I don't ..." she hesitated wondering if she should admit her doubts and then pushed forward. "...believe you."

"I didn't think you would. So I asked a solicitor in the neighborhood to draw a contract. If you would accompany me, his office is just around the corner, he will go over the document with you."

And he had walked with her around the corner to a door in a building. There was no sign on the door or window announcing that there was a solicitor's office inside. Again she hesitated.

"He just moved into the neighborhood. Hasn't had a chance to get things done."

He held the door open for her. Her trepidations were overcome by her lust for the money. Her life would become so much easier. And a trip to Edinburgh! To see the Tattoo!

"How do I get to Edinburgh?" she asked.

"On the Royal Scotsman," Miles Bjornberg answered. "In a private compartment, both ways."

That was all it took. She entered the doorway and found herself in a small office. There was a wooden table in front of which were two metal chairs. As she entered, a black man rose from behind the table and came to greet her.

"Welcome to my humble office, my lady. Ahh, Miles, I thought it might be you."

He showed her to one of the metal chairs and she sat down, leaving her cart beside her.

"Let me move that," the solicitor offered.

"No," she said defensively, putting her hand on the handle. "I like it with me."

"Very well. I am Franklin Weeds," the solicitor said going back around the table.

He picked up a folder and brought it back to her.

"This is a copy of the contract that Miles asked me to draw up."

She took the folder and opened it on her lap and picked up the first page, which she held only a foot in front of her face. She appeared to be embarrassed.

"Cataracts," she explained. "I don't see close up very well."

"I understand," the solicitor said and he commenced to explain the contract line by line. There was a stipulation that Miles had not mentioned but it was minor. That was that no matter what happened while her house was being used, she could only say that she had won the trip to Scotland and knew nothing of what went on. If she adhered to this for one year, she would receive another 5,000 euros.

"I find that satisfactory," she said.

When Miles produced a cheque for 5,000 euros, the balance to be paid upon her return from Scotland, she quickly signed the contract. Miles then accompanied her to her bank just a block away and she deposited the cheque. Outside the bank he thanked her and they parted. He walked back to the solicitor's office and met Franklin Weeds who was locking up. Not a word was said between them and they walked away. The solicitor never returned to his office that he had paid cash for three months rental only the week before.

That morning before Fredek's encounter with the ghost from his past, Agatha Spenser had walked toward the store but halfway there had gotten into a limousine. Five minutes later she (at least to the casual observer) had exited the limousine and returned to her house without going to the grocer's. There were strange changes in her appearance though. She was taller, but with her bent stature this was difficult to discern. She was heavier, but her baggy clothing hid that fact. She was younger, but a good makeup job concealed that fact. She limped, but, again with baggy clothing and slow gait, it was not very apparent. Although she appeared to have the usual difficulties in climbing up her steps, in fact she had none. Safely inside, her house, her stature and countenance changed. Michel Villar quickly shed his female clothing and stepped to the curtained windows. Through a crack in the curtains he watched the street for thirty minutes until he was completely satisfied that no one had noticed anything strange. Then he set about making his preparations for accessing Fredek Gavrilovich Kondrashin's townhouse the next morning.

Chapter 51

The townhouse on the end was the residence of Monica and Lissel Davies. They were twin sisters, Monica the oldest by ten minutes, born at 11:54 New Year's Eve, and Lissel, born 12:04 New Year's day. Actually that made it more fun for them as kids as each had a separate birthday. They were identical twins – well, almost identical. Monica's right eye was green and her left blue while Lissel was just the opposite with her left eye green and her right eye blue. The eyes made it easy to tell them apart.

When they grew up, they discovered they were lesbians – well, Lissel discovered it or, more accurately decided they would be. She had been willingly seduced by a boy when she was fifteen. In the beginning, the seduction had been exciting. It was daytime and they had been walking in the woods and had stopped in a small copse where they were hidden from view. They had kissed and both became aroused and they had sunk to the ground. His hands on her breasts, although clumsy and rough, had been titillating. She had cooperated completely, fumbling just as clumsily getting his zipper down and freeing his erection. At his urging, almost pleading she thought looking back on it, she had performed oral sex briefly. It had not been rewarding and she stopped and brought his hand down to her crotch. She was already wet and helped him remove her panties. She had guided him in and before she could ask him to go slowly, he had pushed into her quickly and deeply, breaking her virginity and lasting only a couple of strokes before ejaculating. It had hurt and she had basically felt nothing but pain.

Rather than try again, she had sought out a girl rumored to be a lesbian. Accepting an invitation to study at the girl's house, she had found that it was more than a rumor. The girl was accomplished and gentle, easily seducing her and bringing her to ecstasy. She had been a willing and eager student and in the course of several weeks had become an expert lover. It was then that she had, in the middle of the night, seduced her sister. It hadn't been a surprise since Lissel had shared her experiences with Monica. Having heard about the painful experience with her male partner, Monica had been hesitant about trying it with her boyfriend although there had been heavy petting. Monica discovered, as Lissel had, that sex with a woman was pleasurable and absent of pain. Thus they had accepted their sexual "fate" and became committed partners.

Probably to express their commitment, they took their physical difference and expressed them outwardly. The right half of Monica's hair – they were blondes – was as short as a military recruit's and the left side, shoulder length, was purple with green highlights to match her eyes. She had a gold chain running from a ring in her right ear lobe to a ring in her right nostril and a ring in her left upper lip. Lissel was her mirror image except her long hair was green with purple highlights and her chain was platinum – after all, being dominant she was more deserving.

They were both artists – struggling, to say the least. Lissel painted and Monica sculpted, mostly in metal. They had converted the upper floor of their townhouse into their studios with Lissel getting the eastern exposure and bigger windows because her painting required it. Being struggling artists, they really couldn't afford the townhouse but their father had made money in the construction business and his company, or one of his companies, had done the renovations.

Their art was mediocre at best but they had friends in the York art world and had managed to get a show of their works in a small gallery run by two male homosexuals. It was there that fate stepped in. Monica had been on duty to answer questions of inquisitive patrons of whom there were few when a black couple had entered. They were dressed in what Monica recognized as African but from what part she had no idea.

"Welcome," she had said holding out her hand. "I'm Monica. The sculptures are mine and the paintings are my sister's."

"Really!" the man had said accepting her hand. "I am Adisa and this is my wife Abeni."

"I love your names," Monica had said. "What do they mean?"

"They are both Yoruba. 'Abeni' means 'we asked for her, and behold, we got her.' "

Monica giggled and squealed, "I love it."

"So do I," Abeni answered.

"What about your name?" Monica asked Adisa.

"It is also Yoruba. It means 'one who is clear.' "

"Wonderful. Sadly I don't know what my name means," Monica said looking a bit crestfallen. "My parents named me after Saint Monica."

"Then it might please you to know,' Abeni said, "it is an ancient name in North Africa and first appeared in

Numidian inscriptions and is thought to refer to Mon, an ancient Libyan god. But nobody knows for certain."

"Oh, goody," Monica exclaimed. "I am both a Christian and a pagan."

Her look became one of puzzlement. "You said the names were Yoruba. What is that?"

"It is the language of an ethnic group from West Africa. There is a large population in Nigeria. That is where we are from."

"So your dress is Nigerian?"

"Yes, largely Yorubian ..."

"You did these sculptures?" Adisa asked having wandered away to stand in front of what appeared to be a lion but could just as well have been an elephant or a pig.

"Yes, do you like it?" Monica said as she and Abeni joined him.

"Oh, my goodness," Abeni said "I certainly do. I have never seen anything like it."

"I call it a Garlion," Monica said and, noticing the puzzlement on their faces, immediately added, "It is a cross between a male lion and a gargoyle."

"Ah, yes," Abeni said. "Now I see it clearly." But she didn't.

Chapter 52

The two Africans wandered the gallery the next ten minutes, Monica trailing behind far enough to give them their privacy but close enough to be able to answer any questions. She turned when she heard the door open and, seeing that it was Lissel, hurried to see her.

"They're from Nigeria," she said. "They like my sculptures, especially the Garlion."

"Monica," Abeni called as though on cue. "Who did this painting?"

"I did," Lissel said as the two sisters hurried to where the Abeni and Adisa were standing looking at a picture.

"You must be Lissel," Adisa said as they joined the two Africans. "I am Adisa and this is my husband Abeni. What was your inspiration?"

The picture they were looking at was a mixture of concentric circles and rectangles with the circles being done in pastels and the rectangles in garish colors.

"Sex," Lissel said.

"Ahh," Adisa said. "So we have breasts and penises!"

"Exactly," Lissel said.

"And the colors?" Adeni asked.

The two sisters looked at each other questioningly. Then Lissel shrugged and started to say something when Adisa said, "Sexual preference!"

Lissel nodded uncertain of what to say.

"What do you call it?"

"Sex."

"I love it!" Adeni said. "Bold and not understated."

The couple continued on through the rest of the exhibition for about ten minutes, communicating in low undertones. Then Adeni motioned the two girls over.

"How long does this exhibition last?" he asked.

"Just through the weekend," Lissel said.

"And then?" queried Adisa.

"What do you mean?" Monica asked.

"Where do these go after that?" Adisa said indicating all the paintings and sculpture.

The two girls looked at each other.

"I guess back to our studios," Monica said.

"What hasn't been sold," Lissel added, which hadn't been anything so far.

"Of course," Adeni said. "What would you think of letting us take it to Nigeria?"

The two girls were stunned.

"We don't understand," Lissel stammered.

"Oh, let me explain," Adeni responded. "We own a small art gallery in Lagos. We would like to put on a show with these," waving his hand and pointing around the gallery, "for about two weeks. We will pay ten thousand euros."

The two girls said nothing, only looked at each other with stunned expressions.

"Of course we will pay for the packing and shipping both ways," Adeni said.

"And your airfare and accommodations," Adisa added.

"You want us to be there?" the girls exclaimed simultaneously.

"Of course," Adisa said.

The two girls shrieked and grabbed each other jumping up and down.

Fifteen minutes later, Adisa and Adeni left the gallery after giving the girls a down payment check for one thousand euros and promising to attend their impromptu party that night.

They walked away about fifty feet and then burst out laughing.

"That stuff is terrible," Adisa said. "Especially that Garlion."

"And that sex painting," Adeni said. "Ghastly. However, if nothing else they took our suggestion for a celebration party without hesitation."

"Young people don't need much of an excuse."

"Wonder what they'll think when there are no more checks and no African show?"

"Maybe they'll learn a lesson," Adisa said.

The celebratory party that evening was exactly what one might have expected Alcohol and drugs – lots of drugs – and the party went on into the wee hours and people of all sorts were coming and going. Despite the lateness of the party, the two girls were up early and off to see "mum and da" to spread the good word of their fortune. What they and everyone else had failed to notice was that two people, notably the Nigerian art gallery representatives, had never left but had secreted themselves in a little used storeroom on the third floor of the townhouse.

An hour after Monica and Lissel had departed, the two representatives, dressed in regular clothes and carrying their African garb in plastic bags, made their way out of the storage room into the studio of Lissel where, in a little closet, they made their way into the attic. This was the one flaw in The Facilitator's careful planning because the attics of the six town houses were all interconnected.

Chapter 53

Tres and I waited in the attic above the sisters' townhouse for almost an hour before Michel Villar stuck his head through the trap door in Agatha Spenser's place.

"I watched him turn the corner and waited five minutes just in case he came back," he said as he started to climb out.

"How did you get up?" I asked.

"Stood on a chair."

"Well, get down and put it back. Clean up any junk that fell from the attic and then I'll pull you up."

He glared at me like a small child asked to do something he didn't want to do but he disappeared.

The attic was filled with cobwebs and dust, not to mention mouse and possibly rat droppings. I doubted that anyone had ever come up into the attic through the trap door in the sisters' place. In order to get into the attic, I had also used a chair. Once in the attic, Tres had moved the chair back and I had dropped a nylon rope with a loop in the bottom and pulled her up until she could grab the frame of the hole and help. Michel was heavier and made the lift more difficult.

While we were doing this Tres used a damp cloth we had brought to clean the cobwebs and other detritus off the door above the Facilitator's place. The surface of the door wouldn't take a suction cup so I used a tripod with three prongs with extremely sticky gunk on the ends and pulled up the door. The space below was a closet as it was in both the sisters' and Agatha's, but this one had an occupant. Michel Villar noticed the look on my face and asked, "What's wrong?"

"Unexpected company," I said motioning him to look. He moved across the intervening space careful to step on the joists. Next to the opening he knelt beside me and looked down.

"A cat!" he said.

Indeed it was. As quiet as we had tried to be, we hadn't been quiet enough to escape the detection of Sasha although we didn't know her name then. She stood in the opening of the door that had been left ajar. She was looking up at us, more curious than scared I judged, but then I don't know cats very well.

"I don't think she'll hurt us," I said.

"How the hell do you know?" Michel Villar sneered. "Friends had a cat who didn't like anyone other than them. Someone broke into their place and saw the cat. Tried to be friendly and reached out to pet it and the cat tore the hell out of his hand and then ran and hid under the couple's bed. He thought he could continue then and wrapped his hand with some cloth. As he was walking by the couple's bed on his way to the dresser in search of jewelry, the cat launched a sneak attack and scratched his leg to pieces through trousers. The guy leapt up on the bed to get away from the cat and didn't dare get off. The couple came home and found him there, cringing up against the headboard with the cat in the middle of the bed. The animal was so upset that it scratched the husband's hand when he picked the cat up."

"I am certain that this is not a cat like that," I said a smile on my face. "But that's why we have Tres along. She can bandage your wounds."

"My wounds!" Michel Villar said. "I'm not going down there until that cat is gone."

"Yes, you are," I said. "This is your show. You go down and secure the area and we'll follow."

"Why don't we just shoot the cat?" Michel Villar asked.

"Don't you dare," Tres said. "It's just a cat."

Trepidatiously, Michel Villar lowered himself through the trapdoor, his eyes never leaving the cat, which stood in the door opening and didn't move. Michel Villar hung there for a minute watching the cat and then dropped to the floor. The cat jumped back a few feet but then came forward until it was a foot from Michel Villar.

"What do I do?" he asked.

"Stick your hand out for it to smell," Tres said.

Michel Villar did this, slowly extending a hand to the cat. The cat sniffed it and then looked up at Michel Villar expectantly.

"What's it want?" Michel Villar asked.

"She wants you to stroke its head," Tres said.

Michel Villar extended his hand and stroked the cat's head. In response the cat move against his legs and rubbed itself.

"He likes you," Tres said.

"What do I do now?" Michel Villar asked.

"Move out of the closet so we can get down," I said.

He started to and almost fell when the cat wrapped itself around his legs.

"He won't let me move," Michel Villar said.

"Pick him up," Tres said and he did and moved out of the closet.

I lowered Tres down and then followed. We found ourselves in an exercise room, several pieces of exercise equipment scattered around, big screen TVs on each wall and a large square padded mat in the middle of the floor.

"Better than a dusty room," I said. "At least we won't leave visible traces."

"Except for what we brought from the attic," Tres observed pointing at prints the three of us had left.

Michel Villar had put the cat down and pulled his Glock.

"Let's be sure the place is clean," he said.

Pulling my Beretta, I joined him and the two of us move stealthily from the room that occupied most of the upper floor. Then we moved down the stairs; at Michel's insistence I went first because the cat kept going between his legs and he finally had to pick it up. He returned to the exercise room and gave the cat to Tres, who was cleaning up the mess we had left. By the time he got to the second floor, I had made certain that it was unoccupied and was waiting at the top of the steps.

I led the way and we cleared the floor, being joined almost immediately by Sasha and Tres.

"Third floor is clean," she said and held up a plastic bag containing a cloth she had used to wipe up our prints.

Then we settled in to wait for The Facilitator to return.

Chapter 54

When The Facilitator collapsed, Tres rushed to his side. Michel Villar had jumped up from his chair dumping the cat onto the floor. The cat appeared to be nonplused and started to clean itself.

"What's wrong?" Michel Villar asked.

"He's cyanotic," Tres answered. "I think he's had a heart attack."

She reached into her pocket and pulled out a capped vial. Opening it, she dumped a pill onto her hand and forced it into his mouth.

"What's that?" I asked as I knelt by her side.

"Aspirin," she said.

The Facilitator opened his eyes and looked around wildly. His breath was ragged. His face was contorted with pain.

"My heart," he gasped.

"Chew the aspirin," Tres said.

"There's glycerin by my bed," The Facilitator gasped.

I held the bottle where he could see it and shook it. He stretched an arm up and I shook my head. It wasn't difficult to do.

"Call an ambulance," he moaned.

"Not going to happen, Fredek," Michel Villar said as he knelt by The Facilitator's side. "At least not until you tell me who hired you to kill me."

A smile flitted across The Facilitator's lips.

"You did," he replied.

"No, I mean who hired you to kill me?"

The Facilitator's body shook. His eyes closed as he winched from pain.

"Tell me, Fedrek, or you won't have a chance. Looks like it's the Widow Maker."

"Never been married," The Facilitator said wryly.

"Tell me," Michel Villar said, trying to grasp The Facilitator's shirt but Tres pushed his hands away.

"Can't," The Facilitator said. "My code."

"To hell with your code," Michel Villar said as he pressed his pistol to the side of The Facilitator's head. "Tell me or you won't die from a heart attack."

"Ask ... Dick ... the ... Butch...," The Facilitator said as his body shook. He raised his head from the floor, shouted something incomprehensible and his body went limp, his head hitting the floor.

Tres felt for a pulse, put her head against his chest and listened. She raised her head and held her hand in front of The Facilitator's nose.

"He's gone," she said.

"Try CPR," Michel Villar said jumping to his feet. "Do something."

Tres put her hands on the floor and pushed herself up. I did the same.

"There's nothing to do, Michel," she said. "We need a defibulator and don't have one. By the time you'll get paramedics here, it will be too late. It's too late now."

"But I need to know. Someone is out there trying to kill me."

"No, Michel," I said. "No one is trying to kill you. You're dead."

"But ... what he said made no sense. Dick the Butch. Sounds like a male dyke."

"No, it's not," Tres said. "It's Shakespeare."

Michel stared at her not comprehending.

"Shakespeare?"

"Yes," Tres said. "Henry VI, Act IV, Scene II. They're talking about starting a revolution and how to proceed. Dick the Butcher says, 'The first thing we do, let's kill all the lawyers.' "

"How do you know that," I asked Tres.

"College. We did the play. I was in it."

"Kill all the lawyers?" Michel said. Then a light seemed to come one and he looked at me. "Did he mean ..."

"I think so," I said. "I think so."

CAT CALLS 999

A strange call was received at the York 999-call center. The operator asked what the problem was and had no answer. She asked again and heard a cat meowing. She repeated her request and had the same answer. Understandably pessimistic that a cat could have called, she dispatched a patrol wagon.

The officer rang at the door but there was no answer. Through a window he could see an arm and near it a cell phone. Rapping on the window and receiving no response, called for an ambulance. Then he tried the door and found it unlocked. Entering he found a man's body lying on the floor and near his right arm a cellphone which was on. He felt for a pulse but found none although the body was warm. He picked the cell phone up and found that he was talking to the 999 operator. The operator asked if there was a cat there just as the officer felt something rubbing his leg. He

looked down to see an orange tabby rubbing his
legs and meowing.
     When the ambulance crew arrived, they tried
to revive the man but to no avail. They took
him to the hospital where he was pronounced
dead. No identification will be released as
the police try to find next of kin.

     We actually laughed when we saw the story two days
later. We had called 999 and then gotten Sasha to meow
rather plaintively. Once we understood that the operator
was sending a patrol car we left. Because of his limp,
which slowed him, down, Michel Villar had left first,
actually before we made the call. We kept tabs on the
story and learned that Sasha was to be the prize in a
lottery. Each ticket was one pound and the proceeds went
to the animal shelter where Sasha had been taken. The
lottery was won by a young couple with two small
children and we knew that she would be happy there. The
story had created quite a stir amongst the populace and
the shelter was the beneficiary of ten thousand pounds.
Of course, no family members were found but there was a
will and The Facilitator was sent home to Russia for
burial. We felt sorry for him because everyone should
have someone and wondered if anyone had attended his
funeral. Of course, we couldn't but we did send a wreath.

Part VII

Kill All The Lawyers

Chapter 55

There were two lawyers to whom The Facilitator could have been referring: Chyrise Callahan, who was the lawyer for Howard Blake, my no-good brother-in-law; and Phil Dombrey, lawyer for my no-good wife. Yes, my no-good wife. After all, the whole thing, at least as far as I could determine, was her idea. If Chyrise and Phil Dombrey were both guilty, her death would probably alert Phil and we wanted to avoid that. We had a pretty good idea that if it was either of them, it was Phil. Let me explain why we didn't believe it was Chyrise.

Despite the fame that the trial on St. Nantes and her defense of my no-good brother-in-law Howard had brought, Chyrise Callahan had not moved her office from where she originally established it. However, she had expanded her staff to include a secretary and a paralegal. She had grown up in the L.A. projects and gone to U.C.L.A. after two years at Los Angeles Community College. Her ambition to be a lawyer was prompted by the inequality she saw while growing up. She took the LSAT and, although doing well, she was not offered admittance except from Thomas M. Cooley Law School in Lansing, Michigan. While very successful, she didn't like the cold Michigan winters and, after a year, sought a law school in warmer climes. She was accepted by Florida State University and Tulane University and chose Florida State because she felt Tulane, being in the recently hurricane devastated New Orleans area, would not offer her the best physical environment. She graduated with honors and secured a job as an Assistant State Attorney with the State Attorney's Office for the Florida Eleventh Judicial Circuit, serving Miami-Dade County, Florida. Three years there, working in a courtroom setting for the last two years convinced her that she wanted to be a litigator. Done with the obligation of law school student loans because of her service with the state, she headed back to Los Angeles. She passed the California bar examination and established her own law office near the projects where she grew up and worked pro bono much of the time, finding enough paying cases to live on, but it wasn't easy. Her first big break came when she successfully defended an indigent white man accused of robbing and raping three black women. It turned out to be a case of badly mistaken identity, since the true perpetrator was a black man. But it made her a name and paying clients poured in. Despite being a diehard bigot, Howard had been one of them. Actually Howard had chosen her because he was a bigot and needed to show those "friggin' faggot frogs" that he wasn't. However, it hadn't helped.

Chyrise had returned from the trial on St. Nantes a bit depressed but much wiser in her chosen field. Those people who heard her summary could really sense that she was on her way to fame and fortune. She didn't want to, but she had returned to St. Nantes for the hanging of her client. Strangely she had stayed clear of Phil Dombrey, Elise's lawyer, going so far as to stay over one extra day because he was on the plane she was scheduled to take.

We decided to entrust her inquisition – for want of a better word – to Jovelyn. She was to act as an aspiring writer who was doing a book on my disappearance and the trial.

***

"I am terrible on being able to tell a person's ethnicity," Chyrise said after Jovelyn introduced herself. She had called ahead and told the secretary what she wanted and Chyrise had set aside an hour in a busy schedule more out of curiosity than anything else. "I know that I should be able to get a clue from your name but 'Gagalac' does nothing for me."

Jovelyn smiled. "I'm from the Philippines. I grew up there, went in the military service and then came here to school. Went to Florida State."

"I did too," Chyrise exclaimed. "But you know that."

"Yes. I know a lot about you but I need more information on you, a deeper insight into your thoughts, to make you appear real in the book."

"I don't understand completely but I will try to help. However, there is one ground rule and it is one I will insist on."

"Yes?" Jovelyn responded smiling. "Only one?"

"There may be others but this one is definite. I will not talk about Phil Dombrey in any manner or form."

"Oh," Jovelyn said dejectedly, trying to look sad. "Your relationship with him is one of the things I had hoped to learn about. I think it is crucial to understand how things went in the trial."

"I'm sorry but that's how it has to be," Chyrise said, starting to stand.

"No, I'll work around it," Jovelyn said feeling that she was about to be dismissed. "No mention of the other lawyer. Fine."

Chyrise sat back down.

"Let me start at the beginning," Jovelyn said, not wanting to give Chyrise time to think. "How did Howard Blake get you to agree to be his lawyer?"

Chyrise laughed.

"He bribed me."

She noticed Jovelyn's quizzical look and then explained.

"Howard called for an appointment and I agreed out of curiosity. I had read about things in the paper. Keith Mitchell, his banker friend, committing suicide – at least that's what the paper said."

"You sound as though you don't believe it."

Chyrise sat silently for a moment, looking at her hands that were clasped on top of the cherry desk in front of her.

"Then I did. It was what the papers said. But Howard had his doubts."

"He never expressed that during the trial. I have read the transcript, of course."

I had gotten a transcript from Michel Villar as part of the agreement to help him. Then it had been out of curiosity, but it had proved useful in preparing Jovelyn.

Chyrise agreed.

"No, of course the proof showed that he had. Despite the confession, both Howard and Elise kept insisting that Keith was delusional and the note was part of that delusion. I almost came to believe that too, but it seemed almost to be a straw they started grabbing at from the beginning."

"Yes, let's get back to that beginning," Jovelyn said, changing the subject.

"Yes, meeting Howard. It was late on a Friday afternoon. He came into this office about 4:00. I didn't have a secretary then. It was just me. I had a bell that sounded when the door was opened. I got up and went out to see who it was although I was expecting Howard. He was standing there just inside the door looking around. '*Mr. Blake*,' I said extending my hand and walking toward him. '*I'm Chyrise Callahan*.'

"He looked a little shocked to see me, I thought. He extended his hand and shook mine, holding it gently. He looked into my eyes, smiled and said, '*Let me cut to the chase. I don't like nig... African-Americans, or chinks, or spics. I don't trust those French frogs because they have no spines. If this means you can't or won't be my lawyer, please say so now and I'll leave*.' I was shocked, naturally, at his bluntness. I knew that bigots still exist in this day and age. I've encountered a few others but none has been as forthright in admitting it. I decided then and there that if he could be that blunt with me, he was someone with whom I could work."

"Did you believe that he was innocent?"

Chyrise was silent for a long time.

"I never could get a good feel of his innocence. There was always something there. Nothing tangible but something blocking an absolute decision on my part."

"What about his sister?"

Chyrise looked at Jovelyn and her right eyebrow raised.

"I've never thought about her because she was ... wasn't my client. But looking back on it, there was this same block. I couldn't get a good read on her. But she was an actress or at least had studied acting. When she testified, I ... didn't... couldn't believe her. Something there was not quite right. But Phil did. He believed her. He wanted ...," she paused, frustration written all over her face. "Damn it to hell. Excuse me, Jovelyn. I just broke my own rule. Well, my fault. Now that that's out, I might as well be completely honest."

Chapter 56

She stopped and reached across her desk and turned off the tape recorder that Jovelyn was using. This was something they had agreed upon prior to the meeting. Then she continued.

" I could tell by the way that Phil looked at her that he wanted in her panties if he hadn't already been in them. And he wanted in mine and almost made it. That last night on St. Nantes, the day after the trial. We had stayed to talk about the appeal and file papers. We didn't go back because the appeals court told us that it wasn't necessary. We went out to dinner, not a celebration, but sort of to mark the end of it all. He was a gentleman. Always acted like a gentleman but I could see him ogling every pretty body in the place. He was practically undressing them with his eyes. Just like he had done me. I didn't think that I drank a lot but I must have because there we were at dinner and then suddenly there I was – flat on my face on his bed. Well, I didn't know it was his bed. My clothing felt strange, my skirt was high and then I felt a tugging at my waist. I was groggy, it took a minute, not really that long, but I suddenly realized that someone was pulling down my panties. I managed to roll over and looked up into his face. He said something about a tiger and liking that. I think. I pushed my hands up into his face and brought my knee up hard into his crotch. He moaned loudly and rolled off me, almost off the bed. I was up in a flash – well, as fast as I could go in that drugged state –and started out of the room. I was halfway out the door when I realized I didn't have my purse. I turned and saw it on the floor at the end of the bed. I raced back and picked up it and when I stood, he was laying on the bed in a fetal position, hands in his crotch and he was screaming at me, '*You black bitch. You're just like all the other whores.*' I turned and fled. That was the last time that I was near him. In order not to leave on the same flight, I made different arrangements and I left earlier than he the next day. When I was back for the execution – never want to see another one of those – I stayed far away from him. Even changed plane reservations out because he was on the flight I was booked on."

She stopped and sat back in her chair. "Wow. That felt good! Getting it out! It's been a long time. However,…" and she looked at Jovelyn quite sternly "if I ever hear or read about this episode, you won't have a nickel to spend the rest of your life."

Jovelyn wanted to laugh but didn't. Instead she just smiled. "You don't have to worry. My nickels are very important to me and your story has nothing to do with mine."

They both seemed to relax. Jovelyn reached for the tape recorder. "May I?"

"Of course," Chyrise said.

"Let me change subjects for a minute. How did you feel about the trial?"

"What do you mean? We lost."

"No, do you think that it was handled fairly?"

"No. Yes. I mean, I didn't like the way it was done, with the judge asking questions and all. I felt that I had no control. It was run his way but that's what the French do. I didn't like it because it is not what I am used to.

However, that said, we were given a fair chance within the rules of the system and we did our best.

"We – I have to include Dombrey in this – weren't given too much to work with by our clients. They kept things from us. Basically I think they lied to us. The story they told at the trial seemed almost connived, almost pulled out of a hat at the last minute. When the trial started, I don't think they thought there was any evidence and then wham." And she held up her hands enumerating. "One – Quentin Baston is miraculously alive with his damning unshakeable testimony. Two – the money. Fingerprints or not, that was damaging. Three – the picture. I felt at that point the trial was over. We had lost. When we had our chance, we did our best but nothing we did, nothing we tried, seemed to work.

"So, I didn't like it and still don't. The judge was fair, given the way it was conducted. I read that he died recently. Some kind of freak accident. I can't say that I'm sorry but no one deserves to die like that. He wasn't that old."

The five of us listened to the tape when Joaquin and Jovelyn returned to Nassau from Los Angeles.

"I don't believe that she had anything to do with it," Jovelyn said. "She was sincere or one hell of an actress."

I agreed, as did Tres and Joaquin.

"I tried to pick her up after the execution," Michel Villar said. "She was civil in her turndown, one of the nicest I ever had. I don't think she was in on it."

"She also doesn't have the money," I said. "I looked at her accounts and 75% of her income goes into helping the people in the projects. If she had enough money to pay The Facilitator, I don't know where she got it."

"So it's on to Miami then," Michel Villar said.

"Yes, but not you."

"Why not," Michel Villar almost screamed.

"Because you're too close. You handled The Facilitator with too much relish."

"But he tried to kill me!" Michel Villar snarled vehemently.

"Yes and you were stupid enough to try to get him to fake the assassination which almost brought about your death. I am not about to let you screw it up again."

"But I managed with him."

"You were in a controlled situation that we set up. One of us was always there with a weapon and we would have killed him if anything went wrong. It is completely unlikely that we will have any such chance with Dombrey. We are going to have to manage it sensibly."

"I AM GOING TO BE THERE," Michel Villar screamed.

"If you are, you are going to be alone."

I could tell that this had stunned him.

"What do you mean?"

"You came and asked me to save your life. To make you disappear. I did, but in doing so, I brought not only myself but also Tres into jeopardy. Since then I have brought Quentin and his family to the brink and now Joaquin and Jovelyn. They are here to help me, and if helping me means helping you they will. But they will not do it if you are present. They are also on the brink being allied with me. One false step and we all die."

Michel Villar looked at Joaquin and Jovelyn.

"We have no reason to help you without Josef," Joaquin said. "My wife and I will walk away if Josef won't help."

Michel Villar looked defeated.

"Okay, you win," he said. "I don't like it but you are probably correct."

"I am," I said and could have crowed in celebration. I didn't tell him about the photographs we have of him reading newspapers with the dates clearly after the day 'his ashes' were spread at sea. "But I think I know a way to do it that you will approve."

"What is it?" demanded Michel Villar.

And I told him.

Chapter 57

The party was in high gear by 7:00 p.m. despite this being a Wednesday. Because it was a Wednesday, it would end early, probably about 2:00 a.m. or 3:00 a.m. at the latest. Wednesday was an unusual night for a bash like this, but it had to be since this was the day that Phil Dombrey's divorce was final. Everyone had expected it ever since he had returned from that trial on St. Nantes. The guilty verdict for his client had left him an empty, bitter person. His persona took an additional downswing when the appeal failed. *"It was a sham,"* Dombrey had told anyone who would listen. *"We didn't stand a chance."* Still he held out hope until he had gone back to St. Nantes to see Elise Andrews and her brother hung.

"Strung up from the yardarms," Phil would exclaim in his most inebriated moments, which were more and more frequent. That part was certainly true because the St. Nantes gallows (hanging was the only option for those given the death sentence) was in the form of a ship's mast. This originated in the 1728 when a pirate ship under the command of John-Paul LaPre had raided the small Village of St. Nantes, as it was known at the time. They were forced to surrender when five fishing boats returned home and seized the pirate's ship while most of the crew were ashore. The Christian populace set the pirates free only to have them return the next year. Overpowering the villagers, the pirates set fire to the church that contained the families of the fishermen who had overcome them the year before. But not before

Genivee Lacour, wife of one of the fishermen, cut Jean-Paul LaPre's cheek with a knife secreted in her skirt. That effort was immortalized by the residents in renaming the small port Genivee. As for LaPre, he and his ship were sunk by a British warship and the seven survivors brought back to St. Nantes for a speedy and unneeded trial. The seven where strung up from the yardarms of the ship and the tradition started.

Phil Dombrey started drinking (more) and, apparently, enjoying it more. He started picking up young girls and women – never a man, at least not to anyone's knowledge. It didn't take long for his wife to have her fill and she filed for divorce. There was no contesting it and Phil started planning the bash to be held on his yacht. This was not a small yacht, but a fairly big one at 180 feet and since the start of the divorce proceedings it had become his home because he didn't stand a prayer of getting his house. Anyone who was anyone in his life was there – except for his wife and kids. And, naturally, there were some who weren't in his life at the time who were there incidentally. These included several young ladies who had panties that he wanted to get into, and the four of us: Joaquin, Jovelyn, Tres and I. We weren't invited, of course. We were working.

Naturally the party was catered and we were part of the wait staff, serving drinks, hors d'oeuvres and the like. Strangely four members of the wait staff scheduled for the party had been taken ill suddenly and recommended us as replacements. Imagine that. Being the only one that Dombrey might recognize, I was wearing a wig and had grown a beard again. Needless to say, the lecherous Dombrey had tried to grope both Jovelyn and Tres but had been warded off.

As the evening progressed, he became increasingly drunker as did many of the other guests. Especially noted was one buxom blonde with deep, inviting cleavage but she seemed more interested in another of the guests and this miffed Dombrey. It was obvious that her panties were the choice of the evening.

Toward midnight, the food started to dwindle as did the guests but the liquor was still flowing freely. Also, judging by the eyes (and noses) of some of the guests, there was more intoxicating stuff to be had somewhere on the boat. In the shuffle of guests departing, the blonde had apparently become separated from her victim of choice who had departed hand-in-hand with someone else and thus laid herself open to Dombrey's advances. He started successfully plying her with glasses of very good vintage champagne. I know that all vintage champagnes are supposed to be good, but they aren't.

Shortly after one a.m., she passed out. At Dombrey's request, Joaquin and I carried her to one of the staterooms that, judging by its lavishness, was his. We laid her on the bed, making certain that she was breathing and left. By one-thirty the guests were gone and we had only to cleanup. Dombrey was not the trusting type and so he hung around making certain that none of the yacht's silver service or crystal ware was missing. Then he tipped us generously and hustled us off the yacht. He stood on the deck watching us until we were in our car and out of sight. Then he went below.

The blonde was lying as we had left her, covered with the bedspread. He pulled this down and eyed her lasciviously, reaching his hands inside her bodice and massaging her breasts. She didn't move. Then he went into the cabin's head and returned wearing only a silk robe. He sat on the side of the bed massaging her breasts with his left hand and himself with his right. Feeling ready he pulled her skirt up above her waist and then pulled down and off her panties. He took a small digital camera from the top of the dresser and took several photographs of her. Putting the camera down, he rolled her over on her stomach and repositioned her dress above her buttocks and took several more pictures. Then he removed his robe and climbed onto the bed spreading her legs in preparation for his moment of triumph. He crawled up above her on all fours and was lowering himself to enter her when he heard ...

"Stop, you pervert. Leave that young lady alone."

Chapter 58

Startled, Dombrey fell off the bed and quickly rose again, grasping for his robe lying at the bottom of the bed, his erection having turned from the Rock of Gibraltar to wilted lettuce. Even the blue pill can't prolong an erection in moments of distress.

"What the ...? Who are you?" he stammered at the man standing in the cabin's doorway. The man he addressed was dressed in eveningwear having been one of the uninvited guests and having stowed away in one of the yacht's other cabins during the party. "Uninvited" is not totally true. True in that Dombrey had not invited him nor had any of the other guests, but I thought if anyone was to savor the vengeance of getting the man who had ordered his best friend killed, then he was the one. And although he was dressed in eveningwear, he had loosened his tie during his wait. Guillaume Martineau (age sixty-seven now) had been a gendarme sergeant major on St. Martin and had come to St. Nantes at age sixty when he retired. At six feet one inch, he weighed 240 pounds, which was thirty pounds more than at retirement. He blamed it on being less active now that he was no longer Michel Villar's bailiff but he still swam daily. He had played tennis regularly with Michel Villar and the two had been "senior" doubles champions two years in a row. His red hair was now tinged with grey and grey-green eyes flashed hostile as he viewed Dombrey.

"How quickly you forget," Guillaume Martineau said, the pistol in his hand never wavering from Dombrey's chest.

Struggling into his robe, Dombrey stared at him and he must have been an imposing sight standing in the narrow doorway. Seeing no kind of recognition, Guillaume Martineau acted as though he was holding a staff in his left hand and made a thumping action with it simultaneously stomping his left foot for effect.

"Guillaume Martineau," Dombrey was virtually speechless. "But ... why?"

"Certainly you can reason that out, you bastard. You had my best friend killed."

Realization struck. "That bastard deserved to die. He railroaded two innocent people to the gallows."

"He railroaded no one. The evidence spoke for itself. The jury vote was more than required for a guilty verdict. The appeal was upheld."

"By one of your frigging frog courts."

"Now you are insulting my county, you swine."

And now, I thought as I heard this, *I understand why Elise chose you as her lawyer. Your background in criminal cases was nil, but you had a hatred of the French that appears to rival Howard's and Keith's and possibly my wife's.*

If this leaves you a little in the dark, remember that Elise was my wife who plotted with her no good brother Howard to kill me. Keith was a friend of Howard's brought in to help. Of course, you might not understand why they tried to kill me. That could be the fifteen million dollar question and also the answer. Both Guillaume Martineau and I were wearing ear buds and microphones in case he needed help either physical or mental.

"Your country?" snarled Dombrey. "Just a bunch of faggot frogs like that Michel Vil…"

"Shut up," Guillaume Martineau snapped. "One more insulting word out of your mouth and it will be the last." As he said this he took a step closer to Dombrey. "You are nothing less than a pig the way you have drugged this woman and sought to take advantage of her."

"This whore," Dombrey said indicating the blonde, "was uninvited to tonight's festivities. All she was looking for was a good time and I am going to give it to her."

"You mean, you were. Not any more. You and I are going to the salon to have a talk."

"I'm not going anywhere with you, faggot."

Dombrey was too drunk to dodge the blow that Guillaume Martineau gave him with the back of his left hand, striking with all the vehemence of a backhand smash on the tennis court. The blow knocked Dombrey back against the dresser and he struggled to stay upright.

"I told you to keep your mouth shut. Don't make me do something that I'll regret. Now move." Saying this he grabbed the front of Dombrey's robe and jerked him toward the door. Propelled roughly forward, Dombrey stumbled but caught himself on the door jam. He started to turn back to Guillaume Martineau, but received a push sending him through the doorway and halfway down the passage way toward the stairway leading to the yacht's main deck.

"Get him in the main salon," I had told him. *"The coffee table will be all set with pen and paper. We'll get*

the girl out and to a hospital. You'll have about half an hour until the cops will arrive."

Guillaume Martineau didn't answer as he had his hands full getting Dombrey down the stairs. After he had Dombrey in the salon, he said, "Okay, we're clear. There's a digital camera on the dresser. He was taking pictures of the girl."

"We'll leave it there for the police to find. More evidence."

With this, Joaquin and I were out the door of the cabin we had been hiding in and quickly into the master's cabin. We had hurried back on board after Dombrey left the main deck. After pulling her skirt down to cover her nakedness, we rolled the girl over and ascertained that she was alive and breathing regularly. We moved her into the center of the bed and then picked her up in the bedspread that we then used as a litter. We left her panties for the police to find to help tie things together. I led the way out of the room, down the short passageway, down the stairs and onto the deck. As we crossed the deck toward the rear gangway, I could see Dombrey and Guillaume Martineau in the salon. Dombrey was seated in front of a coffee table on which I had put pen and paper. Guillaume Martineau was standing with his back to me, pistol trained on Dombrey, left hand gesticulating wildly. Just with this vision, one would have thought him to be Italian.

After getting down the gangplank, we eased our burden to the ground and took a brief rest. "Man, is she ever heavy. She didn't look very big," Joaquin said.

"Dead weight is often heavy," I said.

"She's not dead, is she?" Joaquin asked, fear evident in his voice.

"No, I didn't mean it that way. It is just when a person is asleep – sedated as she is – they are still and consequently they seem heavier."

"Good," Joaquin said, "you have me scared for a moment."

"Sorry. Okay, let's go."

With that we picked up the bedspread and the girl and carried her down the dock and out the gate. Waiting for us were Tres and Jovelyn and a cab they had called in anticipation of our arrival. Tres was also in audio contact with me. We got the woman into the back seat of the cab despite the cabbie's protestations.

"She's alive," I told him, giving him an envelope with a letter I had written while waiting in the cabin. "She's been given a roofie."

"Roofie," repeated the Hispanic cabbie. "No entiendo 'roofie.'"

"Date rape drug," I said.

He shook his head.

"Dope, uh, cocaine."

"Si, si," the cabbie nodded.

"She needs to go to a hospital."

"Si, I know where," the cabbie said.

I gave him a hundred and he got into the cab and left.

"We've got about fifteen minutes before this place is swarming with cops," I said, heading for our car.

"What about Guillaume?" Tres asked.

"He understands," I answered. "He asked to be alone with Dombrey."

We all got into the car and left, heading south for another boat basin where the Banyuhay was docked.

Chapter 59

Guillaume Martineau shoved Dombrey into the main salon. Seizing the opportunity – *It may be my only chance,* Dombrey had thought – he had whirled lashing out with a drunken semblance of a right hook. Had he been sober, he would have been faster – and he would have been more accurate. But he wasn't sober and he missed, his momentum carrying him completely around. Guillaume Martineau gave him a push that sent him stumbling a few feet and collapsing on the divan. Guillaume Martineau reached him in two strides, pulled him up and into a semi-sitting position. Dombrey looked up at him, malevolence in his eyes.

"You friggin faggot frog ..." was all he got out before he was hit with another serve, this one not a backhand and it was harder because in that hand was the gun. Had Dombrey been sober, had his brain worked at all, he would have suspected, and been right, that the gun Guillaume Martineau had was his own. Tres had used a lull in service early in the evening to search the master's cabin and had found the gun in a drawer, fully loaded.

"You watch your mouth, you filthy pig. I know all about you and your predilection for anal sex. Most animals like you don't care what the sex of the person is, all assholes are the same."

"I ...," Dombrey tried to get out.

"Shut up or you'll get another back hand, this time with the gun first."

Dombrey shut up.

"If you had the slightest knowledge of criminal law, if you had paid attention in law school like you should have, you might have done a better job in defending Elise Andrews. That might have made the vote closer, but I think that all you were interested in was getting her in bed on her hands and knees. You tried that with Chyrise but she wouldn't have any part of it, would she?"

"How did you …?"

"Simple. I asked her."

But he hadn't. It had been Jovelyn.

"Then you know…"

"Of course." Guillaume Martineau had no idea what Dombrey was talking about but he kept moving.

"However, that's not the point here and won't be the point at your trial."

Dombrey's head snapped up at this. "Tr … tr … trial. What trial?"

"Yours, for the murder of Michel Villar."

"I didn't kill that fag… I didn't kill him."

"No, but you had him killed. In my country, as in this, that is the same thing. Falls under conspiracy but, once again, probably you were not paying attention. How did you ever manage to pass the bar? I know that and I am not a lawyer."

"You can't prove …"

"Yes, I can."

"What evidence do you have?"

"Enough evidence to get a warrant for your arrest." And he pulled a folded sheaf of papers out of his pocket and flung them on the table in front of Dombrey, who snatched them up.

"But these are in French, I can't read them."

"My mistake," an intentional one and Guillaume Martineau snatched the papers out of Dombrey's hands, folded them and put them back into the pocket. He withdrew other papers from another pocket and thrust them at Dombrey.

Opening them, Dombrey scanned the papers, which indeed appeared to be a warrant for his arrest from the French Embassy in Washington.

"But what is the evidence?"

"We have two things. First, a confession from Fredek Gavrilovich Kondrashin known to most people as The Facilitator. He says you paid him $100,000 to eliminate Michel Villar."

"He squeezed me," Dombrey snarled. "It should have been $50,000 but that faggot ..." he flinched as he suspected another backhand. "But Villar offered him $75,000 to fake it so I had to up the ante."

Suddenly he realized what he had said and stopped. He looked up at Guillaume Martineau, mistake written all over his face.

"Thank you," Guillaume Martineau said reaching into his pocket and pulling out a miniature digital recorder. He hit two buttons and Dombrey's voice was heard, "...squeezed me. It should have been $50,000 but that faggot..." and Guillaume stopped it.

"This is not the only copy of this recording. I am wearing a wire and it is being transmitted to several other spots."

Actually only one, but Dombrey didn't need to know that.

"This will make Huard Jubert's job much easier. It's too bad I am going to be a witness because I would love to be bailiff at your trial."

Dombrey's composure seemed to collapse and he fell back against the divan.

"You know, as Michel said during the trial," and he smiled his best sardonic smile, "it's too bad Devil's Island is closed. You could have been put to great use there. The prisoners were always looking for fresh meat. But our modern prisons offer the same opportunity. When word spreads about how you like it in the ass …"

"But I …"

"You could try to convince them otherwise, but once they get it into their heads, they'll be licking their chops. At least until that noose stretches tight and snaps your neck." Guillaume Martineau grabbed an imaginary rope above his neck and gave it a jerk. He made a cracking sound, his head convulsed, and then flopped over. His eyes closed but for just for an instant and then his head was upright and alert. "They say that most people soil themselves even though they have used an enema beforehand. Always such a mess."

"What's that?" Dombrey said, his head snapping up, listening.

Guillaume Martineau listened and then smiled. "Sirens. Means the gendarmes are on the way. You see the girl was taken to the closest hospital with a note explaining what had happened and where. I think they'll want to talk to you. Also means it is time for me to go."

Picking up the papers he had given Dombrey, he exchanged them for the papers in French that he then dropped on the floor. Ejecting the magazine from the pistol, he caught it and tossed to Dombrey. Being unprepared and very drunk, he missed it and it fell to the floor.

"Clumsy," Guillaume Martineau said, racking the slide of the pistol and catching the bullet that he tossed at Dombrey who, being a little more prepared, caught it. Then Guillaume Martineau set the pistol on the table and moved quickly to the open door of the salon. He stopped and turned back to see Dombrey reaching for the pistol, fumbling it and knocking it on the floor.

"Better hurry," Guillaume Martineau said, "or I'll see you on St. Nantes."

He stretched the imaginary rope, made the cracking sound, then his head lolled and then he was gone. He moved quickly to the side of the yacht opposite the dock, removing the latex gloves he had been wearing and putting them into a pocket in his jacket. At the rail, he picked up a bag I had placed there earlier. Then placing his hands on the railing, he vaulted over it and went feet first into the water.

Chapter 60

"I want to thank you for the opportunity. I feel better now. I am sorry that Michel is dead but at least I had the opportunity to help catch his killer, or the money man behind the killing."

It was an hour after Guillaume Martineau had entered the waters of Miami's harbor. He had gotten his clothes off and into the weighted bag from which he had removed a small rebreathing tank. Then he swam underwater until he was far away from Dombrey's yacht. He let the bag sink into the silt at the bottom of the harbor and swam on until he reached the spot he had selected the previous day. He dropped the air tank in deep water before swimming to shore. There he had gotten out of the water, dressed in clothes left in his rental car and drove to the Ft. Lauderdale airport where he would take a plane out in a few hours.

"You are welcome. You have enough evidence what with the money transfer information and the tape that you should be able to get a conviction if it goes that far. Of course, you might have to wait until he gets out of the American penal system for possession of drugs." (Some his and some we had planted. Hey, the cops need all the help they can get!) "Also there are several cases of rape based on what we saw on the camera. Don't think he ever downloaded any of the pictures. Once word gets out, the victims are liable to come out of the woodwork."

"I don't know why you asked me to help with this."

"I told you that I owed Michel Villar a favor for something he did for me. Let's leave it at that."

"Thank you again. And good-bye." As he hung up the phone, he added quietly, "Josef."

Guillaume Martineau and I had never met face to face. Everything had been arranged via phone calls and I don't believe they were taped. I had paid for his flight to Miami and back but he had done the rest by himself with me providing needed gear. I don't know how he explained his absence to his wife but that is not my concern.

MIAMI LAWYER TAKES OWN LIFE

Miami police responded to call from the Harbor View Hospital with the report that a victim brought into the hospital had been assaulted aboard a yacht belonging to Miami Attorney Phillip Dombrey. When the police reached the yacht they discovered Dombrey in the main salon, dead of a gunshot to the head. A pistol belonging to Dombrey and bearing only his fingerprints was found in his hand. There was no suicide note although papers in French detailed a conspiracy to kill the judge who had sat on the case of Elise Andrews and her brother Howard Blake in the murder of Stuart Andrews, husband of Elise. The papers had only Dombrey's fingerprints. He had been the lawyer defending Elise Andrews in the case. Also discovered was evidence indicating that Dombrey was involved in other assault cases. The number and names of the victims were not released by the police at this time.

The papers that were found were a setup but, truth be told, we couldn't find any evidence other than the money transfer and that had been buried deep, but I have gotten fairly good at tracing the money trail. True there is the audio recording, but it has Guillaume Martineau's voice on it and I wanted to avoid implicating him. Now none of this would be needed. We wouldn't have left the papers there if we had known he was going to take the easy way out. We had left the port of Miami early the morning after the party and we learned about the newspaper article on the web. At least now we were done with the lawyers. That left the Cercle des Frères who were still a threat to me and Michel Villar.

Chapter 61

My head ached. My body tingled. My thoughts were foggy. What the hell happened? I tried to make sense of it. I had been walking back to the yacht after running a couple of silly errands. I had called Tres just before walking through the yacht basin's gate. As I had proceeded down the pier, I heard quick footsteps behind me and instinctively I had reached behind my back under my shirt for the Berretta I now carried out of force of habit. That force of habit being to stay alive. I started to turn to look back when ... blackness.

I opened my eyes, seeing only my pants – dirty, stained. Something red – stained with blood? My blood? I raised my head slowly because I sensed it would hurt to do it quickly. First thing I saw was a wooden floor. Then black boots. Dirty black boots. Military type boots. Above them were camouflage pants. Fatigues, I thought. Military? Then a nasty looking automatic weapon pointed down at the floor. The hand that held it was brown, not tan. Naturally brown. What did I expect? I was in the Caribbean. As I continued to raise my head, I saw a black t-shirt, exposing muscular arms, and behind it a muscular chest. The t-shirt was skin tight. Male. The blackness continued as I reached the neck and face area. A black hood. Maybe a balaclava. I couldn't tell. Everything was hazy. The whites of eyes visible through holes in the hood.

I stared at the eyes and felt – because I couldn't see – gleaming white teeth in a broad evil grin. Suddenly the silence – I don't remember any noise – was broken by a crashing behind me. I saw the automatic weapon start to come up, the body move a step back and simultaneously a red dot appeared between the two eyes and just as suddenly it disappeared, replaced by a black hole which spouted red and then was gone.

A form brushed past me, pausing briefly by the form of the fallen mercenary – what else could he be – before kicking the weapon away and then disappearing through a door in the wall. The mercenary had blocked its existence until his ended. I watched not knowing what to expect. Then the barrel of a weapon appeared in the opening, followed by a form dressed in a black t-shirt, black tactical pants and black boots – dusty black boots. I blinked my eyes and the form's definition sharpened. No hood, but a dark brown face, long black hair held back in a ponytail, white teeth in a broad grin.

"Clear," she said.

"Tres!" I said.

"Who'd you expect? Seal Team Six?"

Tres will be the first one to admit, just beating me, that since all this had started she had become extremely anxious. We were docked in Phillipsburg, St. Maartin, two weeks after the episode in Miami with Phil Dombrey and I had gone to pick up some things at the small store just outside the wharf area. When I had not arrived at the Banyuhay in ten minutes after I had called her from the gate, she had come looking, walking all the way down the pier (around a couple of turns) to the gate. It is not a guarded gate but one you have to swipe a card to enter but not to leave. The gate through which you leave is latched on the inside and is wide enough to permit a cart with luggage or foodstuffs through. I had told her that I was about to swipe my card when I had called. Starting there, she worked her way back to the yacht and it wasn't long until she found where I had fallen. There was blood on the raised portion of the pier, sort of like a gutter from the street to the sidewalk, only there wasn't a sidewalk and the pier was the street. She looked over the edge and on the bottom of the harbor could see a plastic bag. It wasn't dirty so she thought it was recent and recognized it as being from the store to which I had gone to get some stuff. That water was so clear she could read the name on the bag.

Realizing that something had gone amiss, she hurried back to the Banyuhay and turned on the computer and activated the software to track the beacons we both had implanted. There I was, moving away along a street. Quickly she changed into tactical black pants, boots and a black t-shirt. She grabbed a knapsack she loaded with an assortment of weapons, night vision goggles (just in case), and thermal imaging goggles we had recently obtained from Beecher McFalls. We had a motor scooter outside the gate we had rented to get around and she took that and started following my blip on the same type of handheld tracking device I had used to follow her when Richard Barton had abducted her.

It took her an hour but she found the small cottage where I was being held. Twice she had lost the signal. The first time she had panicked, but only momentarily. She remembered what Beecher McFalls had repeatedly drilled into us: *Stay in control! Panic kills.* She kept going and when she reached the spot where the signal had vanished, she acquired it again, the blip moving off the screen to the right. It was only there for a second and if she hadn't looked she would have lost it. There is a small ping associated with the blip – just like a sonar ping – but she couldn't hear it over the sound of the scooter's engine. She cursed the fact that she only had a scooter and then reminded herself that it was all that was available. She had thought at that point of another Beecher-ism: *Keep moving. You become a target sitting still.* She had run the scooter at full speed but when she reached the point of the last signal, there was nothing there. Figuratively she was at a crossroads and literally as well because there was one just fifty feet beyond where she was. She advanced to the crossroads, knowing that they – whoever "they" were – had to come this way. She flipped a mental coin and turned right promising herself at most ten minutes before turning around. At the end of ten minutes there was still no signal and she turned back. Stopping at the crossroads only momentarily, she turned right and soon was out of the city, or at least the heavily populated area. In her mind, this is where she would have taken someone. So even when there was no signal after ten minutes she continued on, promising herself just five more minutes. But the five minutes turned into six and then, just before she turned around, a blip showed on the upper left of the screen. It took her another fifteen minutes to find the house because the screen isn't like a GPS – there are no street maps. Just a black screen.

Chapter 62

At this point I was still unconscious. I had been stunned and then administered something in my arm – we found the bruise later. The cottage was on a dirt road; the nearest neighbor was a hundred yards away. Tres left the scooter behind a bush and hoped it would be there when she returned. She had left the padlock and chain lying back where the scooter had been parked. Despite the relative isolation of the cottage, she didn't want to draw attention, so she used a silenced pistol with a laser sight. The thermal imaging goggles let her know that there were three people in the cottage, two standing and one sitting. That would be me. There was a small car sitting next to the cottage with its trunk lid slightly raised – evidence that I had been brought here in it. Then, relying on our training with Beecher McFalls, she knew she had to separate the two men.

Inside the cottage, I had been administered a drug to counteract the sedative. We knew that because of the disposable needle found lying on the floor. No need to be tidy. They were only here for a short time – a very short time as it turned out. Sometime after that injection, a noise outside alerted the two men. Peering out the side window, one of them saw that the lid of the trunk was closed.

"Better check on it," one of them probably said and so one of them, the drawer of the short straw so to speak, went out to check and left the front door slightly ajar. He was probably cautious as he approached the car from the front of the house. He tested the lid and found it solid. No clue as to how or why it was shut. That was hidden in the trunk – a cord run from the lock mechanism down through a drainage hole in the floor of the trunk. Tres had raised the lid, fastened the cord, slid under the car and then pulled the cord hard. The trunk lid slammed shut and she laid still, pistol at the ready. If the guy had looked under the car – which he should have – he would have been greeted with a bullet. That was his greeting anyway for as he stood by the car looking around, Tres stuck her hand out between his legs, pointed the pistol skyward – make that crotch-ward – and pulled the trigger. She greeted his fall with another bullet, this one to the head.

Then she was out from under the car, moving stealthily to the front door, hoping that was her way in and it was, thanks to the man's sloppiness. The thermal imaging goggles enabled her to locate the other man, who hadn't moved. He should have watched his partner but he failed to do so, and that failing shortened his life expectancy by a little. Or it could have been a lot. Using the thermal imaging goggles, Tres pointed her pistol at the man's head, pushed the goggles up and with her left hand shoved the door hard. Even before it crashed back against the wall, her pistol was moving. You know the rest. Needless to say, she had bested me in almost every aspect of our training with Beecher McFalls. Needless to say, I have never been so happy to be second best.

I had tape across my mouth, my legs were taped to the chair's legs, and my hands where behind the chair held in flexi cuffs. She quickly freed me. After a brief embrace, she helped me to the front door and left me sitting on the steps. She ran around the house and dragged the first man's body to the front of the car to hide it as long as possible and then ran to get the scooter. The trip back to the harbor was uneventful – that is what she said. I was still in a fog and remember very little of it.

Later I asked her why, if she used the heat sensor goggles and knew there were only the three of us in the house, did she check out the back room? She looked at me incredulously and shook her head.

"What is Beecher's number one rule about electronics?"

I stared at her stupidly having no idea what she was talking about.

"No wonder you were number two," she said *"Electronics aren't foolproof – trust yourself first."*

At this point, we had no idea who the men were – there was no ID – or what they wanted. We would find that out much later.

It was several hours after the rescue that the Marchand de Sable (The Sandman) arrived. He parked his rental car behind the other, and then walked to the front door. He rapped on it twice, paused, and then repeated the knock. There was no answer. Pulling a gun from his pocket, he turned the knob and pushed the door open. He was greeted with silence and the smell of blood (but he didn't recognize it). Stepping inside he saw the body. *Where's the other?* he thought. Quickly he checked the back room and then looked outside through a window. He could see feet at the front of the car. Exiting the house and closing the door behind him, he walked past his car and then saw the dried blood where the man had been shot. After ascertaining that the body didn't belong to Josef, he got back in his rental car and left. He would have to find another way to get at the money.

Part VIII

Closing the Cercle

Chapter 65

I was sitting on a bench on the other side of the canal from the bookstore. Basically I was right across from the spot where I had stood – was it just two years ago? – after being told by Dieter, the bookstore clerk, that he couldn't help me. I was dressed like a bum, tattered jeans and tee shirt with a light jacket since winter was beginning to set in. I wished I had some tattered sneakers to wear now because my feet were cold in the sandals, but that is what a lot of bums wear over here. I was lying on a bench (more comfortable than the pavement) playing the role of drunk. I had a bottle in a paper bag and I kept taking "swigs" from it. If anyone were watching they could see that my swigs were taken when someone either entered or exited the bookshop. If anyone took a casual look at my bottle they would see liquid and could even pour some out if they went that far. Closer examination would show that the bottom of the bottle could be screwed off in half a turn and one would be holding a camera in one's hand. The lens was in the middle of the bottom and there was a matching hole in the bottom of the bag. The shutter was activated wirelessly. I held the Bluetooth controller in my other hand. I couldn't afford to be reckless and use binoculars to get a close-up view, but I would have to rely on blowing up images when I got back to my room. I was interested in four people, only one of whom I had seen. The one I had seen was Dieter, the bookstore clerk. I knew where he lived and what he did at night. After three nights of trailing him, I had given up, having discovered he liked to frequent cheap bars selling Mary Jane and undoubtedly other drugs and that his sexual preference seemed to be older men. I had sensed that he was a homosexual when he had found me in that coffee shop and given me the note that put me in contact with Pieter Devenpeck. I doubted that was his real name but it was by that name that I had known him seven years before (it was five at the time). He was the main one of the four individuals I was interested in seeing. The other three would, hopefully, lead me to him. I didn't have names for the other two, only memories of what they looked like. One was a young lady, a brunette whose last name may have been Metternich, at least when I first knew her she said that Allna Metternich was her daughter. That name was written in a children's book I was "supposed to be returning." The other was a muscular young man who may or may not have been her husband. I had no clue as to his name. I don't know what role the three played but I strongly suspected that Pieter Devenpeck was big in Cercle des Frères. Probably based on what I know now, I should call it Cirkel van Broers, which is Dutch for Circle of Brothers. I have no way of knowing if that was indeed the name of the group, if indeed it had a name, but that is what Michel Villar told me.

Getting here was lucky. However, if I had paid more attention I would have known where to go a lot earlier and maybe saved a lot of time and maybe some lives. After leaving Miami, we had gone back to the Bahamas aboard the Banyuhay, dropping off Joaquin and Jovelyn. They were going to sell the boat and take the money and return to the Philippines. They weren't certain what they were going to do there other than raise their family, the first child of which was already on the way. I set them up with enough money to help – actually enough money so they didn't need to work for about ten years. I told them there was more if they needed it but they didn't want the first amount either. We set up a way to keep in contact using email and they had explicit instructions that if they needed help in any way, they were to contact me.

Then Tres and I had taken the Banyuhay to Philipsburg, St. Maarten, where there were a couple of interested purchasers – we had use of it until it was sold. Our main purpose was to discuss how to proceed with Beecher McFalls. Although he was primarily ordnance and planes, he had a lot of ideas. We needed help because we didn't have the faintest idea where to go. Michel Villar had gone to ground, goodness knows where, and there was no trace, absolutely none, of Cercle des Frères. However, we didn't go directly to Beecher (who lives on St. Martin on the other side of the island.) If we hadn't gone to St. Maarten who knows what would have happened. Of course, that was where I got kidnapped and Tres had to rescue me, but that isn't what is really important as far as the Circle of Brothers is concerned. St. Martin and St. Maarten are two counties on the same island, although – and most importantly – St. Martin is French and St. Maarten is Dutch. We were sitting in a sidewalk café in Philipsburg enjoying a sunny afternoon with a round of *Painkillers*, when a young man and woman walked up to the table next to us and the young man asked the people at the table, "Wat gebeurt er?" Tres stopped in mid-sip and almost sprayed me with *Painkiller*. I turned around quickly and stood up, automatically reaching for my Berretta Nano that of late I had carried in a pocket holster. Of course it wasn't there. I reached out and touched one of the people. "What did he just say?" I asked. The young lady looked at me strangely and I thought at first she didn't understand me but she had. The way she looked, I tensed expecting some kind of insult like "Bug off you creep." but instead got "He said, 'What is happening?' " "What language?" I asked. This drew an even stranger look and she said, "Dutch, of course." Before I could say thank you, she was gone.

I sat back down, an obvious look of amazement on my face.

"What did she say?" Tres asked.

"They were Dutch," I responded.

"The kids?" she said gesturing at them.

"Yes, and the men who invaded The House at the End of the Road."

"That explains what we heard. We knew it wasn't French."

When we were on the Banyuhay after the attack and had killed the two "Brothers" lying in wait, we had heard this over a walkie-talkie. For some reason, it had stuck in my memory.

"No, but it should have been," I said. "Michel Villar intimated that the organization for which he worked was French."

"Couldn't they have been mercenaries?" Tres asked.

"They could have been, but I seriously doubt it. I think what it means is that whatever the organization is, it isn't French based but Dutch."

So we asked someone else how to say "Circle of Brothers" in Dutch.

"Why?" the lady had asked.

And Tres quickly responded, "We're playing a game. Like a scavenger hunt but with words."

The shop lady had no idea what a scavenger hunt was, but she told us what we wanted to know: Cirkel van Broers. That is how I got to Amsterdam again. This time by myself until I learned more. Tres had insisted that she come also but I said no. She needed to stay quiet and take care of our growing family.

Chapter 64

I had used a different approach and different disguise every day. Sometimes I was opposite the shop across the canal like today. Sometimes I was on the same side although at least a hundred feet away and sometimes I stood on a bridge as though whiling away the time feeding ducks. The second day I was sitting on a bench on the south side of the shop, same side of the canal. I had tried to dress as much like a native Netherlander as I could but quickly learned that I was not successful. Maybe it was my color.

"Hallo, vreemdeling," said a voice.

I had recognized the "hallo" and turned to see a little old man who couldn't have stood more than five feet tall and weighed less than a hundred pounds. He was wearing old clothes, not shabby but worn. He wore a beret (*Odd*, I thought, *for a Dutch man*). In his right hand he had a cloth bag and in his left what at first I took to be a walking stick. It was too long to be a cane and he grasped it about six inches below the top. The cane was adorned with a blue ball of either plastic or glass. His face was wrinkled and showed signs of weathering as though he had been in a trade where he had worked outdoors.

"Neem me niet kwalijk, ik spreek niet veel Nederlands," I tried to say in the little Dutch I had picked up using a small English-Dutch vocabulary book that I didn't speak much Dutch. Most likely, I murdered the pronunciation.

"Is okay. I not talk much Engels," he answered.

He stood there looking at me and I sat there, in the middle of the bench, looking at him. For a few minutes neither of us moved or said anything.

"What do you want?" I finally said.

He made a motion like I should move over. I felt stupid.

"Het spijt mij," I said as I unhappily moved to the other end of the bench, since I didn't want my view of the shop obstructed. Being so close I hadn't brought a camera.

He sat down and we both looked at the canal for a time with my furtive glances at the shop. He had put the bag down on the ground and his walking stick between us. Finally he picked up the bag and pulled out a chessboard and set it between us and looked at me.

"I don't play chess," I said.

He thought for a minute and then said, "Ik speel niet schaken," pointing at me and then again, "Ik speel niet schaken" and pointed at himself. Reaching into his cloth bag, he pulled out two clear plastic bags, one filled with white checkers pieces and the other with black checkers pieces. He looked at me and then gave me the bag of white checkers pieces. "Edereen speelt dammen," he said and started putting his pieces on the board. I caught the "speelt" but didn't understand the rest. I said, as best I could, "Edereen?" and he waved his hand in a semicircle and I caught it. I picked up one of the checkers and said, "Dammen" and he nodded and smiled. He pointed at the checkerboard and said "Dambord."

And so began a wonderful association which reoccurred every couple of days when I used that guise. I learned two things during our time together: some passable Dutch and that I was a lousy checkers player.

The latter didn't matter. We had a great time. That first day when I was starting to get hungry, he reached into his bag and brought out a big sandwich wrapped in brown paper. The bread was thick and dark, the meat and cheese wonderful. I know because after he got the sandwich unwrapped he picked it up in his two tiny hands and tore it in two pieces and handed me one. Halfway through the sandwich, I put my part down and walked to a nearby store and bought two bottles of water. When I came back, I gave him one and he thanked me. Then he thought for a moment, pointed to himself and said, "Hans Brinker." I laughed at the thought of that old man being the young boy with the silver skates. I made my feet move like skating and he appeared nonplused. Then he waited while I decided what to call myself and then said, for lack of anything better, "Josef Viljoen." Then I pointed at him and said, "Hans" and he pointed at me and said, "Josef."

Days when I was in a disguise such as the vagrant and his wine bottle, I would see Hans walk down the canal and find a place to sit and try to get someone to play checkers with him but it didn't happen successfully very often. He never appeared to recognize me when I was across the canal but I didn't think his eyesight was that good.

For three weeks I kept up this vigil, never seeing anyone I was watching for except Dieter. I was on the verge of trying to get information from him when the unexpected happened. I was sitting on the bench where Hans and I usually met, sitting in the middle to dissuade anyone from joining me and wondering where Hans was. He had been missing for several days. I heard a female voice saying, "Josef?" and I jumped to my feet.

Standing at the end of the bench was a heavyset middle-age woman. The first thing I noticed was her face with tears running down it. The second and third things were Hans' cloth bag and walking stick.

"Ja," I said, "ik ben Josef."

She thrust the bag and cane at me and started to turn away. Then she stopped and turned back. "Hans overleed afgelopen nacht. Hij wilde dat je te hebben deze. Dank u voor het maken van zijn laatste dagen prachtige." Then she stepped forward and kissed me on the cheek.

After she walked hurriedly away, I slumped onto the bench. Hans was dead. He died yesterday. He left me these two belongings. She said I had made his last days wonderful. I felt as sad as she had looked. I enjoyed my time with Hans. It had been the only good thing to come out of this effort so far. Now it was gone. I laid the walking stick on the ground in front of me and picked up the bag. Inside was the checkerboard, the two plastic bags of checkers and something wrapped in paper. I took out the package and stared at what was beneath it. Two plastic bags containing chess pieces. Hans was simply looking for someone to play either with him. I unwrapped the package knowing that inside was a sandwich just as we shared everyday. I didn't feel like eating so I rewrapped it and put it back in the bag.

Then I picked up the walking stick and looked at it. It really was a cane for a taller person, someone like me. I stood up and found that it was perfect, exactly the right height for me. As I grasped the glass knob, it felt loose. Sitting down, I turned and tightened it. No more wiggle. Curious now, I unscrewed it and the knob came off in my hand. I looked inside the knob and noticed a piece of paper stuck at the top of the screw hole. *Probably just to make it tight,* I thought. Then another thought struck me. *Why would he leave me these things?*

I screwed the knob back on, picked up the bag and, walking with the cane as one would, I went back to my hotel leaving my vigil for the first time in three weeks. In the security of my room, I unscrewed the knob again and used a straightened paperclip to remove the piece of paper. It was tissue paper, folded many times and I carefully unfolded it. On the paper was handwritten an address and the word "Succes." I started at the word in disbelief. How had Hans known? My thoughts ran back through the times that I was not with him, that I was in another guise further away or mostly across the canal. I recalled seeing him seeking out people to play checkers (or chess as I realized now), never looking in my direction. But he did more than that. He went in and out of all the stores on that block except for the bookstore. He knew that I was interested in the bookstore! That cagey old Dutchman. I then looked closer at the address "22 Herengracht." The same street where the barge had been when I had come here to get fake papers. But further away and on the other side. My three weeks had not been in vain and I said a silent prayer for the wellbeing of Hans' soul and added a bedankt. Now don't call me a hypocrite. I am not religious – basically an agnostic. But Hans might have been and saying a prayer was the proper thing to do.

Chapter 65

The next morning an old black man shuffled slowly down Herengracht. He was wearing a tattered long black overcoat, brown mittens on his hands. He was bent over and walked, eyes on the pavement, using a cane with a blue knob on top. Where there was a bench or any place he could sit, he took advantage of it and rested. His short-cropped hair was almost stark white matching a thin mustache above his lip. When he reached the doorway of 22 Herengracht, he sat on the stoop and rested for a long time. Several people came in and out of the building during the time he sat there, including a pretty young brunette who paid no attention to him either coming or going. It was obvious that she had been to the grocery when she came back, her cloth shopping bag full.

After about half an hour, the old man stood up and pulled a piece of paper from his pocket. He held it close to his eyes and then turned and painfully climbed the three steps to the door. He peered at the list of names by the doorbells, shook his head, turned and went down the steps to the sidewalk with meticulous care. Then he turned and continued up the street for about a hundred feet. He pulled the paper from his pocket again, looked at it and then crossed a bridge over the canal. He then proceeded back, paralleling the path he had followed on the other side, again taking advantage of every bench. When he was opposite 22 Herengracht, he laboriously climbed the steps and looked at the list of names. Again shaking his head, he carefully went back down to the street and sat on the bottom step. From the depths of one of the coat's pockets he pulled a paper bag containing a wine bottle. He uncorked the bottle and took a swig just as a white haired heavyset man who looked to be in his mid to late sixties came out of 22 Herengracht. He, known as Pieter Devenpeck to some, was also using a cane and was aided in his descent of the stairs by the young brunette woman. Then she kissed him on the cheek and went back inside. The man started walking slowly the way the elderly black man had come. As he walked, he was shadowed on the opposite side of the canal by that same black man who seemed to have been revived by the wine as his steps were a little quicker and quite a lot surer. Pieter Devenpeck walked down Herengracht about an eighth of a mile then turned and walked back that far again past number 22, then turned and returned home. Almost as soon as he arrived the brunette was there to help him up the steps. Over the course of the next two weeks Pieter Devenpeck continued his daily walks; they were a routine both morning and afternoon. As the days progressed, his strength and endurance seemed to grow, his stride lengthened, and the number of laps increased, although he never went beyond an eighth of a mile in either direction. Midway through the second week he had given up the cane and the brunette had ceased to accompany him, as he needed no further help on the steps. It was obvious that he was recuperating from a joint replacement, either hip or knee. He was always observed from the other side by one man during the first week and one of two men during the second. The first a black man in different guises was there morning and afternoon the first few week. During the second he was replaced by another man older, shorter, heavier set, eyes perhaps more vigilant, always scanning, looking, watching.

Finally one morning when Pieter Devenpeck started his walk, the older watcher was already walking in the direction that Pieter Devenpeck was headed although twenty-five feet behind. As Pieter Devenpeck neared the turnaround point that he had been using the past couple of days, a tall black man came down the steps of an apartment building where he had been waiting in the doorway and fell in about five feet behind Pieter Devenpeck, the older watcher beside him. In the matter of a few paces, they were beside Pieter Devenpeck and each grabbed an arm. The black man hissed, first in English and then in Dutch. "Do what we say and your daughter will be fine." Simultaneously with this warning, Pieter Devenpeck felt a poke in the other side that he could not mistake as being the business end of the pistol.

He had known this day would happen and he had expected a threat on his daughter. He would, at least for a time, do as these men wanted. He had thought about it often. Someone moving in to take over his business – to try to take over his business. Or it could be the police working in some different manner. He thought he had the police under control but one never knew. He would say as little as possible, giving out minimal information. He had steeled himself for the time when he knew he was not going to come out alive. At that point he would say as little as possible, knowing that it would not make any difference. Still he had to try to find out what was happening to give him some kind of edge. No sooner had they grabbed him than they turned him toward a narrow alley blocked by a utility work sign. A workman standing behind the sign moved it aside; after the three men passed the sign was replaced.

"What do you want?" Pieter Devenpeck stammered in Dutch "Who are you?"

"We simply want answers to some questions."

"But ..."

"That's enough. Not another word."

As the three men approached the end of the alley another utility worker removed a sign blocking the entrance. The three men exited the alley, crossed a street and started down another alley also blocked by a utility work sign again removed by a workman. The two utility workmen from the other alley carried their signs to a waiting panel truck put them in the back, got into the truck, and pulled away. Halfway down the alley Pieter Devenpeck was guided up some steps and into a building. The room into which Pieter Devenpeck was shepherded was dim, no lights being on and the window shuttered on the outside. He found himself rudely thrust onto a chair, his hands handcuffed behind him using flexicuffs, his feet fastened to the legs of the chair with cable ties, a blindfold put over his face, and his mouth forced open and a gag put in. Then he was left alone.

Chapter 66

Pieter Devenpeck sat patiently as though he was used to this, but he really wasn't. Soon the two men returned. "We are going to remove your gag," one of them said. "If you scream you will only do so once and your life will be finished. Do you understand?"

Pieter Devenpeck nodded and the gag was removed.

"We are calling your home on a cellphone. You are to tell them that you met an old friend and are going for coffee. You will be home in about an hour. If you say any more than that, you won't say another word in this lifetime. One other thing," the voice said, "Hoewel wij Engels spreken, begrijpen wij Nederlands."

Pieter Devenpeck did not wish to tempt fate at that moment, believed that they understood Dutch, and so he did as requested. His daughter told him to have fun. He didn't think he would.

"We are going to ask you questions in English. If you don't understand, tell us."

"You can ask in English, Dutch, French, German. I also speak a little Russian."

For a moment there was silence.

"Now we are going to remove your blindfold and you are to look at a picture."

When the blindfold was removed there were lights in the room, some shining in his eyes and others behind him. A hand put a picture on his legs and he bent his head to look down. After blinking a few times an image swam into view.

"Do you know this man?"

"Yes, his name …"

"Just answer the question."

"How do you know him?"

Pieter Devenpeck knew that if these were the wrong people, the answer could get him into a lot of trouble and he didn't relish a stay in a Netherlands prison.

"I don't want …"

"It doesn't matter what you want. Listen carefully as I will say this once and one time only. What you say here, stays here. No one else will hear your answers. We are not police or any kind of law enforcement. When we have our answers, you can leave here alive. Although how long you remain alive depends on the implications of your answers. And, we know some of the answers."

"You're not police?"

"We ask the questions. We told you we are not police."

Pieter Devenpeck started to look up and his head was thrust back down.

"Don't raise your eyes. We are wearing masks but you wouldn't know us anyway."

Pieter Devenpeck wasn't sure of that but said nothing. He really had no idea who the men were. He knew one was white and the other black – at least that was the impression he had.

"What is your relationship with this man?"

"He's dead. There is no relationship."

"What was your relationship with this man?"

"He handled our money."

"Whose money?"

"My business."

"And what is your business?"

Pieter Devenpeck had to make a decision, which was in part motivated by the click of a pistol's hammer being cocked. He wasn't going to say any more than necessary about the man who had handled the money. His death had cost him nearly $10 million dollars. It seemed to him that having other people handle his money was costing him more than it should. At least when the American had died, the twenty million dollars had been retrieved. His retirement account kept taking the hits.

"Import."

"Importing what?"

"Different things."

The nudge of the gun in his back and the prompting, "Be specific."

"Prostitutes."

"But they are legal here."

"Not young girls."

"Are we talking children?"

"Yes."

"Where do they come from?"

"Countries where people need money. Parents sell them. The girls sell themselves. They need to get away from their life."

"What else?"

Pieter didn't know how much they knew or how much to tell them.

"We import drugs. We don't sell them. We don't pimp the girls. We import them for people who will pimp for them."

"Anything else."

"We provide legal documents for people who need them."

"What kind of documents?"

"Passports, driver's licenses, credit cards, ..."

"And that man whose picture you have. He handled the money?"

"He cleaned it up. Increased it."

"How?"

"I don't know. He just did it."

"Was it profitable?"

"Hell, yes."

"Then why did you have him killed?"

"What?"

Pieter started to raise his head and it was once again shoved down.

"I didn't have him killed. He died as the result of a freak car accident."

"You didn't arrange the accident?"

"No. Why would I? He made money for us!"

"What about Dawoh Mbayo?"

"Who the hell is he?"

"You don't know?"

"No. I have never heard the name."

"That's a lie." The nudge of the gun was harder. He was worried it might go off.

"No. O jee. I am telling the truth. I have never heard that name before."

"What about Jacques St. George?"

"Who?"

Another picture was put on his lap.

"Who is he?"

"Don't you know?"

"Why would I know him?"

"You sent him to get information from Dawoh Mbayo."

"No, I didn't. I don't know either of them."

"Then your boss did."

"I don't have a boss. The business is mine."

"What about this man?"

And another picture was put on his lap.

"Whose he? I have never seen him?"

"He is called 'The Facilitator.' "

"Never heard of him."

"What about Fredek Gavrilovich Kondrashin?"

"A Russian?"

"Yes."

"Never heard of him. Don't like to work with Russians."

"Why?"

"Not trustworthy."

"Who do you have do your dirty work?"

"What dirty work?"

"Taking care of individuals."

"We do it."

"Who is 'we'?"

"People in the organization."

"What's the name of the organization?"

"Doesn't have a name. Why have a name? Draws attention."

"What about Cercle des Frères?"

"Circle of Brothers?"

"Yes."

"Never heard of it."

"In France or here?"

"Neither place and not any place. Like I said, names draw attention."

"So if you wanted to have someone eliminated…"

"Who?"

"Say someone not in the organization. Like me…"

"I'd kill you myself."

"What about Hans Brinker?"

"Who? Hans Brinker? A little boy with silver skates? He didn't exist."

One of the men slapped the back of his head.

"Who handles your money now?"

"We found someone else."

"Who?"

"What are you …"

"What we do depends on what you tell us."

And Pieter Devenpeck told them. After that they replaced the blindfold and the gag and left him alone. The older of the two men went to the front door, opened it, and waved to the two utility workers at the ends of the alley. The one on the right picked his sign up and hurried down the alley past the door to the other end of the alley. The two workers then put their signs into another nondescript panel truck, got in and drove away.

Chapter 67

In the back room of the small house, I waited for Beecher to dismiss his last two men. When I had located the man I called Pieter Devenpeck (for the sake of his anonymity, I shall stick with that name), I devised a plan to talk to him. It would require a grab because I was certain that he wouldn't say much in a straight tête-à-tête. The street along the canal was too narrow to permit a car and make a quick getaway. In fact, the neighboring streets were narrow and the thought of grabbing him, thrusting him into a car, and racing off was tossed out quickly. I spent several hours scouring the neighborhood and found the old house on the alley a block away for rent. I took a long-term lease and other than a look in and bringing some equipment in, it wasn't used at all until the day we grabbed Pieter Devenpeck.

Beecher wasn't any happier with the plan than I was, but once he was on the scene he agreed that it would work. He found four young men in St. Maarten who were in need of work and were fluent in Dutch. We paid for their air flights, a week's worth of work most of which was waiting for us to pick the day and an extra $5000 each. He had admonished them, "If you screw up and get arrested, you are on your own. If you really screw up and get me or my companion arrested, you had better dig a deep hole because when I find you, it will be your grave."

Having dismissed them, they should be on the way to the airport and out of the Netherlands. They knew that if we saw them here after we were done, they would never leave alive.

Beecher entered the room and we discussed what we had learned.

"I believe him," I said and Beecher nodded.

What I had figured out was Michel Villar had me duped from the start. I know now that he knew about me when I got that first fake passport. I don't know how he was turned onto it but he was. From there he could easily have kept a trace on me and turned up all the information he needed. He created Cercle des Frères to keep me guessing, to give me someone to chase but never find. He needed someone to blame for trying to kill him. Once he found out about the lawyers, it didn't matter. But Cercle des Frères served as a good cover for Jacques St. George. The mistake was using Dutch mercenaries rather than French or even American. If I had not heard the one bit of conversation between them that stuck in my head, I could still be looking.

"What happens now?" Beecher asked.

"You go home, and thanks for the help. I am going to see if Pieter Devenpeck will help me find Michel. If he won't, I'll have to find a way. I figure that he has many ties to the European underworld and possibly something will turn up."

"Want me to wait?"

"No, but thanks, Beecher. It's my ballgame now to win or lose. If I fail, I don't want anyone else hurt. I already have put too many people in the path of jeopardy."

Beecher and I shook hands and then he left. I gave him five minutes – also if someone was onto us, five minutes was about all they would wait before busting in. But no one did.

I walked back into the room where Pieter Devenpeck was sitting and turned on the lights. I undid his gag and offered him a drink of water that he gratefully accepted.

"What are you going to do with me?" he asked after drinking half the bottle.

"That depends. You will walk out of here a free man, unharmed except for being detained for an hour or so."

"That's it. Nothing more?"

"Depends on you."

"What do you mean?"

"What would you say if I told you that Michel Villar was not dead?"

His head snapped up and I know he was trying to look at me.

"Not dead! Are you certain?"

"As certain as I can be. I last saw him about six weeks ago."

I handed him one of the pictures of Michel Villar with the dated newspaper.

" I don't know where he is now but unless there was an accident or someone else tried to kill him, he is alive."

"I would kill him with my bare hands. He has some of my money."

Ah, so that's the reason.

"How much money?"

"At least $10 million."

"Probably a lot more. I'll make a deal with you."

"What's the deal?"

"You help me find him and I'll get your money back and more."

"What about him?"

"He is mine."

"Why?"

"I would rather not say."

"I have to know something or there is no deal."

"Okay, let us say that he did to me what he has done to you."

Pieter Devenpeck was quiet for a minute.

"I would rather break his neck with my own two hands. However, before I agree, I have my own condition."

"I expected as much and I think I know what you want. Just sit quietly for a minute."

I turned off the lights shining in his face and moved them out of the way. Then I moved a chair in front of him. I cut the cable ties binding his feet to the legs of the chair. Then I undid the handcuffs, removed them and dropped them to the floor. He didn't move except to move his hands in front of him and starting to massage his wrists. I sat in the chair facing him, my Berretta in my hand.

"You can remove the blindfold."

Pieter Devenpeck stopped massaging his wrists, reached up and removed the blindfold, dropping it to the floor. He blinked a couple of times and rubbed his eyes. Then he looked at me. "I thought it was you. One dead man chasing another."

Chapter 68

I was stunned.

"You said you didn't know me."

"When?"

"Earlier."

"Today?"

"Yes."

Pieter Devenpeck sat and thought. He looked at me, frowned, scratched his head and frowned again.

"Refresh my memory."

"Maybe not. First, who am I?"

"Well, let's see. You could be Josef Viljoen, South African. You could be William David Calhoun or is it David William Calhoun? So many names, sometimes I get confused."

I was nonplused.

"How in the world?"

"Oh," Pieter Devenpeck laughed. "I don't remember them all. Only the ones who really interested me."

"And why did I interest you?"

"Well, the first time you didn't. I say the first time because when you came that second time six or seven years ago, I knew I had gotten you a passport. And, despite your disguise, which I have to admit was quite good, I recognized you. Also we had copies of the pictures and I was able to double check. Yes, I followed the trial but probably not as closely as you did. I could trace the movements, at least part of the time, of Josef Viljoen. But not all the time and I imagine that Mr. Calhoun, whatever the name, appeared only in the Verenigde Staten. Very difficult to trace there.

"I admit I didn't know you were in this country, so you had to use another name to get in. Maybe that name you said that I couldn't remember and still don't. It might come to me but most likely not."

He was right. I had entered the European community using an identity provided by Beecher McFalls, uncertain of what identity that I had in my possession that I could use.

"So, my friend," Pieter Devenpeck said. "Where do you think this zoon van een teef could be?"

"I haven't the faintest idea where the son of a bitch is."

"Where was he the last time you saw him?"

"Nassau, Bahamas."

"When?"

"About six weeks ago."

"Exactly when?"

I thought and gave him the date.

"And do you know what name he was using?"

"No, but he had a goatee, tinged with white. He was using a cane. Said that his leg had never healed properly. We had to move him from the hospital in a body bag and he got jounced around a little."

"Help me understand what has happened. You can leave names out but tell me about him dying."

And I did.

"So someone wanted him dead. Do you know who?"

"Yes, it was a lawyer in a case he had tried."

"Let me guess – it was your case. I mean the one for your murderers."

"Yes."

"And you – or he – got them also?"

"Yes."

"So who knows you are alive?"

"Beside you? Michel Villar."

"No one else?"

I shook my head.

"No wife, no girl friend or significant other?"

"Yes, my ... girl friend."

"You trust her?"

"With my life," I said.

"Good. So just one you need to take care of."

I looked at him and waggled the gun.

"Maybe two?"

"Nee nee. Not me. I need you."

I looked at him not quite comprehending his meaning.

"For what? I can't do money anymore."

"No, but you can supervise the people who do. You know, to insure that what they are doing they are doing right."

"If they're good, I can't trace everything."

"I have made certain that the people I choose now are good but not too good."

"Like your new man."

"Exactly. I don't think he is nearly as good as you."

"He wasn't but now he could be."

"Well," said Pieter Devenpeck, slapping his knees and trying to stand but not making it. I reached out and gave him a hand.

"The old knee still has problems and the new one isn't quite up to par, especially after sitting a while. So, may I finish my walk?"

"Yes, of course."

We made arrangements on how to contact each other and walked out the front door, Pieter first. As we started to part ways he turned around and held out his hand.

"To seal the bargain," he said.

I grasped his hand and he looked down and then into my eyes.

"Always the careful one, aren't you, Stuart."

Then he turned and walked back the way we had come. I turned and walked the other way, stripping off my latex gloves as I went.

Chapter 69

Just as I returned to St. Maartin from Amsterdam following the meeting with Pieter Devenpeck, I had a frantic call from Quentin Baston.

"Zey have taken Pay-Koo," he screamed. Pay-Koo was his son's nickname to differentiate father from son. It was P.Q., the initials for Petit Quentin.

"Calm down," I said feeling about as nervous as he did. "Who has taken Pay-Koo?"

The car had pulled up in front of the maternelle and the man inside sat there for several minutes as though deciding whether to go through with it. However, he was really running over things in his mind. The car had been obtained from the impound lot and wouldn't be missed. The owner was doing time thanks to Michel Villar. The lot had so few cars there was not a regular guard. When it was found, and it would be because he would see to it, there would be questions as to how it was taken but by then it would be too late. He didn't have much confidence in the gendarmerie. He reached into a duffel bag he had brought and pulled out a mask and a wig. The mask went on first then the wig – yellow with curly hair. Opening the door he swiveled so he legs were out of the car and started putting on the one piece costume also pulled from the bag. Puffy legs, arms, and body in garish colors. Standing up he sealed the front with Velcro strips. Then he reached back into the car and pulled from the duffel an Uzi on a strap – at least it looked like an Uzi – and put the strap over his head and his right arm through the loop made by the strap. Then he picked up the duffel. He smiled to himself and thought Marchand de Sable est prêt (The Sandman is ready).

"Some man. I don't know who. He raided the maternelle. He drugged everyone, and took two kids, a girl and Pay-Koo."

As he walked to the maternelle's door, he knew that anyone who saw him would just think he was a clown going to entertain the children. He opened the door and stepped in quickly, closing it behind him. The teacher looked up and seeing him was at first alarmed but then smiled as she thought that some parent had arranged this entertainment. The kids were screaming with excitement and jumping up and down at thoughts of balloon animals or other clever presents that such entertainers usually brought along.

"Have the children lie down," the Sandman said.

"What for?" the teacher asked now suddenly wary but too late – so late.

The Sandman raised his Uzi. "Because I said to."

A panicked look flitted momentarily across the teacher's face but then her training took hold. "It's the Sandman, children," she said clapping her hands excitedly. "We need to take pretend naps so that he can entertain us."

The children obediently and excitedly got their mats and lay down, some closing their eyes but most not.

"Take one of these for each child and hold it over their faces until they sleep," the Sandman instructed, handing her a plastic bag with enough chloroform-laden cloths to put the children to sleep. She looked at the cloths and stammered, "But ..."

"Do it," the Sandman said.

Reluctantly the teacher did, putting each child into an anesthetized sleep. As she was holding the cloth over the last child's face, the Sandman took one he had prepared for her. When she started to rise, he grabbed her and held the cloth over her face. She struggled briefly and then succumbed. The Sandman put the duffel on the floor and went to the mat where Pay-Koo lay. Picking him up, he put him in the duffel and chose a small girl and put her in also, adding the Uzi water gun. He zipped the duffel, picked it up effortlessly and exited the maternelle. He put the duffel in the back seat, took off the clown's clothing, and got into the car. Inside he removed the wig and mask. He glanced around and saw no one looking at him so he started the car and drove away.

"The girl was found in the car he drove away. It was near a dock."

At the pier where he had tied up his runabout, he unzipped the duffel and took the little girl out and laid her on the floor of the back seat. He put the clown clothes, wig and mask into the duffel, zipped it, and carried it to his runabout. He unfastened the painter, started the engine and nonchalantly motored away, heading for his own pier where a small yacht was docked. There he tied up the runabout and carried the duffel onto the yacht and below to the single cabin. He took everything out of the bag, laying Pay-Koo on the bed. Putting everything else back in the bag, he carried it topside. Untying the lines, he started the yacht and motored out and away from St. Nantes.

"What did the man look like?" I asked.

"Zey say he was dressed as a clown."

"Big man?"

"Yes, but ze mademoiselle was so frightened he could have been a midget."

"Did he have a gun?"

"She zinks so but she was scared."

Half an hour later he took out a satellite phone and dialed a number. When the call was answered, he asked to speak to Celesse Baston. When she picked up he said, "Listen to me carefully. I have your youngest son. Quiet. He is fine and he will stay fine as long as you do as I say. The children and the teacher at the maternelle were given chloroform. One girl is missing," and he told her where she could be found. She had been his insurance. "You tell Josef that you want ten million Euros. He has thirty-six hours to get it. I will call you at home then and give you instructions on where to bring the money. Don't tell the gendarmes about the money. If I see gendarmes other than at the maternelle or where the girl is found, you will not see your son again." He cut the connection, removed the chip and tossed it overboard.

"What's he want?"

"Ten million Euros."

"How is the transfer to be made?"

"We don't know. You have thirty-six hours to get the money and then he will call and give instructions."

Chapter 70

After the call to Celesse, the Sandman breathed a sigh of relief. The most difficult part of the plan was over. He had been lucky. No one had spotted him, questioned his movements and called the gendarmes. *People were too damned complacent.* He smiled to himself. *Fortunately,* he thought. The hardest part over, the most tedious part began. That of taking care of the kid. He had never really liked kids. His wife had wanted them and he had agreed. He had discovered that he loved his own kids, especially his grandchildren none of whom he would ever be able to see again. Nor his wife who happened to be taking care of a couple of grandchildren and gave him the chance to do what he needed to without intervention. He had purchased diapers but the little nipper would have to wear the same clothes. He had the kind of food most two-year-olds eat, plenty of juice boxes, and a collection of DVDs brought from home and previously used by his grandchildren when they visited infrequently. Usually he and his wife, she mostly, went to visit them in their homes. If needed, he would put the kid to sleep again but he knew that could be risky. He had to keep him alive and reasonably well until he made the exchange. Well, until he had his money.

Almost precisely thirty-six hours later, Quentin called. "He says to take a boat – just you – to a spot wiz GPS coordinates he gave me. You put ze money in a rubber raft and back off. He will collect it and zen put Pay-Koo in the raft. When he is away, you can get Pay-

Koo. He says if zere is a bug, he will dump Pay-Koo in ze ocean. Oh, yes, he says zere better no be a plane."

So here I was, ten million euros in counterfeit money, well most of it was counterfeit thanks to Pieter Devenpeck who had couriered the money to me in a private plane. There was about one million in actual Euro notes in case he checked, but I doubted that he would.

"Why are you doing this?" I yelled across the intervening distance between my boat and his as mine coasted to a stop.

"Why do you think?" came the retort. "That arrogant prig used me all those years and then left me with nothing. Just vanished and took it all with him."

"But he's dead," I countered.

"That's what they say, but you're supposed to be dead too, aren't you, Josef?"

Not much I could say to that. But the fact that he knew me as Josef said a lot. The only way he could know was that Michel had told him. And that made sense. He obviously was part of Michel Villar's plot.

"Put the money in the raft and back off," Guillaume Martineau shouted.

"Show me Pay-Koo first," was my retort.

"Certainly. Glad to get rid of the petit bâtard."

Guillaume Martineau bent down and picked up Pay-Koo by the back of his shirt. He was screaming his head off, kicking his arms and legs. He was put back down quickly.

"Don't want to drop the petit bâtard in the water, do I? Now the money." As he spoke he was scanning the skies.

"Don't worry," I said. "There is no plane."

"I'm not looking for your plane," he retorted cockily, "I'm looking for mine."

So that was his getaway plan. Had to admit it was a good one – if it worked.

I put the rubber raft into the water and set the bag with the money in it. Then I backed away about fifty feet. Guillaume Martineau backed up and then motored over to the raft and picked the bag up using a boat hook. He ran some electronic device over it checking for bugs – but there weren't any. I watched as he unzipped the bag and pulled out a packet. I held my breath as he looked at it.

"It's real," I shouted or as good-looking counterfeit and Pieter Devenpeck could get me that quickly.

"It had better be."

"Put the boy in the raft," I almost pleaded.

Guillaume Martineau reached down and picked Pay-Koo up by the back of his shirt and held him over the side kicking and screaming.

"In the raft," I screamed.

He released Pay-Koo and gunned the engine, the prop starting to make waves almost at the same time Pay-Koo hit the water and went under. I knew there was no way I was going to reach him in time. I watched Guillaume Martineau roar away without a look behind as almost miraculously Pay-Koo was set into the raft by hands raising him out of the Caribbean. Beecher waved to me and started towing the raft toward me, Pay-Koo lying on the bottom kicking and screaming. As I had approached, Beecher had been in the water holding onto a rope on the side away from Guillaume Martineau. He was wearing scuba gear fitted with a rebreather and had moved under the boat when I stopped. When I put the raft in the water, he had moved under the raft and held onto specially fitted handles so as not to be seen. When Guillaume Martineau was alongside the raft, he had released his hold and affixed a bomb to Guillaume Martineau's boat. Then he waited to catch Pay-Koo because we didn't think that he was going to be put into the raft. He told me that Guillaume Martineau had literally dropped Pay-Koo into his arms. He had quickly covered his mouth and nose to prevent any further intake of water and surfaced as quickly as possible. I picked up the detonating device and flipped a switch. A red light came on and blinked, the device searching for a signal. The blinking red light turned to solid green just as Beecher reached my boat. I put the detonator down and took Pay-Koo from his hands and held him tightly as Beecher clambered aboard. Then I gave Pay-Koo to him, picked up the detonating device and looked at Guillaume Martineau's rapidly disappearing boat.

"See you in hell," I said pressing the button. The boat disappeared in a ball of fire seconds before the sound of the detonation reached us.

"One rat down, one to go," I said taking, Petit Quentin so that Beecher could get out of his gear. I got Pay-Koo out of his wet clothes and filthy diaper – I didn't think he had been changed since his abduction just 40 hours before. I was just putting a dry shirt on him when Quentin's boat eased along side. I passed Pay-Koo over to Celesse and he immediately stopped his crying.

"Thank you," Celesse said. "We owe you much, Josef."

"You owe me nothing," I said. "It is my fault that this happened. Until I am certain that this is over, I will have people watching your family constantly." And indeed they had been since a few hours after I had received Quentin's call. I was furious with myself because I had never expected Guillaume Martineau to be a bad guy. That was another score to settle. And with that thought, I realized, that if you didn't count Quentin and Celesse who were not actually involved, it had happened again: Four went out. Three came back. We know what happened!

Chapter 71

It was a beautiful Miami morning – clear sky, no breeze. It was exactly the kind of day that Miamians use to get outside: go to the beach, take a walk, go sailing, fishing, or watch the Marlins or the Dolphins, depending upon the season. It was not a morning to be inside. So why was Alan Murphy headed for his place of business? The markets were all closed; there was nothing to do there. Nobody else would be there. And that was the reason. Alan Murphy had things to do and preferred that no one was around who could possibly witness anything.

Preferring to remain as anonymous as possible, he parked a block away in an indoor lot where his car couldn't be seen. He locked the car and started the short walk to his office. He was wearing jeans and a Marlin's tee shirt, sandals on his feet. Definitely not the look of someone ready to make a client ten million dollars richer with a couple of key clicks at the computer keyboard. And definitely not dressed like someone who was about to make himself one million dollars richer. With that prospect looming ahead, it still didn't explain why Alan Murphy's palms were sweating and why his stomach was churning. What was really causing his anxiety was the simple fact that what he was about to do, what he had been doing for several months, was illegal. That simple fact explained why he was doing this on a Sunday morning in an empty office.

Lost deep in his thoughts about what he was about to do, Alan Murphy suddenly found himself looking at the frosted glass double doors leading into his office complex. The name on the door seemed to shout back at him: Andrews Investment Management. The acronym AIM had become "Alan's Investment Management" in his own mind but he had left it alone. When he had taken over the business after Stuart's demise (*How fortunate that had been*, Alan thought) he had given thoughts to changing it. But it had been the name and the excellent image that it conveyed that had kept the majority of the clients that had been left hanging and brought new ones in. Although he hadn't the financial wizardry that Stuart had, he had done well for his clients and they, for the most part, were extremely pleased. There were the disgruntled few who had left for what they hoped were greener pastures. But in the still unsettled markets of today, most of them were happy with their returns.

Alan Murphy unlocked the doors, entered the office complex, then closed and locked the doors behind him. After entering the code in the security system panel, he had stood there in the dim light provided by the security system for several minutes. This was more to ascertain that he was alone in the complex than to dwell on the quiet solitude. Satisfied that all was well and that he was truly alone, he entered his office. Sunlight streamed through the floor to ceiling windows on the two outside walls. His big desk was positioned cattycornered so that he sat with his back to the windows preferring natural light to the florescent ceiling lighting.

Settling himself in his red leather captain's chair, he entered a few clicks into his keyboard. The computer screen lit, bringing up the security message. No one had been in the complex since he had left Friday evening and the computer system had remained secure. A few more taps of the keyboard activated internet access and he waited, watching the progress as connections were checked and security assured. Elbows resting on the arms of his command chair, chin resting on the points of his fingers, hands together as in prayer, he stared at the screen. It wouldn't take much to make the transfers, quick key entries he could do with his eyes closed, he sat there savoring the moment. In a few minutes he would be a rich man. Richer than he had ever hoped. Richer maybe than Stuart had been. Stuart, Mister Goody Two Shoes, would never have taken the chance he had been offered. Stuart would have notified the FCC, not that it would have done any good. These guys were too good he knew. He didn't even know who had contacted him. It had all been done via secure emails and phone calls. They knew about him head to toes and had let him know that. Every dalliance, every affair. Screw up and they could ruin him. He really wasn't any worse than most of his associates but … .

Shaking those thoughts from his mind, he entered the investment site, accessed the account, and transferred ten million dollars to his client. He stared at the numbers remaining on the screen: $1,547,232.46. It was all his. He would leave half a million in the account, it would soon have more funds that he would move from other accounts, accounts which seemed never ending as his clients passed money to him. Money he would "invest" and cleanse and then return with a profit. Rather than dwell on the prospects, he quickly entered the codes necessary to transfer funds to one of his own accounts, and in a few moments the numbers on the screen read $547,232.46. Smiling to himself he closed the account and moved on to his own account. Starting balance:

$132,456.23. He sat there watching the screen. Suddenly it refreshed. Deposit: $1,000,000. Balance $1,132,456.23. He smiled. He was rich. Rich beyond all his dreams. Suddenly the screen refreshed and he stared disbelieving at the new entry. Transfer, $750,000. Balance $382,456.23. What had happened? His money was gone. Transferred out as effortlessly as he had transferred it in. But how? Frantically he ran his security program trying to trace what had happened but found nothing.

Sinking back into his chair, no longer feeling in command, he stared at the screen. His wealth had suddenly disappeared, heavily taxed by someone. But who? Where?

A chime announced the arrival of an email into his secure mailbox. Reflexively he opened it. Subject: For Your Eyes Only. He scanned down to the one line message: "Don't be greedy. We are watching."

* * *

Several thousand miles away, a smile flitted across my face. With help, I had managed to insert a program into Alan's computer system using many different emails to several different associates. Once compiled and running, it kept track of Alan's computer activities and let me know everything he did – sites, usernames, passwords, etc. The program had alerted me that he was working on this Sunday morning and I had watched his progress. When he moved that money into his account, I moved the "unlawful vig" to mine. This was per agreement with Pieter Devenpeck and I would accurately report it, forwarding half to him – I was not going to risk another inquisition. In fact, I had no doubt that there was someone keeping an eye on me to make certain I did my job. My job was to keep Alan on the up and up. If he moved his operation elsewhere, I would be out of luck, but I didn't think Alan would do that. If he did, I would know because I wouldn't have any tracking when money was put into Pieter Devenpeck's accounts. To get rid of my tracking in his office, he would have to replace every computer and I doubted that he could afford that. I knew Alan pretty well and figured that this one warning would keep him on the straight and narrow, at least for the near future. That taken care of, I turned my attention to other things.

Chapter 72

Quentin and his family were safe now. As safe as I could make them. They had money and could live a peaceful life but I knew that Quentin would keep fishing. Joaquin and Jovelyn had sold the Banyuhay and gone back to the Philippines to raise a family already started. In fact, their child would be born about a month before ours. I wasn't concerned about Beecher McFalls as he was more than able to take care of himself. Tres wasn't happy with me leaving again.

"But Daws, where are your going?"

"I can't tell you where or why, my beloved. If I did, you would want to follow."

"But I love you ..."

"I know and that is why I cannot let you go with me."

"But certainly I can ..."

"No," I said gently touching her rounded stomach that just now was beginning to show. *"I cannot risk any harm coming to our child. You must stay safe and let me do what I must do."*

"But ..."

"I started this alone and alone I must finish this. Please trust me."

There were tears at the corners of her eyes.

"I do," she said.

"You go to our new home. I will join you soon."

I kissed her and with that I walked away.

Now I sat in his living room waiting. It had taken only a few weeks for Pieter Devenpeck to track him down. I had taken a circuitous route to get to his hiding place and didn't think it could be easily traced. I don't know who would want to. A few days' surveillance and I knew his pattern and had my opportunity. I believe that he had misjudged us, misjudged me – and that was not at all like him.

I heard the key in the door, one lock and then two. The door opened. There were footsteps. The door closed and then several quiet beeps as the alarm was disconnected. I had thought about changing the code to confound him but that would require me to enter it. That would put me close to him and he would be quick to seize on the opportunity.

I heard him remove his rain jacket, shake it out and hang it on the doorknob to dry. I heard the first drips of the rain from the coat hitting the tile. Then a few quick steps and he was at the entrance to the room. A pause and then the lights went on, or at least the ones near him did. I had unscrewed the ones that would have illuminated my position.

I noticed him pause, wondering what was wrong and peering at the dimness where I was sitting. I hit the remote that turned the lights on in the foyer. The sudden brightness made him start, glance behind him and then he froze, looking straight at me.

"Hello, Michel," I said.

He just stared at me momentarily and I knew that I had caught him completely off guard. Then he smiled that trademark sardonic smile.

"Stuart," he said starting to move toward me.

"That's far enough, Michel," I said as I stood and made the gun in my hand obvious.

He stopped immediately.

"I thought we agreed not to contact each other again," he said quizzically.

"We had," I agreed, "but then I got to thinking. Bad habit of mine, but not in this case."

"What do you mean?"

"How long were you planning on letting us live?" I asked.

"What ...," he half stammered. He was beginning to realize that he had been found out.

"Have you already hired someone or are we still in a grace period."

"Grace period? Hired someone? Stuart, you are being paranoid."

"Am I really? Was St. George investigating on his own or on instructions from the grave? I am not quite certain."

Michel stared at me, finally, I think, beginning to understand.

"Why would I send St. George after you?"

"Oh, come now, Michel. I admit that I may not be as worldly in matters of the dark side as you are, but you must give me some credit."

Michel stared at me.

"It's been a long day, Stuart. Do you mind if I have a drink?"

"No, go right ahead."

I had been in the house for over an hour and had removed everything I thought he could possibly use as a weapon. I had found a Beretta Nano in the liquor cabinet and rendered it useless but I left it in place for him to find.

He got a crystal tumbler and removed the lid of the ice bucket. I hadn't known that Royal Selangor made an ice bucket, but it didn't surprise me. The ice was pristine when I looked at it earlier and I was certain that it still was. Michel seemed to pause before taking ice, then shrugged slightly, filled the tumbler, and then paused as he started to replace the lid.

"You won't be joining me, will you, Stuart?"

"I think not."

Michel nodded imperceptibly, replaced the lid on the ice bucket, and reached for the crystal decanter of vodka. The stopper was halfway out when he stopped and replaced it.

"Do you mind if I get a fresh bottle?"

I had expected this ploy. The Beretta was in the cabinet with the extra bottles.

"Of course not."

Michel opened the cabinet door and reached in. He paused, looked, and then pulled out a bottle of Presidential vodka, which seemed to be his current drink of choice, and closed the cabinet door.

"You found the Beretta."

A statement not a question.

"What do you think?" was my response.

"I don't think I want to gamble with you."

"I agree. The gambles you have taken have not turned out favorably."

Michel opened the bottle and poured himself a stiff drink. He lifted the glass as if to toast "To life" and took a long drink. So long that he refilled his glass when he finished.

"I guess I'm not driving tonight so I don't have to worry."

Yes, you do, I thought.

I watched him to see if there was any immediate reaction but there didn't seem to be.

"So when did you first begin to suspect?" Michel Villar asked.

"Oh, looking back on it, I have to say that day you visited me on the Zàkpa."

"Yes, that was a mistake."

"I agree. You came to gloat."

Michel Villar nodded.

"Yes. I should have left well enough alone."

"You knew too much for a simple go-between for Circle of Brothers as you called them. Then there was The Facilitator's familiarity with you. You were surprised when he didn't take your bribe. Almost got you killed."

"Yes, that was foolhardy."

"What was really foolish was not being satisfied with the money you had taken from Pieter Devenpeck."

He really looked surprised.

"I should have guessed by your appearance here. How did you figure that out?"

"Pure accident." And I told him about the encounter on the Banyuhay and the subsequent event on St. Maarten. "You know if you hadn't sent St. George after me, I wouldn't have suspected. You could have gone off and lived the life you wanted to live."

"There wasn't enough money."

"So you sent St. George after me. Pure greed, Michel. Probably sent those two thugs in St. Maarten also or was that Guillaume Martineau's idea?"

Michel looked at his drink, then at me, and there was a look of surprise on his face.

"May I sit?" he asked moving toward the nearest chair.

"I think it would be best," I said.

He sat clumsily, the drink falling from his hand and spilling on the carpet, the liquid spreading out and the ice rolling like dice on green velvet.

"The decanter too?" he asked, his speech slurred.

"Yes," I said, getting up from my chair. "It wouldn't have mattered"

"What if I chose scotch?"

"You wouldn't, Michel, you are too much a creature of habit in your drinking."

"I left papers with my lawyer."

"No you didn't. You wouldn't take that chance."

He shrugged.

"How long?" he asked.

"Not too much longer," I answered. "It is working faster than we had thought."

He raised an eyebrow questioningly.

"McFalls," I answered. "It's a combination of drugs. The first paralyzes, the second puts you out so you won't feel any pain, and the third ..."

"Autops...," he tried to get out.

"Untraceable after three hours and you really have to know what to look for. It's so new, I don't think it has a name yet. It was developed for Iraq and Afghanistan although it never got used in Gitmo."

"I should have known from the start ... well, from your first visit to me in St. Nantes after I had the house. You trusted me too much. You knew too much about what was going on just to be a go-between for the money."

As I was talking, I started cleaning up. His eyes followed me but nothing else; the paralysis was taking effect quickly. I opened the bag I had brought and got out two bottles of his vodka. One I put in the cabinet and I put the bottle he had opened in the bag. The decanter I took into the bathroom, poured it in the toilet and flushed three times. I then went to the kitchen and poured water into the decanter rinsing it several times and letting the water run. I filled the decanter halfway from the second bottle, which then went into my bag. If they got really curious, they would wonder why his prints were not on the bottle in the cabinet but since it was unopened, I doubt they would go so far.

When I was done with the bottles, I made certain that all the lights worked properly. Then I went and stood before him. His eyes were still following me but starting to glaze over.

"I am sorry, Michel. I really liked you. But it has to be this way. I want to live and, to be honest, you don't deserve to."

I pulled a small flashlight from my pocket and shone it into his eyes. The pupils didn't react.

"Good bye, Michel," I said and picked up my bag and walked to the kitchen. I looked around to be certain that I had left nothing behind. Then I opened the back door and stepped out into the night and the rain.

PAINKILLER RECEIPE

Tres and I drank a lot of *Painkillers* in this book so I thought I would give you a recipe.

Painkiller® recipe
Scale ingredients to servings

2 oz dark rum
1 oz cream of coconut
4 oz pineapple juice

Shake or stir ingredients, and pour over ice in a tall glass. Sprinkle nutmeg on top, and serve.

However, this is not how we do it. We buy a concentrated mixture of orange juice and pineapple juice and use a coconut flavored rum. The concentrate makes half a gallon (64 ozs). So that means (at a ratio of 5:1) 13 oz of rum which is about half of a 750 ml of rum. We eyeball it, leaving about half of a new bottle. Most of the time we forget the nutmeg.

According to Wikipedia: "A **Painkiller** is a famous rum cocktail trademarked by Pusser's Rum, their signature drink. The Painkiller® is a blend of Pusser's Rum with 4 parts pineapple juice, 1 part cream of coconut and 1 part orange juice, well shaken and served over the rocks with a generous amount of fresh nutmeg on top. It may be made with either two, three or four ounces of Pusser's dark rum.

"Reputation has it [per Edward Hamilton's 1997 book The Complete Guide to Rum p. 47] that the original Painkiller® was created in the 1970s at the Soggy Dollar Bar at White Bay on the island of Jost Van Dyke in the British Virgin Islands."

I have never been to the Soggy Dollar Bar but I have been told that you get there by boat. At three square miles, Jost Van Dyke is the fourth largest of the British Virgin Islands.
Enjoy,
Stuart Andrews

~*~*~

The Payback Series

If you enjoyed reading this, the second book in the Payback series, you will enjoy the initial volume, *Payback is a Bitch*, which will introduce you to the dynamic Stuart Andrews as he begins his quest for vengeance and revenge, available in print from A-Argus Books at www.a-argusbooks.com, or free in the ebook version at
https://www.smashwords.com/dashboard/edit/221914

*****

The third volume in the action-packed adventure series, *Payback is Bitter Vengeance* will continue the traumatic quest for survival for Stuart and the love of his life, Tres, in the most dynamic chapter of their action adventure thriller series. Available from A-Argus Books October 2014. Order from best bookstores everywhere.

Available in ebook from amazon.com (Kindle), barnesandnoble.com (Nook), Kobo, Smashwords and other ebook sellers.